Praise for *The Changelings*

"A richly drawn fairy world that will have readers staying way up past their bedtime to read what their plucky heroine, Izzy, does next."

—Jen Calonita, author of the
Fairy Tale Reform School series

"Fresh and imaginative—new inventions on every page. I loved every ingenious twist and turn right up to the wonderfully satisfying ending."

—Katherine Catmull, author of
The Radiant Road and *Summer and Bird*

"*The Changelings* is charming! Perfect for readers who love stories full of magic, adventure, mystery, and fairies, topped off with a satisfying and very happy ending. Soontornvat's debut sparkles and delights!"

—Nikki Loftin, author of
The Sinister Sweetness of Splendid Academy

"This well-paced novel full of likable characters will attract fantasy lovers, especially those interested in fairies."

—*School Library Journal*

"An engaging story with unusual twists and a thought-provoking conclusion."

—*School Library Connection*

"A fantasy adventure with [...] plenty of action, a bit of danger, and a happy ending. Incorporating a few elements of the Pied Piper legend, Soontornvat emphasizes the importance of family, whether it's the one you're born into, the one you find yourself in, or the one you create for yourself."

—*Booklist*

ALSO BY CHRISTINA SOONTORNVAT

The Changelings

IN A
DARK LAND
A CHANGELINGS STORY

CHRISTINA SOONTORNVAT

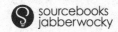

sourcebooks
jabberwocky

Published by Sourcebooks Jabberwocky, an imprint of Sourcebooks, Inc.
P.O. Box 4410, Naperville, Illinois 60567-4410
(630) 961-3900
Fax: (630) 961-2168
www.sourcebooks.com

Library of Congress Cataloging-in-Publication data is on file with the publisher.

Source of Production: Maple Press, York, Pennsylvania, USA
Date of Production: August 2017
Run Number: 5010097

Printed and bound in the United States of America.
MA 10 9 8 7 6 5 4 3 2 1

for
Elowyn and Aven

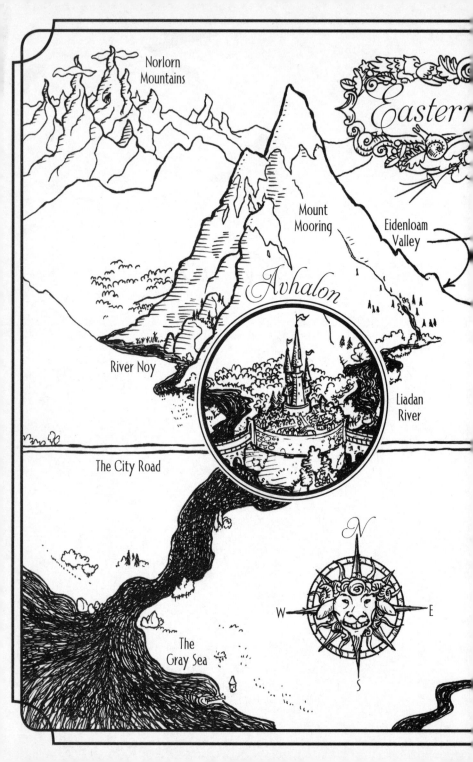

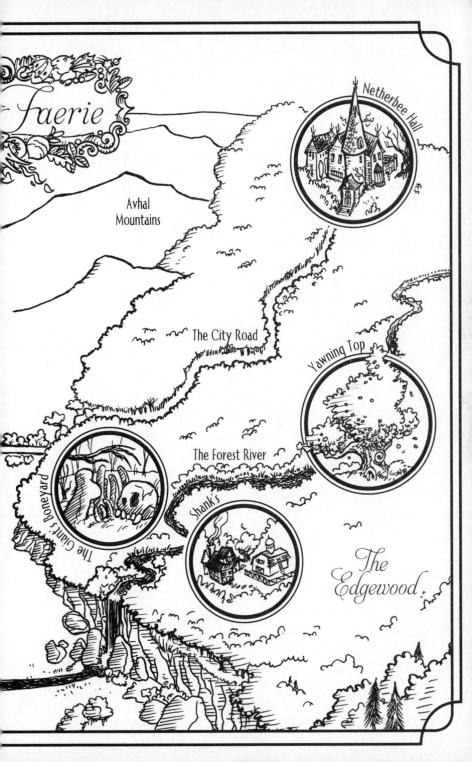

VISITORS TO CAMP KITTERPINES

LEAF, STONE, LEAF, STONE, leaf, stone, leaf, stone...

Izzy carefully layered the last leaf and dark-gray rock on top of the others. She leaned back onto her heels and looked down at the other four towers she and her little sister, Hen, had just built. The towers wobbled. Overall, it was a pretty sorry attempt, but it wasn't entirely their fault. The rocks here weren't smooth and flat like the ones they could find in the woods back home.

Hen stood up and raised her arms out at her sides. She shut her eyes and tilted her face to the sky. "Oh, Good Piper," she intoned. "Hear our call. We salmon you here..."

"Summon," corrected Izzy.

Hen wrinkled her nose and then continued her chant. "We summon you here. Come forth, o' Piper, and cross into our world!"

Hen stood perfectly still, her blond curls ruffling in the slight breeze.

Izzy allowed what she felt was an extra-long dramatic pause. "I told you. This isn't going to—"

"Shh!" Hen's eyes popped open. "You hear that? Could it be the sound of a fairy flute?"

Izzy listened. The brassy spurts of a bugle rang out from the direction of camp headquarters. It was time to rotate activities.

Hen slumped, one hand on her hip. "Oh man. I was sure making these towers would work."

Izzy sighed and straightened a stack that had fallen over. "We've been making them for months. I don't know why you expect anything different to happen now."

Hen spread her arms again and spun around. "Because look at this place! This forest is so Faerie, it's not even funny."

Izzy looked up at the trees towering over them. Hen had a point. The forest preserve that surrounded Camp Kitterpines hadn't heard the swing of an ax since Davy Crockett was alive. Colossal oak trees stretched up and out of sight, their trunks as wide around as a baby swimming pool. The last time Izzy had seen trees that big was when she stepped into the Edgewood, the forest that covered the eastern border of Faerie, nine excruciatingly long months ago.

A part of Izzy was happy to be in such a magical-feeling place. But the rest of her couldn't help resenting it. This forest was the reason her parents had abandoned them at Camp Kitterpines for the summer.

"We picked this place just for you, Izzy," their mom had

said during the long, winding drive through the Cherokee National Forest. "You love the woods, and that's exactly what this camp is all about. There'll be hiking and swimming and all sorts of nature activities. The lake even has a waterslide."

"Waterslide? That's so cool!" Hen bounced on her seat, singing the official camp song for the one hundredth time. "*Hi-ho, hi-ho, it's to the woods we go...*"

"Izzy, look at what a great attitude your sister has," said her dad.

True, but then again, Hen would have a great attitude about marching to her own beheading. Izzy's parents were so clueless. They had no idea that the reason Izzy spent so much time in the woods behind their house wasn't because she'd suddenly become a nature lover.

She was waiting for her chance to go back to Faerie.

At first, it had been great to be home again, to sleep in her own bed with her dog, Dublin, at her feet, knowing she was safe with her parents in the next room. Izzy had learned firsthand that for all its wonders, Faerie was a dangerous place. She and her sister were lucky to have survived their adventures at all—being kidnapped by an evil witch, hunted by goblins, trekking halfway across Eastern Faerie. Sure, when Izzy returned to Earth, she'd had to leave her best—make that her *only*—friends behind. But she had told herself she'd see them again soon.

But now an entire school year had blown by, and there had

been no sign, no message from any of the Changelings. Izzy worried. Had something bad happened to them? Or maybe they were just too busy. They had each other. Maybe they didn't miss her the way she missed them. That thought worried her even more.

And then recently, in the weeks since school had let out, Izzy had started to feel differently whenever she went into the woods behind her house. It was hard to explain. The air smelled greener, the light seemed sharper, and goose bumps ran up the backs of her arms, the same way they did when she crossed into Faerie the first time.

Just when Izzy was sure her friends were about to finally make contact, her parents had whisked them away to sleep-away camp so they could take their first solo vacation in twelve years. They'd even put poor Dublin in a boarding kennel. Parents could be so selfish.

Izzy frowned and plucked a leaf off a vine she hoped wasn't poison ivy. She handed it to Hen, who'd started gathering more tower materials.

"I think we should build just a couple more," said Hen, cradling a rock under her chin. "If Peter sees them, he'll know we're here and come find us."

"Who are you talking about?" asked a voice behind them.

Izzy spun around. Long-legged Larissa stood on the trail with her arms crossed. The other girls from the twelve-year-old cabin stood behind her, watching Izzy and Hen with curiosity.

Larissa held up one pinkie, the camp salute. "Hi-ho."

"Hi-HO!" responded Hen, pinkie extended with glee.

Larissa glared at Izzy until she limply held up her finger. "Hi-ho."

Larissa's mother and grandmother had gone to Camp Kitterpines and had donated enough money to have the dining hall named after them, which Larissa made sure no one forgot. She strode toward Izzy and Hen, knocking over three of the towers with her long, floppy feet.

"Who's Peter?" she asked. "Your boyfriend?"

Hen, who never got sarcasm, chuckled. "Ha, of course not! Good Peter is the Piper. He's the one who lures human children away from their homes and switches them with Changelings. He's, like, a thousand years old. And last September, he stole me away into Faerie because he was pretending to work for this wicked witch named Morvanna. Izzy and the Changelings had to rescue me…"

Izzy kept silent while Hen spilled all the details of their entire adventure in Faerie. When they'd first returned to Earth, she'd tried to keep her little sister quiet about it. But she soon realized that the more Hen blabbed, the more everyone, including her parents, thought it was all just an elaborate make-believe game. Even now, the camp girls smiled indulgingly at Hen. Izzy could tell what they were thinking: *What a cute little girl with a great imagination!*

Larissa was the only one who rolled her eyes. "Come on,"

she said to the others, cutting Hen off. "Let's go before someone changes us into a troll."

She knocked over another stone tower and started walking back toward camp.

The other girls patted Hen on the head and turned to follow Larissa. One of them tapped Izzy on the shoulder. "You want to come? Our last activity is sand volleyball. You can be on my team."

Izzy glanced at the girls trotting away. Larissa was a snob, but most of the others were pretty friendly. Izzy told herself she should go with them. She should be friendly back for once and give this camp a shot instead of being a loner like she usually was.

But she just couldn't. There was something depressing about the thought of playing volleyball moments after trying to summon a fairy to take you away to a magical world.

Izzy smiled and shook her head. "Thanks, but I'll meet you guys in the dining hall."

The girl shrugged and left.

Hen picked her backpack up off the ground and swung it over one shoulder. "I've got to go too. Our cabin's last activity today is fire building, and I've got to show them how to do it. Yesterday, our activities counselor couldn't get one going. Not even with a bow drill!"

Izzy laughed. When it came to fire, her little sister could teach a college course. Their parents had to check her duffel bag three times for smuggled fireworks before they dropped them off. The fireworks were pretty tame—Crackle Caps and Fizzy Twirlers—and Hen was always super careful. But the camp handbook strictly prohibited incendiary devices of any kind.

"OK," said Izzy. "I'll see you after dinner for the marshmallow roast."

She watched her sister sprint back along the trail, her backpack bobbing up and down as she ran. With a sigh, Izzy picked up the rocks Hen left behind and began repairing the towers Larissa had knocked over.

Izzy glanced back in the direction of camp. She could hear the faraway sounds of laughter and happy shouting, but no one was near enough to see her. There was another reason she hadn't wanted to hang out with the girls in her cabin. She didn't belong with them.

Not just because she was awkward or introverted. Because she wasn't even a human.

Izzy was a Changeling.

She'd discovered this during the last few days of her journey in Faerie. It had come as a complete shock. Even now, the thought that she was a shape-shifting fairy switched at birth with a human baby sounded so crazy that Izzy could hardly believe it wasn't a bedtime story she'd made up for her little sister.

Izzy shut her eyes. She knew she had the ability to Change into a fox, a mouse, and a blackbird. She'd done it before but without fully realizing what she was doing. When Izzy returned to Earth, she had promised Good Peter she wouldn't Change. It was a promise she'd tried to break almost immediately. She was trying to break it now.

Izzy took a deep breath. She imagined herself as a fox, tail swishing, ears twitching, shiny black nose pointed to the sky. She imagined the breeze tickling her stiff whiskers and parting the fur down her back.

But when she looked down, hoping to see paws, she saw her own hands. She had no fur, no whiskers. She wasn't a fox. Just her plain, ordinary self.

Izzy let a slow puff of air out the side of her mouth. Despite trying almost every day, she hadn't Changed into anything since she'd been home. For some reason, Changing just wouldn't come to her. The more she tried, the more she felt like that part of her was all just make-believe.

Another bugle song blasted out from camp. Izzy slowly got to her feet. Time to get ready for another delicious meal of sloppy joes and canned beans.

A draft of air ruffled the leaves overhead. They swished against each other like sheets of tissue paper. The sound made the hairs on the back of Izzy's neck prickle. The wind stilled, but the shuffling noise remained. Izzy stood frozen. The noise didn't come from the treetops. It was somewhere in front of her on the ground.

Someone was coming closer. It couldn't be a camper. Those

girls crashed through the woods like elephants. Whoever was coming took slow, careful steps, like they didn't want to be heard.

"Who's there?" Izzy asked, her voice sounding higher than normal.

The steps shuffled closer. Izzy heard a wet snorting sound.

Adrenaline and memory rushed over her like a wave. The sound was unmistakable.

Izzy still dreamed of them. No, not dreams. Nightmares.

Unglers.

STUCK

THE UNGLERS WERE MONSTERS—EYELESS, boar-faced beasts that Morvanna had bred to hunt down Changelings. But they couldn't be here. This was Earth, not Faerie.

Izzy held still. She tried to listen over the sound of her own heart beating in her ears. Ahead, the undergrowth along the hiking trail parted.

Four bony gray fingers tapped along the ground.

Izzy turned and bolted. Behind her, a piercing squeal rang out. She tore down the trail, swerving as the path curled through the trees. She didn't dare slow down to look over her shoulder, but she heard the sickening thud of the Unglers vaulting themselves forward on knobby hands.

"Help!" screamed Izzy. "Someone! Help me!"

Ahead, she glimpsed the cabins through the trees. She was close now. She could make it.

Izzy burst out of the woods into the sunlight. She ran

across the grass, past a group of girls in brightly colored camp T-shirts, straight into the arms of the camp director.

Miss Madrone dropped her walkie-talkie and stumbled backward. "What on Earth? Doyle, what's gotten into you?"

"In the woods!" panted Izzy. "It's these—creatures!"

Miss Madrone held Izzy by the shoulders. "Hon, you've got to calm down!"

Izzy gasped for breath. "Please...we've got to...get everyone out!"

The campers standing nearby looked frightened. Some whimpered and huddled together, and others looked confused.

"Go!" Izzy shouted at them. "Run!"

The younger girls screamed and ran to their cabins. Frantic squealing and snorting came out of the woods, and the branches of the trees broke apart. Izzy clutched Miss Madrone's arm.

Four rangy pigs with gray and brown spots ambled out into the sunshine.

"What?" gasped Izzy. "No...it can't be."

Gasps rippled through the crowd of campers, followed by giggles and then full belly laughter.

"Girls, girls! Calm down!" Miss Madrone blew her whistle and clapped her hands. "Hi-ho, girls, hi-ho! Or I'll take points away from your cabins!" She extracted her arm from Izzy's grip. "Didn't you read your handbook, Doyle? Camp Kitterpines has a feral pig problem. This is why we've got to keep all food strictly in the dining hall. Someone's obviously been breaking that rule. Now we've got to corral those pigs and get them out of here before they poop all over the tennis courts! Hobson! Bennett! Come on, ladies, you're on pig duty!"

Miss Madrone and the junior counselors waddled after the pigs, shooing them down the gravelly road that ran through camp.

Izzy stood bent over with her hands on her knees, keenly aware that two-thirds of Camp Kitterpines was staring at her. She would not look up. She would just wait until all the girls went away to archery or papier-mâché or whatever activities they were wonderfully good at.

She heard the noise of jangling plastic and saw her sister's rainbow-laced tennis shoes standing on the grass in front of her.

Hen's face was smeared with black ashes. She held a bow drill in one hand and a brown cardboard box in the other.

"Hey, are you OK? I just passed Miss Madrone, and she said you were really upset."

Izzy looked at the scattered pig tracks leading out of the forest. There was no way she had confused pigs with Unglers. Unless she'd been thinking about Faerie so much that it was making her hallucinate. But those horrid gray fingers. She did not imagine them.

Hen looked at her worriedly. "What's wrong?"

Izzy knew if she said what she was thinking, Hen would go berserk and make an even bigger scene.

"It's nothing. I'm fine," said Izzy.

"Miss Madrone asked me if our family read the camp handbook." Hen shifted her backpack straps and looked over her shoulder. "You don't think she's going to search our bunks, do you? Like, for counter bands?"

"Contraband," corrected Izzy. She raised one eyebrow at her sister. "Why? What are you hiding?"

"What, me? Nothing." Hen scratched a streak of ash off her nose and held out the package. "Here, Mom and Dad sent this to us. Half's for you. They said they got your letter."

Izzy took the package and looked inside. It was a plastic bag of double-chocolate sandwich cookies, way beyond half-eaten. "But I didn't send them a letter."

Hen shrugged. "Whatever you did, do it again so they'll send more snacks."

Izzy slid the letter out of the box before handing it back to Hen. "You can have the rest of the cookies. But you better eat them in the dining hall, or Miss Madrone will have a fit."

Hen skipped off across the grass with the box tucked under her arm.

Izzy sniffed the letter from her parents, hoping to catch the scent of her mother's perfume, but the paper just smelled like chocolate cookies. The letter said Bangkok was wonderful, the resort was gorgeous, and they'd bring the girls presents from the markets. They said they were so glad to get Izzy's letter and hear what a fantastic time she was having at camp, and they were happy that she was making friends. Izzy hadn't written them any such thing.

She crumpled the letter into a ball and threw it in the trash can. "Now who's the crazy one?"

Back in her cabin, Izzy locked herself in the bathroom. She heard the bugle call for dinner, followed by the laughter and chatter of girls as they passed her cabin on their way back from the lake. She heard one of them say, "Can you *believe* she did that?" And another: "No kidding. She's crazy!" The others broke into peals of laughter.

Izzy knew who they were talking about. She grimaced at her reflection in the rust-edged mirror. Maybe she was going crazy. But if the alternative was that there actually were Unglers in the forest, then Izzy would rather be crazy.

Tennis shoes thudded up the porch steps and into the cabin. The bathroom doorknob rattled, making Izzy jump back from the sink.

"Hey, who's in there? I need to get ready for dinner!" It was Larissa. "Quit hogging the bathroom!"

If Izzy could have Changed, she would have turned into a blackbird and flown away. Maybe if she flew far or fast enough, she could zip right out of this stupid world and into another one.

The door rattled again. Izzy looked into the mirror and

narrowed her eyes at her reflection. Just because she couldn't Change didn't mean she was completely out of tricks.

It was a big risk for Izzy to use any of her powers in front of people. If anyone caught her, there would be questions she couldn't answer without sounding even more crazy. But Izzy knew she could pull this trick off. And Larissa had it coming.

The bathroom door jerked open, and Larissa staggered backward.

"Oh, Miss—Miss Madrone!" Larissa stammered. "I didn't know you were in there!"

Miss Madrone scowled down at Larissa.

Of course, it wasn't Miss Madrone at all. It was Izzy, doing a dead-on Likeness of the camp director. A Likeness was different from a true Change. Compared with Changing, it was a thin and temporary disguise, like pulling on a mask. But for some reason, even though Izzy couldn't Change, she could do a Likeness with the best of them.

The Likeness of Miss Madrone whipped out a pad of paper and a stubby golf pencil from one of her vest pockets. "Larissa, your rudeness has earned your cabin five demerits."

The other girls groaned.

Larissa gaped in shock. She'd probably never gotten a demerit in her life. "But, Miss Madrone, that's not fair!"

Izzy pointed the golf pencil straight at Larissa's nose. "Talking back, are we? Now you've got cafeteria cleanup duty, young lady."

Larissa's lip quivered. "But it's sloppy joes tonight," she whimpered.

Izzy nearly started laughing, which would have been a disaster. You had to concentrate to hold on to a Likeness. Breaking into giggles was one sure way to lose it.

She straightened her spine and jammed the pencil back into her pocket. "I don't want to hear one word about it, or you'll have it tomorrow too. Now you girls get on down to the dining hall. Double time! Hi-ho, hi-ho!"

She clapped her hands, and all the girls fled the cabin, running across the field to the dining hall.

Izzy shut herself back in the bathroom. She slid down the door and fell into giggles, while the Likeness of Miss Madrone faded away.

If only the Changelings could be there to share in her triumph. Selden would especially enjoy seeing Larissa get what she deserved. Izzy stood up and leaned over the sink. The reflection in the mirror was her own again: round-eared, human-looking Izzy. Hadn't Alice found a way back to Wonderland by going through the looking glass? Izzy poked a finger at the cheap mirror. It didn't budge. She leaned her elbows on the counter and let her forehead thump against the glass.

She was a fairy who couldn't find her way back to Faerie.

She was a Changeling who couldn't Change.

In every way that mattered, Izzy was Stuck.

COLLECTING SPECIES

LARISSA CRUNCHED THE STRAIGHT pin into the beetle's iridescent shell. Pale yellow liquid oozed out of its back onto the foam collection board.

Izzy turned away so she didn't have to watch the beetle's legs pedal helplessly. "Do we really have to do this?"

Larissa finished pressing the pin into the board and reached into her collection jar for another specimen. "Why did I have to get teamed up with the one girl in our cabin who's afraid of bugs?" she grumbled.

"I'm not afraid of bugs," said Izzy. "I just don't like skewering them alive. It seems cruel. Besides, should we be doing this? I mean, what if we accidentally kill an endangered species or something?"

Larissa rolled her eyes so hard that it made her lids twitch. "There are hundreds of species of beetles in Tennessee. They're the most common insect in the world, which is why I picked them for this nature collection project. It was supposed to be easy, but I didn't think I'd have to do everything *by myself*."

"Fine, I'll go look," said Izzy, standing up and brushing off her knees. "But I'm bringing back one that's already dead."

"Oh sure," said Larissa sweetly. "You'll find lots if you look under fallen logs. Of course, you'll have to go into the woods for that." She pushed the tip of her nose up with her finger and snorted.

Izzy pretended not to hear. She'd tried to forget all about the pig incident. It would have been easier if it hadn't been the one thing all the campers kept talking about. That afternoon at lunch, Larissa had held up her ham sandwich and shrieked, "It's after me, it's after me!" Everyone got a good laugh at that one.

"I'll be back," said Izzy. "With beetles."

She crossed the grassy field in front of their cabin, past the girls swishing rackets on the tennis courts, and up to the trailhead that led into the woods. Knowing Larissa was watching her, Izzy strode casually onto the trail. But once she reached the shade of the forest, she paused.

The air smelled different today, greener and sweet. And the woods were quieter than she remembered.

Izzy's heartbeat started to speed up. If she really had seen Unglers yesterday, then the counselors would find her half-chewed corpse on the trail, and at least everyone would know she had been telling the truth. But if Izzy really had just imagined them, then she needed to get over it. She couldn't spend the rest of the summer being the butt of Larissa's pig jokes.

Izzy squared her shoulders and kept walking. She'd only gone a few yards into the forest when she heard the thwack of a ball against a tennis racket behind her. Someone on the courts shouted, "Aw, shoot!"

A lime-green tennis ball bounced over Izzy's shoulder and rolled to a stop a few feet ahead of her.

Izzy exhaled. She was saved. Those girls needed their ball. She could go back out to the safety of the sunshine—not because she was afraid but because she was being helpful.

"I'll get it!" she called over her shoulder.

Izzy walked up to the ball. She must have accidentally flicked it when she bent to pick it up, because it rolled off the trail and came to a stop against the trunk of an oak tree.

She followed the ball. As she tried to grab it again, it rolled out of reach and wound around the other side of the trunk. Izzy stared at the ball, then looked into the trees, listening for any sound of snorting. But all she heard was Larissa yelling for her to hurry up.

Izzy lunged forward and swooped for the ball. Just as her fingers grazed the neon fuzz, the ball hopped over a tree root and rolled deeper into the woods.

She held her breath. This time, she did hear something, but it wasn't snuffling or snorting. At first, she thought it was a bird call. When she recognized what it was, her heart started fluttering like a moth caught in a jar.

It was the quick, cheerful notes of a flute.

Izzy squeezed her fingers into her palms and made the same wish she'd wished for nine solid months. Then she ran after the ball. It rolled and skipped over the undergrowth, always just out of her reach. The flute played on, faster and faster. No longer afraid, she laughed as it led her farther from the trail, farther from Camp Kitterpines. Izzy knew this flute.

The same instrument had been playing the day Hen was taken into Faerie, but it had played a different melody then. This time, the flute played a happy tune to match the soaring feeling filling Izzy's chest.

The tennis ball rocked to a stop in a fluffy patch of ferns. A slender man with raven hair and long, pointed ears stood in the patch of sunshine. He lowered the flute from his lips and nodded politely.

"Hello, Izzy."

Izzy rushed up to him but stopped just short of hugging him.

The Pied Piper was not one for hugs.

THE ROAD BACK

IZZY ONCE LOOKED UP the word *pied* in the dictionary. She had laughed when she read that it meant "multicolored" or "patchwork." The Piper—or Good Peter, as she and the Changelings called him—wouldn't be caught dead in a patchwork suit.

Peter had always reminded Izzy of a classy actor from the old black-and-white movies her mom loved to watch: never a hair out of place, always ready with something witty to say. Today, he wore a perfectly tailored silk jacket the color of a ripe blackberry.

"Peter, what are you doing here?" blurted Izzy.

Peter tucked his flute into his jacket pocket. "You are always shouting questions at me. Don't I even get a 'good afternoon' first?"

"I'm sorry," said Izzy. "It's just that I—well, I can't believe you're really here!"

Peter showed Izzy a flat stone he held in his palm. It was one of the rocks she and Hen had used to make their towers the day before. "I saw your message."

"But we've been leaving those towers all around my house for months. I was sure you'd find us there, not here in the middle of nowhere, USA."

Peter tossed the rock over his shoulder. "On the contrary, there are quite a few very ancient fairy roads that run through these woods. If I remember correctly, the Crockett homestead is just a mile north of here." Peter sighed. "Those were the days. Humans were so preoccupied with surviving the winter and not getting eaten by wild animals. I could snap up their children and swap them for Changelings with hardly any effort at all."

"Hold on," said Izzy. "Are you saying Davy Crockett was really a *Changeling*?"

Peter looked at her like she'd asked if the Earth was round. "He killed a bear when he was only three, didn't he? What did you think he was?"

He had a point. Izzy wondered what other famous people from her history books were really Changelings, switched at birth by the Piper. But she put that thought aside. She had more important questions.

"Please tell me you've finally, finally come to take us back to Faerie for a visit!"

Peter smiled. "That is precisely my errand."

Izzy felt like her little sister, bouncing on her toes. "You've got no idea how badly I wanted to hear that!" She stopped, reality rooting her back to the ground. "But wait—what are we going to tell the camp counselors?"

"I've already begun all the arrangements." Peter took one step to the side. "Meet my colleague, Mr. Smudge."

Izzy hadn't realized they weren't alone. A small man no higher than her waist with his hair drawn back in a ponytail bowed to her.

"Good afternoon, miss," he said in a crisp, professional tone.

"Oh, good afternoon," said Izzy, bowing in return.

"Smudge, you have all the documents in order, I presume?" Peter asked him.

Smudge held up a packet of envelopes in his ink-stained fingers. "I have prepared all the necessary papers as you requested."

Peter took the packet from Smudge and slid out one of the envelopes. He handed it to Izzy. She took out the sheet of paper inside and read it to herself.

It was a letter from her parents addressed to Miss Madrone saying that they were pulling Izzy out of camp immediately so she could attend psychological therapy for her intense fear of pigs. Her parents had both signed it, and there was an accompanying note from her pediatrician back in Everton.

Izzy flipped the paper over in wonder. "But how did you get Mom and Dad to write this?"

Peter took the letter from Izzy and handed it back to his colleague. "Smudge here is a Scriber, an elf trained in the high art of forgery. We had to raid your house for a writing sample, but the rest was easy."

Izzy looked down at Smudge. "You've already been sending them letters from us, haven't you?"

Smudge smiled proudly and handed Izzy a different packet of envelopes.

These were all addressed to her parents at their resort: half from Izzy, half from Hen. They were perfectly written in each girl's handwriting, detailing how much fun they were having at camp and all the wonderful friends they were making. The elf had even smeared some peanut butter on a few of Hen's letters.

"Nice touch," said Izzy, handing the packet back to Smudge.

Peter looked down at the letters and chuckled. "You know, this postal service of yours really is extraordinary. You put a little stamp on anything, and you can send it anywhere in the world. It's actually quite magical if you think about it." He adjusted his jacket cuffs and cleared his throat. "Now, Smudge will stay behind to remove your things from your cabin. Over the next few weeks, he'll post these letters and intercept any real correspondence from your parents so there is no confusion." Peter tapped the panel of his jacket, where he'd stored his flute. "I've taken care of the Madrone woman and her junior counselors. We shouldn't have any problems with them doubting any part of our plan."

On Earth, Peter's flute could play some useful tricks on the minds of humans. He had a certain song he played for human families whose babies he switched with Changelings. It helped keep them from being so suspicious of the little strangers in their cribs. It was also how he'd managed to deal with Izzy's parents when she and Hen returned from Faerie after being gone for a week. Their mom and dad had never asked a single question.

Izzy couldn't stop the giant smile from spreading across her face. "This is amazing! I can't believe you're here and we're actually about to go back to Faerie. If you wait here, I'll go find Hen. It might take me a minute, because I think she's all the way on the archery field…"

Peter held her back by the arm. "I'm afraid there isn't time. We have to leave right away."

Peter's face was composed as it always was, but underneath, Izzy caught the slightest ruffle of anxiety.

"Right now? But not without Hen. I can't leave her behind."

Peter tugged down on the hem of his jacket. "We'll arrange a trip for your sister another time, I promise. Besides, she's having a good time at camp, isn't she? Don't spoil it for her."

Izzy frowned and looked over her shoulder. True, Hen loved camp, but she would love sitting in an empty warehouse as long as she got to eat sloppy joes every night. Izzy knew her little sister would be devastated if she ever found out that Izzy had gone to Faerie without her.

Peter had already turned and started walking deeper into the woods. "I'm in a hurry to get back," he called over his shoulder. "If you want to come at all, you've got to come now."

"Go on, miss," said Smudge with a short nod in Peter's direction. "I'll take care of the logistics, and no one will ever be the wiser."

Izzy felt pulled both ways. But she'd been waiting for this chance too long to let it slip past her now. Before she ran to follow Peter, she turned back to Smudge.

"If you can figure out a way to send Hen more cookies from our parents, that would be really nice of you."

Smudge winked. "Good as done." He tucked the envelopes under his shirt and trotted in the other direction, toward camp.

Izzy raced after Peter. "Wait for me, I'm coming!"

Peter paused to let her catch up to him before continuing on. Izzy struggled to match his pace. He wove through the trees, somehow not once snagging his nice clothes on any briars. He led Izzy on a twisting route, clearly knowing where he was going even though Izzy couldn't see any symbols marking their path.

"You told Hen and me not to go looking for a way back," said Izzy. "But we tried anyway."

Peter looked down at her out of the corner of his eye. "I suspected you would. I suppose you broke your other promise not to Change?"

Izzy twisted the hem of her T-shirt. "I haven't Changed at

all since I've been home," she said, which technically was the truth. "I just wanted to go back to Faerie. But I could never figure out how to get there."

"You just didn't know what you were looking for," said Peter. "Ah, here we are."

He stopped so suddenly that Izzy nearly slammed into him. She looked around. This part of the forest looked no different from every other part they had just tramped through.

She tilted her head up at him. "Where? I don't see anything."

Peter took his flute out and played three long notes. He motioned for her to stand near his shoulder. Bending down slightly, he pointed one finger straight ahead. "Right there. You see?"

Izzy followed his gaze. "Holy moly," she whispered.

It was the strangest optical illusion Izzy had ever seen. It looked like the forest had been painted onto panels, like scenery in a theater. A moment before, she had been in the audience. Now it was like she had stepped onstage, into the wings, and could see the scenery for what it really was.

Between the "panels," a square opening was cut into the ground. Polished stone steps led down into darkness and out of sight.

Izzy shook her head in awe. "And all this time, I've been looking down muddy holes."

"I don't do holes," said Peter. He held out his hand and led Izzy toward the steps. "Go slowly. The stone is quite worn."

Izzy took it slow, careful not to slip on the stairs' rounded edges. The steps must have been climbed by hundreds of thousands of feet to be polished so smooth. But for now, Izzy and Peter were the only ones. The passage was still and silent inside. Izzy counted thirty steps before they reached the bottom. A hallway stretched out ahead into complete darkness. Izzy followed Peter as he started walking down the hall. It was cooler farther in but not damp. She could hear her breath echoing softly off stone walls to either side.

Peter didn't play his flute but held it out in front of him like a torch. As they walked on, lanterns set in the walls flared alight, putting themselves out once Peter and Izzy walked past. Farther in, the passage grew larger, wide enough that a car could have driven down it. A line running down the center gave the impression that once upon a time, there must have been traffic going in both directions.

Every so often, they passed other halls that branched off from both sides of the main corridor. Most of the halls were unmarked, but some had words carved over the entrances: *Bavaria, Ayutthaya, Shenandoah.*

"This is pretty different from the last time I came through," she whispered.

Back then, Izzy had slid on her bottom down a narrow dirt tunnel, terrified of what might be at the end. Even though she knew what to expect this time, her heart was still drumming against her ribs.

"This is a proper fairy road," said Peter. "Part of the original network of passageways built between Faerie and Earth when they first separated. The hole you wriggled down was a back door, the equivalent of a drainage ditch designed to keep the main roads from flooding when it rains. It's a good thing you went that way though. If you'd found your way into one of these passages, you'd certainly have gotten lost." Peter stopped walking abruptly and waved his arm in front of them. "And then there's the matter of these troublesome cave-ins."

Up ahead, the walls on either side of the passageway had collapsed in on each other. A pile of broken stone blocked the way, floor to ceiling.

Peter sighed, annoyed. "These roads are so old. They're in desperate need of repair. When I have time, I try to come down and shore them up. But since hardly anyone but me travels between our worlds anymore, it doesn't seem worth the effort of keeping things maintained."

Izzy looked up at the enormous pile of rock. It would take a construction crew weeks to move that much material out of the way.

She was just about to ask if they had to turn around when Peter held his flute to his lips. A train of slow, rising notes filled the hall. Peter repeated them over and over, picking up the tempo each time. The stones on the pile began to tremble and shift.

Izzy stepped back and covered her ears. The rocks scraped and crunched against one another as they floated back into place. It was all very smooth and orderly. The stones snapped back into the walls and ceiling, like they just needed a reminder of where they were supposed to be. The whole thing took less than a minute. Even the rock dust swirling in the air settled right where it should be.

Peter lowered his flute and continued walking, as if clearing fifty tons of granite was something he did every day.

Izzy hung back. It'd been a long time since she'd seen fairy magic. She forgot how impressive it was. And how easy. A rockslide couldn't stop Peter. So what had taken him so long to come find her?

"I was waiting for you," blurted Izzy. She hadn't meant to sound upset, but her voice crackled bitterly.

Peter stopped and turned around. He looked confused at her sudden change in mood. "Now please don't be—"

"Almost every day," Izzy interrupted. "I went out into the woods after school, thinking that was the day you were going to come. But you didn't. No one did. We thought Marian would come back at least. She told us she loved us, but obviously, she didn't. She forgot us."

Marian Malloy, Izzy's neighbor, had been her grandmother's best friend and Izzy's first guide into Faerie. The girls had begun to think of her as an adopted grandparent. Hen had taken Marian's disappearance especially hard, running down the road every other day to see if the old woman had returned to her house.

Peter folded his hands over his flute. "Now don't start blaming Marian. She wanted to go back and see you, but she can't. She can't go back to Earth again, Izzy."

"What? Why?"

Peter sighed. "Always questions with you." He glanced nervously over his shoulder at the way they had come. "It's a long story I really don't have time to go over at the moment."

Izzy folded her arms in front of her. "We can walk while you talk."

"Oh, very well then." Peter rolled a shoulder forward, motioning for Izzy to follow him. He walked on, tapping his flute against his knuckles. Finally, he said, "Managing the Exchange is quite a bit of work. Tedious things that no one appreciates. Everyone thinks it's all about playing a little tune on my flute and skipping into the forest with a child at my heels. But it's a tremendous responsibility. I make my selections with great care. I have to be sure that the human families I send the Changelings into will be good matches for them. I usually make the right choice, but it's impossible to be accurate all the time."

Izzy nodded, thinking about her friends: Selden, Lug, and Dree. All of them had been rejected by their human families.

She started to ask what that had to do with Marian before remembering that Marian was a Changeling herself. The old woman had gone to Earth many years before and had lived most of her life in the human world.

Peter continued. "Likewise, once I bring human children into Faerie, I have to make sure they get adopted by good fairy families. That part of the arrangement is trickier." He fell quiet for a moment. His mouth twisted on one side, then the other, like he was wrestling with some private thought. He glanced at Izzy, cleared his throat, and kept going. "Humans have a reputation for being hard workers, and there are some fairies who think that when they adopt one, they're getting a free servant. They think they'll be able to kick their feet up the rest of their lives. What they don't realize is that humans are too independent to abide by that sort of treatment. Some humans also have quite a capacity for vengefulness."

They passed an open hall, and a puff of cool air blew onto Izzy. She shivered.

"I've had more than a handful of humans run away from their fairy families over the years," said Peter. "Some of them find new homes on their own or make their lives elsewhere in Faerie. But some grow bitter. They head north, into the lawless Norlorn Mountains. They learn magic. They become—"

"Witches," whispered Izzy.

"Indeed. Humans have no innate magic of their own, but they have a keen skill for learning fairy magic and turning it to their own uses. Most of the time, the result is fairly harmless—love potions, garden tinctures, and the like. But some learn deep magic. They learn to write their own spells, and they grow very powerful. In the early days, it was quite a problem.

Witches took their new knowledge back to Earth. They had too much power over their fellow humans, who had no magic to fight them. There were plagues and wars, and other humans burned anyone they thought was a witch. Those were dark, dark days that nearly destroyed both our worlds."

Peter tapped his chest with his flute. "It took help from both sides to finally subdue the witches. We burned their spell books and scattered the ashes. But we knew we had to prevent such a thing from ever happening again.

"So I set a ban on all the fairy roads, big and small. If a witch sets foot on the paths between the worlds, that path will close up. With them inside."

Izzy suddenly felt very claustrophobic, like she could sense the millions of tons of rock surrounding her. She quickened her pace.

"But Marian isn't a real witch," she said. "She's a Changeling, not a human."

"She's not technically a witch, no. But she performs magic that isn't her own. And she's been learning more spells while you've been gone. It would be too great a risk for her to chance it."

"Will I get to see her?" asked Izzy.

"Yes," said Peter cautiously. "But not right away. She's very busy. You know Marian. Always working on some project or other."

"So Marian can't go back to Earth," said Izzy. "But that doesn't explain why you never came to see me. You could've come anytime."

Peter ran a finger along the inside of his collar. "I've been so busy—busier than I have been in centuries. Besides, I thought I should give you some time to settle back in the place you belong. It was your decision to go back to Earth, after all."

"I know, and I'm glad I decided to go back. I wanted to stay with my family. With Hen." Izzy felt another pang of guilt for leaving her sister behind at camp. She dragged her fingers along the cold stone wall beside her. "But the place I belong? I'm not sure that's on Earth."

"Well, take comfort then. You're about to leave it behind. At least for a little while."

Peter took a sudden turn into the dark archway on their left. At the end of a short hall, a shimmering puddle of green liquid threw dappled beams up onto the stone walls. When Izzy's eyes adjusted to the brightness, she realized the puddle was actually light, shining up through a square opening cut into the floor.

She stood beside Peter and leaned over the opening. Dizziness overtook her, and she clutched his sleeve to keep from falling in. On the other side of the hole, the trees of a lush forest swayed far below them.

Or was it far above? It was all very confusing. Everything on the other side was upside down.

"Is this normal?" whispered Izzy.

"Every doorway into Faerie opens at a different angle," said Peter, bending down and placing his hands on the edge of the hole. "Now this part is just a little tricky. It helps if you hold your breath."

That wasn't a problem. Izzy was hardly breathing anyway. She watched as Peter swung himself over the lip of the opening and flipped into the green light.

She heard his voice from the other side, but his words were too muffled to understand. He sounded even more annoyed than usual. And then she caught the sound of other voices. Her heart skipped a beat when she recognized them.

The sleek silhouette of a cat's head appeared over the opening. Its long tail swished back and forth. The cat spoke with a girl's voice.

"It's just like you to be sneaking around, hiding in holes."

A wolf with thick black fur joined the cat. "What do you think, Dree? Should we leave her down there?"

"Make room!" called a booming, kind voice, and the head of a large bear appeared, blocking out the light. Lug's smile stretched the whole length of his face. "Dearest Izzy! Get up here this moment!"

He reached his furry arms through the opening. Izzy grabbed his paws. In one swooping motion, Lug pulled her down—or up, she couldn't tell which was which—headfirst into Faerie.

5

REUNIONS

Izzy wondered if it were possible to be hugged to death. "Lug…" she stammered. "Hey…I can't breathe!"

Lug eased up and held her out at arms' length. "Sorry, forgot about all this fur!" He waggled his shoulders and Changed from a bear into his normal form, which wasn't much smaller and almost as furry. "There we go. Now where were we?" He smooshed Izzy into another embrace.

Izzy had never quite figured out what Lug was. Unlike the other Changelings, he didn't look like a child in his normal form. He was some mix of boy and beast, with a wide face covered in dark-brown fuzz and a black furry stripe across his eyes like a raccoon. Like all fairies, he had pointed ears.

"My word, Izzy, we have missed you!" he said.

Izzy laughed and patted his hairy arms. "It's OK. I missed you too." She took a step back to get a better look at him and nearly stepped right into the hole he had pulled her out of.

"Careful!" said Lug, grabbing her by the elbow. "Don't want to break an ankle your first day back in Faerie, do you?"

Back in Faerie.

Izzy took a deep breath and looked around. All her senses felt sharper, like she'd been living the past nine months on a flat page and someone had suddenly folded her into shape. This was the Edgewood, the sprawling forest that covered the eastern border of Faerie. She'd been gone so long, she had forgotten the scale of things. The trees around Camp Kitterpines looked like saplings compared with the massive ones that towered overhead, filling her whole view with green.

Dree Changed into her girl form and pushed Lug aside. "All right, all right, we know you're cuddly, Lug, but quit hogging her."

Dree gave Izzy a tight but brief squeeze. She wasn't as affectionate as Lug, but then again, not many people were. She stood back from Izzy and smiled, her eyes shimmering in the sunlight. When Dree was in her girl form, she was translucent. Izzy could see through her body as if she were made of cloudy glass.

"I bet I've missed you more than anyone," Dree said to Izzy. "I've had to put up with these smelly boys all by myself."

Lug dipped his head and sniffed his armpit. "I know you're not talking about me. I rolled in a rosemary bush just this morning."

Selden hung back in his boy form, running his fingers through his twisty black hair. He wore his shirtsleeves pushed up past his elbows. His dark-brown arms were covered in scratches and scars, probably from climbing trees. A look of mischief glinted in his dark eyes.

Izzy walked up to him. "Hi. You got taller."

Selden grinned and shoved his hands in his pockets. "Can't say the same for you, shrimp. Don't they feed you anything on Earth?"

Izzy tried to push him in the shoulder, but he side-stepped her and flicked her on the forehead. Still the same old Selden.

"What are you all doing here?" she asked. "Peter didn't say you guys were coming to meet me."

"It's a surprise for both of us," said Peter. He stood a few yards away with his arms folded, glaring at Selden. Peter was almost always annoyed about something, but this time, he looked genuinely angry. "I told you to wait for me to bring her back," he snapped.

"Why am I the one you always get mad at?" asked Selden.

"Because you're the one I left in charge."

Selden nodded importantly. "Yes, and as the one in charge, I made the decision that we needed to bring Izzy these."

He reached into a cloth bag slung over his shoulder and pulled out a pair of worn leather boots with brass buckles on the sides.

"My boots!" Izzy reached out for the familiar brown leather. "You kept them?"

"I knew you'd come back wearing useless shoes," said Selden, nodding down at Izzy's sneakers.

Izzy smiled as she sat down and unlaced her shoes. She slipped into the boots and wriggled her toes inside the soft leather. Selden was a real snob when it came to anything made on Earth, but he was right about shoes at least.

Izzy sprang to her feet and marched in place. "I could walk for miles in these."

"Wonderful," grumbled Peter. "The farthest you'll be walking is a few hundred feet."

"That's it? We're not going to Avhalon?"

"We are." Dree hooked one arm around Izzy's elbow. "Just wait till you see our ride."

"Race you there!" Selden jumped up and arched into a backflip. When he landed, he'd Changed into a sleek black stoat.

"Show-off," said Dree as he scampered ahead through the trees.

Izzy and the others followed, crossing a dry creek bed. Up the other side, taking up most of the room in a wide clearing, sat a huge lumpy basket draped in folds of dark-purple fabric. From a distance, it looked like a giant blackberry pie that had oozed out of its crust.

As they approached the basket, a man with curly brown hair and rosy cheeks popped up from behind the rim, holding a pair of pliers in one hand. It was Tom Diffley.

"Izzy! Bless my bones, it's good to see you!" He leaned over the side to give Izzy a hug.

"Hi, Tom," said Izzy, stretching up on her toes to reach him. She patted the basket. "This must be your latest invention."

"Finished it this spring. I call her the *Muscadine*." Tom caught Peter's angry glare and fiddled with the pliers in his hand. "Sorry about the kids," he said, nodding at Selden and the others. "I didn't know they'd hitched a ride till after we landed. Should've known we were carrying extra weight when we left Avhalon."

Lug rubbed the back of his neck. "Don't be mad at Tom. I did a Likeness of one of the sandbags."

"I got here on my own, thank you kindly," said Dree, Changing into a butterfly with one graceful swoop of her arms.

Peter rubbed the bridge of his nose impatiently. It looked like steam might start coming off the top of his head. "May we proceed already? This was supposed to be a quick trip. Touch down and back up." He lifted up a fold of purple cloth with the end of his flute. "Why are these deflated?"

"You said to be quiet while you were gone, so I turned the pumps off," said Tom. "Don't worry. Won't take a minute to get it all up and running again."

"A minute too long," said Peter.

Tom ignored him and ducked under the sagging fabric. It heaved up and down as he worked some hidden machinery underneath. Tom was a shepherd by trade, but his true passion was for building things. He attributed his skill at invention to the human blood running through his fairy veins.

"Just got to start the pumps up!" he called.

They heard a series of metallic bangs, followed by a rhythmic wheezing and finally the low-pitched whir of gears engaging and taking over. With a loud hiss, the fabric began to billow and puff up with air.

"Is this made from your sheep's wool?" shouted Izzy, pointing at the purple cloth.

"No," Tom answered. "Wool's too heavy. This is Wispworm silk." He grinned. "I had it dyed purple. What can I say? I like the color."

Soon, the silk had filled enough that Izzy could tell there were three separate balloons, each one the size of a school bus. Tubes connected them to a complicated-looking copper contraption in the center of the basket. A tiny glass window in the machinery showed a bright flame flickering inside.

The flame made Izzy think of Hen. It felt wrong and weird to be there without her sister. She wondered if she could beg Peter to go back and get her. But the purple balloons had fully inflated. They tugged impatiently at the ropes that attached them to the basket. Lug and Peter reached up to make sure the rigging didn't tangle while Dree supervised from the air.

Tom settled himself behind a wooden frame he could tilt and pivot in different directions. He checked a few gauges and then called out to Selden. "We're almost ready! Cast off those lines!" Tom pointed to the ropes tethering the ship to the trees around the edges of the clearing.

"Give me a hand, Izzy," said Selden, Changing back into a boy and jogging down the length of one of the ropes. "You get that line over there while I get these two."

Izzy circled around the basket, following one of the tethers to where it was tied to a tree trunk. She pulled the rope in and clamped it under her arm to give herself some slack to work with while she untied the knot. As she freed the last loop, she glanced up into the bushes.

A face stared out at her.

Izzy gasped and fell onto the ground on her back. She propped herself up on one elbow and looked again. The face was mostly hidden by leaves, but she could clearly see a pair of unblinking green eyes watching her.

"Hey, you guys?" Izzy's voice was drowned out by the hiss and thrum of the *Muscadine*'s machinery.

The eyes blinked once, but the face didn't move. Cautiously, Izzy reached out for a long stick lying near her foot. She picked it up and held it pointed in front of her.

"Who-who's there?" she asked.

"Izzy? Are you all right?" Peter called out behind her.

The green eyes shifted in Peter's direction. A rush of air swept over the clearing, fluttering the bushes and sweeping away a scattering of tiny, bright-green leaves.

Peter hurried over to Izzy. He knelt down beside her, his flute ready in his hand. "What is it? What's wrong?"

Izzy jabbed the stick into the bushes, pushing the leaves

aside. Her stick struck a large mossy stone that had been hidden by the branches. What she had thought were eyes watching her were really two round patches of lime-green lichen.

Izzy exhaled. "Sorry, I thought I saw something."

Peter tilted his face. "What was it?"

Izzy hesitated. First Unglers and now a face. Maybe she should say something about her visions. But Peter was already in such a hurry. What if she worried him and he canceled her visit or cut it short?

"No, it was nothing," said Izzy. "Really."

Peter scanned the woods as he helped Izzy to her feet. "Come on. We should go."

They hurried back to the *Muscadine*. The other Changelings were already waiting for them inside the basket.

"All right, Lug," Tom called as Peter helped Izzy climb over the side. "Now for the anchors!"

Lug went to each corner of the *Muscadine* and heaved up the heavy stones that anchored them to the ground. He tipped them over the side easily, as if they were made of foam.

"You can fly with me anytime," said Tom with a smile. "Gave me a backache just watching you."

Three corners of the basket rose up, but the spot where Lug stood stayed pinned to the ground.

"Oh!" Lug chuckled. "I almost forgot."

He shimmied into the form of an overgrown badger with a long stripy tail. He was still large—taller than Izzy when he

43

stood on his hind legs—but it was the smallest form he could Change into. Steadily, the *Muscadine* rose.

"Come on, Izzy. Us too," said Selden, Changing back into a stoat.

Izzy curled her toes under. She'd have to tell her friends about her problem eventually, but she had hoped it wouldn't come up on their first day back together.

"I—about Changing…" Izzy began.

"Hurry it along, please," called Peter.

Izzy swallowed. "There's something—"

"Actually, Izzy, hold up," called Tom, leaning forward to check the gauges above the steering frame. "I need you to stand between Peter and Lug to balance the weight. If we get off balance, the whole basket will tip over. It's something I've still got to work on."

Relieved, Izzy took her place on the other side of the basket.

Selden climbed up onto the rim beside her. "Just wait," he said. "You've never seen anything like this."

"I've flown in a plane before," said Izzy.

Selden huffed. "Trust me. It's better."

Izzy leaned over the side and watched the trees of the Edgewood recede beneath them. Soon, they had risen high enough that she could see the forest stretching out to the east in an endless sea of green.

Tom flipped a switch that powered a fan at the back of the basket, and the wind blew Izzy's hair back. They began coasting west, speeding over the rim of the Edgewood plateau, where the forest abruptly stopped and gave way to miles of flowering meadow.

Dree Changed into a silvery scissor-tailed bird. She flew straight up, then turned and dove back down, spinning, pulling up at the last minute to land gracefully on the lip of the basket.

"Now who's the show-off?" said Selden.

Dree stuck her tongue out the side of her beak.

The *Muscadine* was flying fast now, and the wind whistled in Izzy's ears. But it clearly wasn't fast enough for Good Peter. He looked down, clocking the distance while his black hair whipped around his head. He really must have been in a rush if he didn't care that his hair got tangled.

Dree and Selden wanted to hear all about Izzy's life back home. The three of them crouched against the side of the basket while Izzy told them about her school back in Everton, aware of how mundane it must sound compared with living in a castle in Faerie. But they listened intently, and she did have a few highlights, like winning first place in the science fair.

"You actually *made* a machine that creates light?" asked Dree. "Was it magic?"

"It's called a generator," explained Izzy. "And it's not magic. It's science. I just wound about a million coils of wire around a magnet. I found the instructions on the Internet."

"What kind of net?" asked Selden.

"Never mind." Izzy laughed. "But you don't want to hear about all this. It's so boring. I'm sure it's nothing like all the fun adventures you've been having."

"We haven't had adventures," said Selden. He looked over his shoulder at Peter, then lowered his voice so only Izzy and Dree could hear. "He keeps us on too tight a leash. We're practically prisoners in the castle in Avhalon."

But as he told Izzy what they'd been up to since she left, it didn't sound so much like a prison as paradise. The Changelings had spent the last nine months playing games, throwing parties, swiping pies from the castle kitchens, and generally driving Peter up the wall. Avhalon held a festival or holiday every other week. Some of them sounded familiar, like Day of the Dead and Mayfest, but others she'd never heard of: Lambing Day, Thripplemas, Feisting Feast.

"And in a few more days, it'll be the Summer Solstice," said Dree. "It's one of my favorites."

"You just watch," said Selden. "I bet Peter won't even let us go this year."

Izzy glanced at Peter. "Has he always been so strict with you?"

"He's always been irritable," said Selden. "But this time, something else is going on. I think he's up to something, but I can't figure out what."

"He's been gone more than usual," added Dree. "I think he's having a secret romance, but no one agrees with me."

Selden made a gagging face, then clutched his throat and fell over like he just choked and died.

Dree rolled her eyes and pecked at him with her beak.

Selden revived, wearing a grin of sharp little stoat teeth. "Dree's been reading sappy love stories. They're eating away at her brain."

"They're *novels*." Dree turned to Izzy. "Avhalon's got a good library. You'll appreciate it even if no one else does."

"Look!" called Lug from the other side of the basket. He pointed down over the side. "We're almost there!"

Izzy stood up and leaned over the edge. A heavy wave of memories rolled over her as she looked down onto Avhalon. The island immortalized in the King Arthur legends wasn't an island at all but a city surrounded by rivers. It wasn't even much of a city, more like a country village with a high stone wall enclosing it all the way around.

The elegant white castle in the center of town seemed very out of place among the other rattletrap buildings. It looked too perfect, like something out of a fairy tale. And Izzy had learned all too well that fairy tales were rarely what they seemed in Faerie.

The castle was a recent addition, courtesy of Morvanna. Izzy spotted the tower where the cruel woman had kept the other Changelings prisoner for years before Izzy and Selden had rescued them. The ballroom where they'd fought Morvanna was just below. The windows had all been replaced with new glass, but Izzy knew exactly which one the witch had fallen out of, down to her death on the stones below. She shuddered at the memory.

"Doesn't living in the castle give you guys the creeps?" Izzy asked her friends.

"Peter is sleeping in Morvanna's old room," said Selden. "Talk about nightmares."

"I think he does that because he knows everyone will be too scared to bother him," said Dree loudly.

Peter surely heard her, but he didn't respond. Deep frown lines creased his smooth forehead. "Where the devil are they?" he grumbled, surveying the town below.

"Who are you looking for?" asked Izzy.

"The Watch. I haven't even been gone a whole day, and five of the guards I set up have left their posts." He rubbed the space between his eyebrows with one finger. "This is what three hundred years of peace get you. Laziness."

The heavy whir of the air pumps faded as Tom steered the ship slowly down toward a large open plaza on the eastern side of town. Below, the Avhalonian fairies gathered together to wave up at the *Muscadine*, scattering once they realized it was about to land on top of them.

"Selden, the lines!" Tom shouted.

Selden Changed back into his boy form. He leaped up to the rim of the basket and started reeling in ropes and tossing anchor cables down to fairies waiting on the ground below.

The ship was still six feet from the ground when Peter jumped over the side. Izzy waited until they landed to climb out after him.

"Lufkin!" called Peter. "Where is that lazy excuse for a mayor?"

As Peter stormed across the plaza, a fairy man with deep dimples and a receding hairline hopped toward him on bare feet. The man had been reclining on the ledge of a stone fountain with his toes in the water when they landed, and he left a trail of puddles in his path.

"Peter, you're back!" called Lufkin, holding his arms wide. He wore a too-tight jacket with wilted flowers stuck through the buttonholes. "I wasn't expecting you until nightfall."

"Clearly," said Peter. He watched in disgust as Lufkin squeezed his wet feet into dry shoes. "Where's the Watch? I only saw one guard at the Orchard Gate."

Lufkin pointed to a group of men and women in red uniforms hanging paper lanterns across the street. "Well, we needed help with the Solstice decorations, and they're the only ones with ladders, so…" He cleared his throat and adjusted a bronze medal pinned to his jacket. The word *Constable* was engraved into it. "Now see here, Peter. I'm the elected official, and one of my duties is preparing our fair city for the Solstice Celebration—"

Peter jabbed a finger into Lufkin's sternum. "I elected you, you frivolous fool. And I did it because you said you'd help me restore some order to Avhalon. It's no wonder Morvanna stormed in here and took over the way she did. It would be like taking control of a pile of puff pastries."

"Speaking of that," said Lug. He jumped down from the basket. The *Muscadine* bobbed up again. "Did we miss supper?"

"That's the attitude, my boy!" said Lufkin, slapping Lug on the back. "Now, Peter, don't worry yourself so much. As usual, the Watch haven't seen anything out of the ordinary. If anything, they're bored out of their minds." He clapped his hands overhead and called loudly to the decorating team, "My friends, carry on without me! I'll be dining with these fine—"

Peter stopped Lufkin with another chest jab. "You aren't dining with anyone tonight. You're setting the Watch back in their posts, and you're joining them on the night shift."

Lufkin frowned and walked away muttering something about how sour apples spoil parties.

Selden jumped down from the basket. He gave Peter a sideways look as they crossed the plaza toward the castle entrance. "Why are you so mad about the Watch? What have you got them looking out for?"

"For sneaky Changeling children slipping out of the castle when they've been told to stay put," said Peter. Before he could go on with his lecture, a riotous cry echoed out from the castle doors. Peter grimaced. "The next time I leave, I'm locking everyone in their rooms."

A square brown kite zipped out through the castle doors and glided toward them. It wasn't until it was a yard from

Izzy's face that she realized it was a flying squirrel. The squirrel smacked into her chest and clung to her shirt, then Changed into a little girl with long black pigtails.

"Izzy's back!" she cried.

Fourteen Changelings poured out through the doors like marauders raiding a fortress in reverse. They swarmed around Izzy, hugging her and high-fiving her, something Hen had taught them before she left. The littlest ones tried to climb on her back, switching to Lug when they realized she couldn't hold them all.

"Hi…Olligan! And Hale!… Ow, Sibi, you're pulling my hair." Izzy tried greeting everyone, but they kept Changing, which made it hard to keep track of who was who.

The Changelings talked over each other, asking a hundred questions all at once. They swept her up like a wave, pushing and pulling her through the open doors into the gleaming white halls of the castle.

Izzy had daydreamed of this moment for months. Back in Faerie, back with her friends. It would have been just as perfect as she'd imagined had she not glanced behind her and seen Peter swing the heavy castle doors shut and bolt them with thick iron bars.

Was he trying to keep the Changelings from leaving? Or were the iron bars there to keep someone else from getting inside? But she couldn't give herself much time to worry about it. Fourteen pairs of hands were dragging her through the halls, straight to dinner.

SECRETS

I ZZY'S MEMORIES OF MORVANNA'S castle were of stark, orderly rooms scrubbed as clean as a dentist's office. The entry hall was still bare, but as the Changelings led Izzy up the stairs to the floors where they lived and played, it became obvious that the castle had new and very different masters.

Garlands made of acorn shells and mismatched buttons crisscrossed the windows. Good Peter clearly employed some servants; they'd passed fairy men and women dressed in uniforms on their way in. But either they didn't take their jobs very seriously or they'd just given up on trying to clean up after the wild children under their care. Dirty laundry lay strewn across the stair railings. Most rooms had pillow forts constructed in the corners. One hallway even had a fairly substantial real wooden fort built across it.

Park, a dimple-cheeked boy who could Change into a

raccoon, pointed to the fort. "Rusk and me are making an impenetrable fortress."

"Wow," said Izzy. "A fort within a castle. You'll be extra secure."

Park grinned and wiped his nose with two fingers. They were bound together with a makeshift bandage. With a wink, he Changed into a small rodent with big ears and a long, wiggling nose. "You've got to try out the slide."

He scurried to the top of the fort and rocketed down a tiny slide made from a hammered sheet of tin. "Come on, Izzy! Change into a mouse and give it a try!"

Izzy smiled and cleared her throat. "Well, maybe not right this min—"

"Later, later," said Lug, pushing Izzy gently toward the next room. "First things first, and dinner is always first."

Izzy's mouth watered the moment she stepped into the dining room. She remembered fairy food. And after days of oversalted sloppy joes and dry tuna fish sandwiches, she was ravenous for it.

A long wooden table stretched down the center of the dining room. The castle servants had just finished lighting the candles in the chandelier overhead. Auburn-haired Olligan pulled out a seat for Izzy. Mote and Mite, the twins, hopped into the chair beside her.

"Move over! I want to sit next to Izzy!"

"No, I was here first!"

Hale untangled the boys and took them to seats at the other end of the table. "If you fight over it, you're both going to sit in the other room." She swung her long braid back over her shoulder. "Besides, I want to sit by Izzy, and I'm the oldest."

Hale was fifteen, older even than Dree and Selden. She'd never been Exchanged. Years ago, when it had been her turn to go to Earth, Selden had convinced her to let him go first. Izzy had always assumed Selden had tricked Hale or twisted her arm to get her to switch. But seeing her now with Sibi and Yash in her lap, Izzy wondered if Hale had actually wanted to stay behind. She seemed like she genuinely loved taking care of everyone. Hale was the perfect stand-in for a parent, at least as close as the Changelings would come to having one until they went for the Exchange.

Across the table, a chipmunk poked its head out of the top of Olligan's overalls pocket. Olligan cupped his hands gently around the little animal and set it beside his plate. Izzy waited for it to Change into one of the children before she remembered that Ollie had a special way with animals.

Ollie leaned down so the chipmunk could chatter in his ear. "Yes, I told you, we're about to eat," said Ollie. "Just be patient." Then he made a very high-pitched chirping that must have been a chipmunk joke, because the little animal rolled onto its back squealing.

Yash Changed into a lizard with a collar of sparkling green scales. She climbed up Izzy's chair leg and sprawled across her lap. The twins buzzed back and forth across the table as fat dragonflies. All the younger Changelings were so excited that they Changed from one form to another in rapid succession. Izzy tried to keep track of who was who among the menagerie, but it was overwhelming, like sitting down to dinner with escaped zoo animals from a dozen different zoos.

Hale stood up and clapped her hands. "Hey, hey, where are your manners?" she said loudly. The little ones went quiet under her commanding gaze. "That's better," she said, flipping her braid from one shoulder to the other. "What did we talk about this morning at breakfast? No Changing at the table. Look at Izzy, what good manners she has, staying in her normal form while she waits for the food to come. You could all learn a lesson from her."

Izzy blushed as the other Changelings mumbled apologies and Changed back into children. She was glad when the kitchen door swung open and the servants brought in the food: a golden pie filled with cheese and baked apples, potatoes roasted crispy brown and glittering with salt, crunchy sweet beans from the castle garden, and, for dessert, cups of berry pudding heaped with peaks of whipped cream.

Izzy looked around and realized for the first time that Peter wasn't with them.

"Where did Peter go?" she asked Lug, who had taken the seat to her left.

Lug shrugged as he wiped his mouth with the napkin tied around his neck. "He doesn't ever eat with us for some reason."

Selden leaned back in his chair and kicked his heels onto the table. "See what I mean? He's avoiding us. It's because he's hiding something."

"Peter's always avoided us," said Dree. "And he doesn't eat with us because I don't think he eats at all."

Lug shook his head. "Can you even imagine such a thing?"

No, Izzy couldn't, especially not with food like this. She had second and third helpings. The little ones finished their dinners in less than five minutes and started to squirm in their chairs. Sibi, who climbed like a monkey even when she wasn't in her chocolate-colored monkey form, scaled the back of Izzy's chair and swung down into her lap.

"Izzy, will you show us? Please?"

"Show you what?" asked Izzy.

"You know!" said Phlox.

"Yeah," said Luthia. "Show us a really good one!"

"They're talking about a Likeness," explained Hale. "Selden and I have been teaching them how to do it. He told them how good you are at it, and I think they're a bit in awe of you."

Little Sibi's dark eyes grew wide. "Did you really do a Likeness of Morvanna?" she whispered.

Izzy nodded slowly. "I really did."

"We heard it was so good that it put her under a spell," added Rusk.

Izzy rubbed the back of her neck. "I don't know if it was that good…"

"It was," said Selden, picking salad out of his teeth. "But only because she learned how from me."

Izzy rolled her eyes at him. Selden was the one who'd given her the idea to trick Morvanna with her own Likeness, but he hadn't actually taught her anything. For some reason, Izzy had a natural talent for pretending to be someone else.

"Now don't do anything that will give the little ones nightmares," warned Hale. "Or else they'll all be crawling into my bed tonight."

Yash covered her eyes with her dimpled hands. "I don't want to see a wicked witch!"

Izzy smiled at her. "Don't worry. I don't want to give myself nightmares either. Let me see if I can do someone else." She handed Sibi back to Hale, knocking her fork off the table. "Oops, let me get that. Hold on…"

Izzy knelt down under the table where no one could see her. She took a deep breath and imagined what it would be like to be a very unkempt boy with terrible table manners. When she stood up again, everyone gasped, and their eyes went back and forth between Selden and her. She must have nailed it.

Izzy—who didn't look like Izzy any longer—jumped onto her chair and rifled her fingers through tangled black curls.

"Everyone listen up!" she ordered in her best Selden

impersonation. "All of you are wearing ridiculous shoes! What are you? Humans? Don't make me gag!"

Laughter erupted around the table, and everyone pointed at Selden, who sat with his arms crossed, glaring up at his double. "Oh, come on. I don't sound like that. And I'm taller." He Changed into a leopard and playfully swiped a paw up at Izzy's Likeness of him.

Izzy jumped back and landed on the floor, back in her own form. She could have held onto his Likeness for longer if she hadn't lost her concentration, but it had been good enough to please the table. Izzy bowed as everyone applauded. Dree whistled through her teeth.

"Encore, encore!" called Olligan. "Do another one!"

Izzy shut her eyes. To do a Likeness, she had to feel some connection to the person she was impersonating. It was usually a phrase or a gesture that would help her get into character. She held her chin up high, very snobby, very haughty. No, that wasn't quite doing it. She smoothed her hair back off her forehead and tugged down on imaginary jacket cuffs. That did the trick.

When she opened her eyes and held out her hands, they were pale with long slender fingers. "Whatever are you staring at?" she said, holding her nose in the air just like she'd seen Good Peter do a hundred times. "You children are forever staring at things you know nothing about."

Her Peter Likeness got a standing ovation. Even Selden stood up and gave her the slow clap.

"One more!" shouted Park, wiping tears of laughter from the corners of his eyes.

"Oh yes, please do one more?"

Izzy thought for a minute. She snapped her fingers and whirled around on the ball of one foot. When she stopped, the lacy hem of a dress spun around her, flaring in a wide circle at her knees.

Izzy put her hands on her hips and rolled her eyes. "Don't be a beetle brain. Don't you know all humans are spies?"

Izzy didn't understand why no one was laughing this time. She knew she'd gotten the Likeness of Dree perfectly—she could feel it. But when she looked down at her arms, she realized she hadn't gotten it right all the way. Her skin was opaque, not see-through the way Dree's was.

"Oh, whoops! I guess that was trickier than I thought." Izzy looked up. She lost hold of the Likeness the moment she saw Dree's face.

Dree stared up at her like she'd just been punched in the stomach. Tears shimmered in the corners of her eyes.

Izzy realized she'd just done something very stupid. "Oh, I'm sorry—I didn't mean…"

Dree jumped up, knocking her chair over, and bolted from the room.

Izzy started to follow her, but Lug held onto her arm. "Give her just a minute by herself, dear. Here, have a potato."

Hale cleared her throat and shifted Sibi up onto her

shoulder. "I think the little ones are getting tired. Mote, Mite, you come up with us. You've both got to have baths tonight."

Mote gasped like Hale had suggested electrocution. "But we had one three days ago!"

"No complaining. Come on." Hale Changed into a chestnut-colored horse. The littlest Changelings helped each other onto her back, and she clip-clopped out of the room with them hanging onto her braided mane.

The rest of the Changelings made lunges for the last remaining pudding or started sword fighting with their forks. Ollie and his chipmunk were engaged in a serious conversation about walnuts.

No one said anything about Dree's Likeness to Izzy, but she still felt like sliding down the seat of her chair and hiding under the table. "Ugh, why did I do that?" she groaned.

Selden slid into Hale's empty seat and used his finger to wipe the leftover sauce off her plate. "Don't get too mad at yourself. Dree's pretty sensitive about the way she looks."

"But I love the way she looks," said Izzy. "It's part of what makes her so special."

Lug squeezed Izzy's hand. "We all have our secret little hurts that we hide from everyone else," he said softly. "Even the toughest of us."

Her appetite gone, Izzy rolled a potato around on her plate until the servants came back to clear the dishes. While the others started getting out decks of cards and a chessboard, Izzy slipped out of the dining room. She wandered upstairs, past servants lighting lamps in the dark hallways, and found Hale dragging Mote and Mite into the large tiled bathroom.

"Do you know where my room is supposed to be? The one I'm sharing with Dree?"

Hale pointed the way up another flight of carpeted stairs. "Last door on the left. Boys! If you try to run away again, I'll cut your fingernails too!"

As Izzy climbed the stairs, she heard loud splashes followed by howls. She found the door to her room and knocked.

"Come in," said Dree softly.

Izzy opened the door and pulled it shut behind her. The room was spacious, with a high ceiling and two canopy beds set along one wall. The moonlight streaming in through the tall windows filled the space with a soft silver glow. At first, she didn't see Dree at all. Then she spotted her wavery form, sitting on the floor in a beam of pale light, her arms wrapped around her knees.

"This place is a step up from Yawning Top, isn't it?" said Dree without looking up. "It was hard to get used to such a soft mattress after so many years of living in a tree trunk. Did you know Lug still sleeps on a pile of sticks on the floor?"

Izzy sat down beside her. "Dree, I'm so sorry. I hope you didn't think I was making fun of you back there."

Dree stared at her fingers, flipping them back and forth, in and out of the moonbeam. "I didn't think that at all. I'm not mad at you. It was just seeing myself like that—the way a person's supposed to—" Dree cleared her throat. One corner of her mouth ticked up without making a smile. "You know something funny about me? Whenever I Change into one of my other forms, I'm normal, solid. I've never figured out why…"

They sat in silence for a long moment. When Dree spoke again, her words caught. "What's wrong with me, Izzy?" she whispered. "No one else looks this way."

"Nothing's wrong with you. You're different, but that isn't bad."

Izzy struggled to think of what else to say. Like all Changelings, Dree was an orphan, so there was no way to know if she inherited her ghostliness from her parents. When Dree had gone to Earth for the Exchange, she hadn't been able to make herself look solid. Her "mother" on Earth was afraid of her, and she'd tossed Dree into a river. Dree had survived, of course, but she didn't like to talk about it. It must have been terrible.

Dree put on a stiff version of her usual sarcastic smile. "Sometimes, I wonder if one day I'll just fade away completely. I'll just wake up and not be there. And no one will even notice."

Izzy grabbed Dree's hand. "Don't say that! Of course we'd notice. And besides, that's not going to happen anyway."

Izzy thought about what Lug said at the dinner table, that everyone had their secret hurts. Maybe her friend should know she wasn't alone.

Izzy swallowed. "At least you can Change," she said.

Dree brushed a tear off her glassy cheek. "What do you mean?"

Izzy took a deep breath and let it back out slowly. "I think I might be Stuck."

Dree leaned back and tilted her head. "Stuck? Like in one form? But that's not possible. In the dining room, I just saw you…"

"Oh, I can do a Likeness any day of the week. Just say the word." Izzy smiled, thinking of the trick she pulled on Larissa. "You should've seen what I did in my cabin at camp. But *Changing* is different. I've tried. A lot. And I can't do it."

Dree stared at Izzy long and serious. Being Stuck wasn't something the Changelings took lightly.

"So that's my little secret," said Izzy with a sigh. "I don't belong with humans, but I don't belong with you either. I'm a Changeling who can't Change."

Dree brushed the hair back from her face and blinked her last tear away. "If you can do a Likeness, then you can Change," she said firmly. "You just need some practice, that's all."

"I don't think that's it. I've *been* practicing."

"Not with us you haven't. We'll start tomorrow first thing. You'll do drills every day. Each of us can rotate, taking turns teaching you what we know. By the time you leave Avhalon, you'll be Changing in your sleep. Sound good?"

"It sounds a little like camp."

Dree grinned and nodded. "Yup. Changeling camp."

Dree held her hand up, fingers spread wide in the moonlight. It took Izzy a beat to realize she was waiting for a high five. Izzy gave her one and smiled.

"Hi-ho."

CHANGELING CAMP

"DON'T HOLD YOUR BREATH," said Dree. "Let it flow, in and out."

"And don't shut your eyes so tight," said Selden. "You're trying to Change, not disappear."

"Focus."

"But don't think about it too hard."

"I always find it helps me to wiggle my bottom," said Lug. "Ever so slightly."

Izzy opened her eyes and let out a sigh. "You guys are giving me too much advice. It's confusing."

She stood on a plush carpet in the center of the parlor, across the hall from the dining room. Selden, Lug, and Dree stood in front of her, staring expectantly, like parents trying to get their toddler to take its first steps.

In the room across the hall, Izzy could hear the happy screams of the younger Changelings, who were playing a modified game of tag. Every time someone got tagged, they had to Change into a different form. When they ran out of forms to Change into, that child was it. It was a game Izzy obviously couldn't play, which was why she'd spent the entire morning shut inside the parlor, her friends doing their best to teach her something they could do in their sleep.

"Don't get discouraged," said Lug. "You Changed into your fox form this morning and stayed in it for almost a whole minute. Tiny steps climb mountains, as they say."

Izzy rubbed her knuckles into her eyes. "If I take steps any smaller, I'll start moving backward."

"Lug's right. Any progress is good," said Dree, flopping into one of the parlor chairs.

Dree had been patient so far, but Izzy could tell she was tired. They all were. It didn't help that the day had turned muggy and hot, and fairies had yet to invent air-conditioning.

Selden flicked a toothpick from one side of his mouth to the other. He pulled it out and pointed the chewed end at Izzy. "I don't get it. You've Changed before. What were you doing then that you're not doing now?"

Izzy shook her head. "It's like I told you. I didn't realize what I was doing. I never even knew I could Change until Peter told me I was a Changeling."

"Fox, mouse, blackbird," said Selden, counting on his fingers. "You've got to have at least one other form you can do. All the rest of us can do four."

"Yash can do six," said Lug.

"Yeah, but three of them are different kinds of lizards," said Dree.

"We could find your poem in *The Book of the Bretabairn*," said Lug. When Izzy stared back at him blankly, he added, "You remember. It's the old book of poetry that describes each Changeling and the creatures they can Change into. If we knew what your fourth form was, you could try that one too."

Izzy rubbed her temples. "Now you want me to try to Change into more things? I can barely even do one."

"I thought perhaps they're all related," said Lug. "If you knew what all your forms are, it might help."

"I think Izzy's right," said Dree. "We should take things one step at a time. Let's focus on what you *can* do instead of what you can't. You're better at Likenesses than any of us. So what are you doing when you put on a Likeness?"

Izzy thought for a minute. "Well, I just imagine what it's like to be that person. I put myself in their shoes, try to think like them. So when I did the Likeness of Selden…"

"You tried to empty your mind completely," said Dree.

Izzy giggled as she dodged the spittle-covered toothpick lobbed at her head. "Hey, come on. You know we're joking."

Izzy knew she shouldn't tease Selden. He hadn't teased her once about not being able to Change, which for him was practically a miracle. In fact, he'd taken the whole thing very seriously. He'd been the one to coach her into the fox form earlier in the morning. It helped that one of his forms was a wolf.

From his perch on the back of the parlor sofa, Hiron cleared his throat. Izzy turned. She'd almost forgotten he was there.

Hiron had golden-brown skin and thick black hair, and he was the only Changeling who wore glasses. He pushed them farther up the bridge of his nose with one finger. "Maybe I should come back later? I mean, it seems like you're still on a very rudimentary level, Izzy."

Izzy gritted her back teeth together and tried not to be offended. Hiron wasn't mean or snobby like Larissa. He was just a serious sort of person who said exactly what he was thinking. Even if it was kind of rude.

Besides, he was right. She was rudimentary, through and through.

"No, Hiron, you should stay," said Selden. "It'll be good to mix things up. She's practiced the mouse and fox all morning. Izzy could use some help with her blackbird form."

Izzy had thought Dree would be the one to teach her how to Change into a bird. But they'd enlisted Hiron for the job, because all his Changed forms were birds: a kingfisher, a crane, a mockingbird, and an enormous gold eagle with a wingspan the length of a minivan.

Hiron hopped down from the sofa and began pacing in front of Izzy with his hands behind his back. When Hiron talked, he had a habit of looking up, like he was reading invisible words written in the air.

"To connect with your bird form, you must connect to your inner flyer. The soul of every bird is flight. The noble eagle, the humble pigeon—"

"The ostrich," said Dree. "The dodo."

Hiron blinked a few times. If he got the joke, he didn't think it was funny. "Even the flightless birds have flight in their hearts. You should know that, Dree. Now, Izzy, if you want to Change into a bird, you'll need to take to the sky." He crossed to the far end of the room and patted the top of a wooden desk. "Hop up here."

Izzy took a breath and walked to the desk. She was ready to be serious. She could do this. She could Change into a bird. It was every kid's dream. To fly.

Izzy climbed up on top of the desk. She stood in the center, feet apart. The others stared up at her.

"Maybe it'd be better if you guys turned around," she said.

Lug lumbered slowly around, making a complete circle.

Izzy sighed. "I meant face the other direction."

"Oh!" Lug chuckled. "Of course."

Everyone but Hiron turned their backs to her. "All right, raise your arms up," he instructed.

Izzy held her arms to the side and shrugged her shoulders to loosen them up. She closed her eyes but not too tight. She let her breath flow naturally. She wasn't wiggling her butt though, no matter what Lug said.

"Now move your arms up and down slowly," said Hiron. "They aren't arms. They're wings. You feel the air ruffling your feathers."

Izzy held her chin out as her arms rose and fell. She knew she must have looked silly, but she didn't care. If this was what it took to Change, she'd do it.

"Your heart is light," said Hiron softly. "Lighter than air. Your bones are light too. Just like paper."

Lighter than air. Bones like paper.

Izzy heard a gasp from Dree. She knew her friends must be watching her, but she didn't open her eyes. She didn't want to lose focus. She'd done it. She could feel the slight tingle of feathers, the quills tugging at the places where they attached to her skin. She was a bird.

"Good, excellent," said Hiron slowly. "Now step forward. When you get to the end of the desk, you'll leap up and take flight."

Izzy walked forward, her scaly feet tapping lightly on the wooden desk. When her claws felt the edge, she took one big breath, held her arms high, and jumped.

Izzy instinctively pumped her wings. The air lifted her. She rose up, up. It was magic.

And then she opened her eyes.

Izzy flapped her arms, a pointless move since they were just plain arms now. She landed with a heavy thud on the parlor carpet.

During the long pause that followed, Izzy could feel the embarrassment pulsing from her face out to the rest of her body. She finally raised her head and looked at her friends.

A strained smile stretched across Lug's face. "That was really very good, Izzy! You held that for almost one entire second!"

Dree, who never sugarcoated anything, looked as disappointed as Izzy felt. "I really thought you had that one."

Selden walked over and pulled Izzy to her feet. "I think I figured out what your problem is," he said.

Izzy winced at the pain blooming in her left hip. "I've got just one?"

"You're not *Changing* at all," said Selden. "I think you were doing a Likeness of a blackbird just then. That's why you couldn't hold it."

Hiron's eyes widened, and he snapped his fingers. "You know, I think you're right! That makes perfect sense."

"A Likeness of a Change," said Dree. "I didn't even know you could do that."

"So what am I supposed to do now?" asked Izzy, not even trying to hide the frustration in her voice. "I mean, what's the difference?"

"It's like you said yourself," said Selden. "With a Likeness, you're imagining being something else. It's not you. But a

Change is still you. You can't imagine being you. You just *are* you."

The parlor door clicked open, and Olligan peeked his head around the door. "Oh, there you are, Izzy. Peter's looking for you."

"For me? Why?"

Ollie shrugged. "He told me to come find you. He's in his room."

"I guess that means our lesson's over for now?" asked Hiron.

"It was over anyway," said Izzy.

She walked past the others, out the parlor door, and started up the stairs.

You just are you. Easy for Selden to say. He'd known who he was all his life. Izzy hadn't found out she was a Changeling until last year. All her life, she'd felt like the oddball, the one who didn't quite belong with everyone else. But as much as she hated to admit it, she didn't belong with the Changelings either.

If Selden was trying to tell her to just be herself, which self did he mean?

When Izzy reached Peter's room, she knocked on the door. "Peter? Ollie said you wanted to see me."

"Come in," Peter answered.

Izzy swung the door open. Peter's study—Morvanna's former sitting room—had a cavernous vaulted ceiling and windows covering most of the walls. Up here at the top of the castle, a limp breeze found its way in past the open curtains. There was one couch in the room, which didn't look like it had been sat on, and one side table that held a bowl of fruit so perfect that it looked plastic. The only evidence the room was used at all was the desk at the opposite end, piled high with a messy stack of papers.

Peter leaned over the desk, his back to Izzy. It was strange to see him working. Izzy always had the impression he spent his free time combing his hair or sorting his vast collection of silk neckties. But today, he was absorbed by the materials on his desk. His hair stuck up at the back, and his fingertips were stained indigo from his pen. He even had a blotch of ink on his otherwise pristine white shirt.

"I've had a message from Smudge," he said without looking up at Izzy. "There's a bit of a hiccup in our scheme."

Worry tangled up like a ball of yarn in Izzy's stomach. What if she had to go home early? "The counselors didn't believe his note?" she asked.

"Oh, it isn't them," said Peter. He waved Izzy closer to his desk. "They didn't question a word of it. It's your sister. Smudge thinks she's suspicious. After the counselors told her your mother had come to pick you up, she ran straight out to the woods. She's been snooping around ever since. This was the last letter from her that Smudge intercepted on its way to the post office."

Peter handed Izzy a letter written in turquoise crayon:

Dear Izzy,

Sounds like you're enjoying the psychedelic institute. Funny, but I never knew you were scared of pigs before. Guess you were hiding that from me. DON'T YOU HATE IT WHEN PEOPLE DON'T TELL THE TRUTH? HA HA. Mom's been sending lots of cookies.

                         Love,

                         Hen

Izzy smiled as she handed the letter back to Peter. She couldn't help feeling proud of her sister. "Hen's pretty smart when it comes to stuff like this."

"Well, I don't want her causing a stir. Those ludicrous camp workers haven't asked questions, but they might start if Hen makes enough of a fuss about you." Peter took a sheet of paper from his desk and a pen and held them out to Izzy. "While I'm fully confident in Smudge's forgery abilities, I think it would be best if we could send her a letter from you directly to dispel any doubts. Write something only you would say. Make it convincing."

Izzy looked down at the blank page, then back up at Peter. "You want me to lie to her?"

"Is that a problem?"

"I just wish I didn't have to, that's all."

Peter exhaled out his nostrils. "The only reason you're here at all is because of a lie. My very existence—and yours, I might add—is built upon a mountain of lies. You want to start being honest now?"

"OK, OK, I guess you're right." Izzy took the pen and paper from him.

Peter moved the books and papers on his desk to make some space for her. A thin leather journal fell off the top of the stack and landed splayed open at Izzy's feet. She bent to pick it up, but Peter grabbed it first. He snapped it shut and tucked it quickly into the middle of a pile of other notebooks.

Izzy thought it was a clumsy, jerky sort of move for Peter, who was usually so graceful in everything he did. But she let it go and started on the letter to her sister.

Dear Hen… Izzy began. It wasn't like she was telling Hen a lie that would hurt her. But she still felt bad doing it. She wished she could tell Hen everything, but not if it meant she'd have to go back to camp. She couldn't go back—not yet.

Her pen scratched against the page as she wrote. Peter sat, one leg crossed at the knee, rolling his flute back and forth across his desk.

"Here," said Izzy when she had finished the letter. "I wrote her a story. It's one of her favorites. She'll know this is from me."

Peter's eyes scanned the page. "Rumpelstiltskin?"

"Hen calls it 'Rumpled stilt man.'"

Peter smirked. "That old story always amused me. The ridiculousness of it."

"You mean the whole turning straw into gold thing?" asked Izzy.

"No, no, the part about guessing his name. It's actually a very common name in Faerie. There's a whole village of Rumpelstiltskins on the other side of the Dunla River."

Peter folded Izzy's letter and sealed it in an envelope. He opened his desk drawer, revealing an impressive array of earthly office supplies—paper clips, staples, and a roll of stamps from different countries. Izzy watched him peel a U.S. postage stamp off a reel and stick it on the envelope. "I'll send this to Smudge, he'll stick it in a mailing box for us, and all will be well."

Peter played a quick, fluttery song on his flute. The envelope lifted off the desk, into the air, and sailed through one of the open windows, zipping fast through the sky like a paper moth.

"Thank you for your help," said Peter. "You may go now."

He turned his back to Izzy and resumed his writing. Izzy crossed the room but stopped when she reached the door.

"Peter, can I ask you something?"

"No."

Izzy planted her feet. "I want to know more about me."

Peter held his pen still but didn't look up at her.

Izzy swallowed. "What I mean is, I want to know who I really am. Where did I come from?"

"You are an orphan. Just like all the other Changelings."

"Yes, I know, but…"

Peter turned, one eyebrow arched sharply. "I hope you're not under some grand illusion that you're the last descendant from a fairy royal family or something absurd like that."

Izzy blinked. "No, I didn't think that. Wait, *am* I?"

"No."

Izzy took a breath and started again. "It's just that I'm having trouble Changing, and I thought…"

"Good," said Peter. "You don't need to be doing any Changing. You've already been Exchanged, which means the best thing you can do for us all is to get Stuck like you are. Fewer chances to raise people's suspicions."

Izzy shifted and squared her shoulders. She was not going to let this drop. Peter had dodged her questions a million other times, and he wasn't doing it again.

"This isn't just about Changing," she said. "When I'm on Earth, I don't really feel like I fit in with everyone else. And now that I'm here, I don't really fit in with the other Changelings either. You told me that when I was a baby, someone brought me to you and asked you to hide me on Earth, right? I thought maybe if I knew more about my past, if I knew who I really was…"

Peter had gone back to writing. It was like Izzy wasn't even there.

"Peter, please?"

He snapped his head up angrily. "Do you know how many Changeling babies have been left on my doorstep over the centuries? How many squealing infants I've taken in and taken care of every day of my vastly long life? If you are wondering if you're special, the answer is: you're not. You're just like all the others. A problem for me to deal with, a commodity in a trade. That's it."

With the afternoon sun shining directly onto his face, Peter looked washed out and tired. For the first time, Izzy noticed faint whiskers of wrinkles in the corners of his slender eyes.

"You children always ask more from me no matter how much I do for you," he said, waving his fingers over the tall stacks of papers. "And meanwhile, the work never stops piling up." Peter picked up his pen and turned back to his writing. "Now if you'll excuse me, I have work that must be attended to."

Izzy turned and left the room, shutting the door behind her without looking back. She walked quickly down the hallway to the stairs. A few stubborn tears leaked out of her eyes. She brushed them away, annoyed at herself for even making them. What had she expected from Peter? Hugs and a lullaby? He would never understand. Peter was like a robot, programmed to do one task. As long as he kept the Exchange going, he didn't worry himself about the details.

He'd said she was just like all the other Changelings. But she wasn't.

Izzy could bear being different on Earth if she knew she fit somewhere. But the thought of being a misfit in two worlds just wasn't acceptable.

She was a Changeling. And she was going to learn how to Change no matter what it took.

Izzy walked straight back into the parlor and swung open the door.

"I want to read it," she said.

Her friends looked up at her, confused.

"Read what?" asked Lug.

"*The Book of the Bretabairn*," said Izzy. "Where is it?"

Selden groaned and flopped onto his back on the carpet.

Dree smiled. "It's at the library."

THE BOOK OF
THE BRETABAIRN

"You sure you can pull this off?" Selden whispered.

Izzy carefully peered around the corner into the kitchen. Two fairies of the Watch stood on either side of the door that led out into the street. "As long as you're sure Peter won't catch us."

"Lug's keeping an eye on him," whispered Dree. "If Peter comes out of his room and asks for us, Lug's going to tell him we're playing hide-and-seek. Whenever I've snuck out to the library before, it's taken about an hour. We should get going."

"OK," said Izzy, taking a deep breath. "Whatever you do, just don't make me laugh."

She rolled her shoulders back and did the same cuff adjustment she did the other night at dinner. When she felt Peter's Likeness snap into place, she sauntered around the corner and walked up to the guards.

"Come along, you two," she called over her shoulder to

Selden and Dree, trying to achieve Peter's tone of undisguised annoyance. "You children never appreciate the concept of being on time."

The Watch leaped to attention, looking much more watchful than they had just a moment before. "Afternoon, Good Peter, sir!"

"Hmm," said Izzy snobbishly. She patted her jacket pocket and hoped the guards wouldn't notice it was empty. She could imitate Peter and his clothes almost perfectly, but the flute was one thing she couldn't do. "I'm taking these two to the apothecary. They're unwell."

On cue, Dree coughed into her hands, and Selden wiped his nose against his shoulder.

Izzy flared one nostril in disgust. "The last thing we need is disease spreading throughout the castle. We'll be gone one hour. Do not leave this post or speak to anyone until we have returned."

"Yes, sir!" The Watch stepped aside so Izzy could pass. As Selden walked out, he hacked up a wad of phlegm and rolled it around on his tongue. The guards gave him extra room.

The three crossed the street and rounded the corner. When they were sure no one could see them, they ducked into an alley between two shops. Exhaling, Izzy dropped Peter's Likeness.

"That was perfect!" said Dree, squeezing Izzy's shoulder. "Now let's get moving. We've got to make the most of this hour of freedom."

The city of Avhalon was decked out in full festival mode for the Summer Solstice. The Avhalonians might not have paid much attention to whether their houses were structurally sound, but they took their parties very seriously. Lanterns and pennants hung crisscrossed between the rickety buildings lining the streets. Wildflower bouquets decorated every windowsill. They passed a team of pixies laying a thick carpet of rose petals on top of the sidewalk pavers.

The three rounded a corner and came to one of the few brick structures Izzy had seen in the city. Most of Avhalon's buildings were wood, but this one had been built of white bricks, all irregular shapes and sizes. A hand-painted sign over the front read, *Libraria et Artifactus Museum du Earth.*

"Earth?" asked Izzy.

Selden shook his head. "Just wait."

They pushed open the door and walked inside. If Izzy had been blindfolded, she would still have known where she was. The air smelled like crackled paper, leather, and old glue. It smelled like books.

Izzy's family had moved around almost once a year before finally settling in Tennessee. In every town she'd ever lived in, the first place she made sure to find was the library. And now here she was in a library in Faerie.

The library was a two-story building with books lining the walls on each level, floor to ceiling. A skylight illuminated an atrium open in the center. In the middle of the atrium was a very solid-looking circulation desk, and behind the desk, wearing a tweed vest and a beret tilted awkwardly between its horns, stood a goat.

The goat looked up at them as they approached. He adjusted the reading glasses that wrapped around his narrow face. "Good afternoon," he said regally. "Welcome to the Earth Library and Artifact Museum. I am the head librarian, Dr. Nettle. Are you members?"

"Remember me?" asked Dree, stepping forward. "I'm not a member, but I do come in a lot."

"Ah yes!" said the goat with a bleating laugh. "Hello again, dear girl. We get so many visitors here, but you will find that I never forget a face."

Izzy looked around the dusty, empty building. The library didn't give off the impression of having many visitors at all. Dr. Nettle pulled a pocket watch out of his vest and shook it back and forth like he was rattling a cup of dice. The sproingy sound of a busted spring rang out from the contraption.

"Let me see," said the goat. "Ah yes, you're just in time for our noon program."

Izzy looked at Selden, confused. It was long past noon.

Selden tapped a finger near his temple as if to say, *Warned you. This guy is nuts.*

"Today's lecture is about the history of washcloths…" Dr. Nettle began.

A look of terror flashed over Dree's face. She'd obviously

sat through Dr. Nettle's lectures before. "Not today, please," she said quickly. "We don't have that much time. Our friend wants to look at your books."

Dr. Nettle's eyes lit up, and his back hooves clopped excitedly on the wooden floor. "Of course, of course. Allow me to orient you to our collection, my dear."

He came out from behind the desk and sidled up to Izzy, walking carefully on his back legs. He wouldn't have been especially fat for a goat, but standing up, his belly bulged way out in front of him, and the buttons on his vest threatened to pop off and hit Izzy in the nose.

"We have the greatest collection of Earth-bound books in all of Faerie," said Dr. Nettle proudly.

"Earth-bound?"

"Oh yes," said Dr. Nettle. "Everything in our library was written on Earth."

Izzy frowned. "Oh. I thought there would be fairy books here."

Dr. Nettle laughed, wheezing. "Oh my goodness, no! Most fairies can hardly write their own names. If we had a library dedicated to fairy books, it could fit inside a closet."

He waved Izzy over to a section marked *Classics*. The shelves were crammed with cookbooks, old handwriting textbooks that looked like they were about to crumble to dust, and a set of encyclopedias made entirely of *J* volumes. Not everything looked ancient. There were car owner's manuals and Taiwanese shipping logs. One set of shelves was filled with phone books from San Antonio, Texas.

"Wow, this is really some collection," said Izzy.

"It's taken decades to curate," said the goat proudly. He picked up one of the *J* encyclopedias and flipped through the pages clumsily with his left hoof. "This one," he said with a sigh. "A masterpiece."

When he leaned down to replace it on the shelf, Izzy noticed it was upside down. She wondered if the head librarian even knew how to read the books in his collection.

"We haven't had a new addition to the library in quite some time," said Dr. Nettle. "You wouldn't believe some of the ridiculous books that used to come through here. I have had to go through and cull quite a few unworthy ones." He stifled a burp. "I do keep a few more frivolous items around, just for posterity."

"Those are the ones Dree reads," whispered Selden loudly.

A short bookshelf in a neglected back corner of the library was dedicated to fiction. Izzy recognized a couple of titles: a copy of *The Adventures of Tom Sawyer* and *Winnie-the-Pooh*. Some of the older books had been written in other languages Izzy couldn't read. A very thick copy of *War and Peace* had a suspicious chunk missing in the shape of a bite mark.

Dree slid out a book called *Wuthering Heights*. The author had the same last name as the one who wrote the novel Dree kept next to her bed back in the castle.

"This one's really good too," she whispered to Izzy. "I come in and switch them out, and old Nettle never notices."

"I heard you have a copy of *The Book of the Bretabairn*," said Izzy. She had scanned over all the books and hadn't spotted it yet.

"There is only one copy in existence, and yes, we have it," said Dr. Nettle, lifting his chest. "We have a small collection of books written by humans while they were visiting here in Faerie." He waved his fore hoof toward a stack on the upper level. "Peruse as long as you wish, my girl, but remember that we only lend materials to members."

"How do you become a member?" asked Izzy as she climbed the stairs.

"Oh, it's quite a simple process," said Dr. Nettle. "You just need to fill out a short application…" He held up a scroll of paper that unfurled to his hooves and rolled across the floor.

"Now you know why I just take the books," whispered Dree. "That application is complete gibberish."

At the top of the stairs, a narrow bookcase sagged in the corner. Izzy immediately spotted *The Book of the Bretabairn* on the bottom shelf.

It looked different from every other book in the library. A curly gold letter *B* had been embossed on the spine. The cover was made from thick black leather, shiny around the edges where readers had polished it smooth with the oil from their fingertips. Dr. Nettle said it had been written by a human, but to Izzy, it gave off a very fairy feeling, a feeling of magic. She slid it carefully off the shelf and laid it on a nearby reading desk.

Izzy ran her hand over the cover, where the symbol of two clasped hands had been burned into the leather and painted gold. Her fingertips tingled like the book held an electric charge. "A human really wrote this?" she whispered.

Dree leaned over Izzy's shoulder and opened the cover. She pointed to the title page.

The Book of the Bretabairn
Writ by Ida Green

"We think she was related to Master Green," said Selden.

Selden had told Izzy the story of Master Green before. According to legend, a thousand years ago, Faerie and Earth were one. Master Green and the fairy king, Revelrun, had worked together to split the two worlds apart. At the time, they envisioned fairies and humans traveling frequently back and forth between the two worlds. But instead, Earth and Faerie became more and more separate. Peter started the Exchange to make sure the worlds weren't severed completely.

"This is amazing," Izzy whispered, afraid her breath might blow the brittle pages away. "How old did you say this book was?"

"Old," said Selden, pulling a chair up beside her.

"Five hundred years old," added Dree. She sat cross-legged on the floor beside them and started reading *Wuthering Heights*.

Izzy turned to the first page. Ida Green had the most perfect handwriting she'd ever seen, all loops and flourishes. The first poem was an introduction and didn't belong to one Changeling in particular.

> *Wee Bretabairn, born in the caul,*
> *Child of none, mime of all.*
> *With dimpled cheeks and fine white teeth,*
> *Mother won't guess what hides beneath.*
> *Father, too, will never know*
> *His babe's a fey in man-child clothes.*

"This book is so thick," said Izzy, running her finger down the spine. "If there's a poem on every page, then there must be hundreds of poems in here. But there are only eighteen Changelings. How do you know when you find yours?"

"You just know," said Selden. He leaned over and turned past a few pages. "I think Lug's is one of the first ones. Let's see… It would have helped if old Ida could've drawn some pictures."

Izzy gasped. "Here it is!"

She wouldn't have known it was Lug's poem from the title. In fact, the titles didn't seem to have anything to do with the actual verses. But Izzy recognized it from the last line, which Lug had recited for her once before. She read it aloud:

Ox, badger, ram, and bear,
No trace of malice dwelling there.
A nose for growing, living things,
An eye for what the kind deed brings,
Arms to gather what has come apart,
And a stout body for a strong heart.

Izzy shook her head in amazement. "Gosh, that is Lug, up and down. I don't understand how a woman who lived five hundred years ago could write something that fits him so perfectly."

Selden, who rarely admitted to being impressed—especially not by something done by humans—scratched the back of his neck and smiled. "Somehow, each of us has a poem that fits. I've never figured out if the poems were written to match us or if we grow up to match the poems. Either way, it's pretty wild."

Izzy looked at Selden. "So? Where's yours?"

He flushed and pressed his hair flat with his palm. "We're here to find your poem, not mine."

"Oh, come on. Please?"

"All right," he said. "It's near the back."

They gently turned the pages until Selden found it. Izzy read it silently to herself.

Enemies, shield your throats,
From wolf, leopard, stag, stoat.
Strongest, bravest, when wounded deep,

From the battle you cannot keep
Him from charging in, flag unfurled,
Baring sharp points against the world.

"What do you think?" Selden asked softly. "Sound like me?"

Izzy watched him as he twisted one section of his hair around and around his finger. Dree had once told her Selden's story. He had wanted to be Exchanged so badly that he'd skipped his turn in line to do it. But once he got to Earth, his human family gave him up for adoption. Selden was tougher than any kid Izzy had ever met. But now she wondered what wounds he was hiding underneath all that armor.

Izzy smiled at him. "Yeah. I think it does sound like you."

The tingling in Izzy's fingertips spread up and down her arms. This book was magic, pure and simple. And she was a part of it. Somewhere in this book, she would find herself.

Izzy went back to the beginning and began flipping through each page. She found Dree's poem and one for Hale, Olligan, and Chervil. The one with the line *Heavy footed but light in the air* had to be Hiron's.

The poems called out what was special about each Changeling. It was incredible how their true selves, the essence of who they were, could be boiled down into just six lines. Izzy flipped faster through the book, the anticipation of finding her own poem growing with every page turn.

But when she reached the end, she still hadn't found one that suited her or described the creatures she could Change into. Izzy started all over again from the beginning, reading more carefully this time. There must have been something she missed.

She was halfway through her second reading when Dr. Nettle clomped heavily up the stairs wagging his broken pocket watch. "Children, I am afraid it's almost six o'clock, and the library is closing for the day."

Izzy looked at the bright afternoon sunlight streaming through the window. It was nowhere near six. "Please, can we have just a little more time?"

"We've got to get back anyway," said Dree. "We told Lug we'd only be gone an hour."

"You may come again tomorrow," said Dr. Nettle. "We open promptly at nine."

Reluctantly, Izzy closed the heavy book and set it back on the shelf. When Dr. Nettle turned around, Dree hid *Wuthering Heights* in a fold of her dress. Izzy was tempted to do the same with *The Book of the Bretabairn*, but it was too big and heavy to hide.

Dr. Nettle led them out through the empty building and to the front stoop. "Do come again," he said, holding the door for them as they stepped out into the blinding sunlight. "But be warned that you should plan to arrive at least an hour early so as to avoid the long lines." The door shut behind them.

As they wound their way back to the castle, Izzy looked over her shoulder. "*The Book of the Bretabairn* doesn't seem like it belongs there with all those old car manuals and phone books. Shouldn't it be somewhere safe?"

"Are you joking?" asked Selden, back to his superior self. "I can't think of a safer place in Faerie than that library. No one in their right mind goes there. Ever."

Dree brought out her novel. "I'd go more often if Nettle would get a new book more than once a century."

Izzy followed behind them, only half listening to them argue about Dree's romance stories. Her fingertips buzzed as if she still held *The Book of the Bretabairn* in her hands. Izzy had felt something in the library. It was like a small light had been switched on inside her. But that one light wasn't enough. If only she could find her own poem, she was sure it would illuminate everything.

For now, she was still in the dark.

STILL A FOX

BACK INSIDE THE CASTLE, they went to find Lug. On the way, they were nearly bowled over by children carrying armfuls of craft supplies.

"We're getting ready for the Solstice Celebration," explained Park.

Rusk wiggled beside him, trying to shimmy out of the twine wrapped around his torso. "Tonight's the Gathering of Masks in the city center. Park and I are going to be gorgons." He held a pair of long stockings up over his head and waggled them. "These are our snakes."

"What's the Gathering of Masks?" asked Izzy.

"It's a tradition the night before the Solstice," explained Dree. "Everyone wears masks and capes and stands around the fountain in the center of town. At dawn, you take your mask off, and if you've done a good enough job, no one knows who everyone else is." She picked a dried glob of paste out of

Rusk's hair. "But Peter's not going to let you go to the Solstice Celebration in a million years. You know that, right?"

Rusk and Park both looked crushed.

"We could have our own little Gathering inside the castle," said Lug, patting their shoulders. "I always loved the mask making. What do you think, Selden? Should we all make some too?"

"Aw, that's baby stuff," said Selden. "Besides, I've already got my mask."

He rubbed his hands over his face, like he was scrubbing it clean, a ritual Izzy was surprised he knew how to do. When he took his hands away, he still looked somewhat like himself but with grayish-green skin and a warty nose that twisted in a long curlicue. He was a Selden goblin.

"I'm gonna get you, Bretabairn!" Tongue lolling out, Selden chased Yash, Mite, and Mote, who ran squealing gleefully down the hallway.

Izzy went up to her room and sat down on the bed to take off her boots. She couldn't stop thinking about *The Book of the Bretabairn* and when she could get back to the library again.

Her fingers still tingled from turning the pages. She could almost smell the leather cover, feel the weight of it in her hands. Reading the poems written for the other Changelings, she had felt something stirring inside her. It was like looking through an old photo album filled with baby pictures, knowing she was too young to actually remember doing those things but having some feeling of memory all the same.

Suddenly, she smelled the sharp vinegary odor of Lug's feet.

"Lug, it might be time to roll in the rosemary bush again," she said, turning around. But Lug wasn't there. She was still alone. Izzy went to the door of her room and stepped out into the hall.

The hallway was empty as well. Izzy could hear the sounds of the Changelings downstairs, busy with their mask making. But she could distinctly smell Lug, like he was waving his toes inches from her face. His scent mingled with the golden, crackling aroma of toasting bread. But the kitchens were three floors down. How could she smell bread toasting all the way up here?

Izzy looked down at her hands and gasped. Fine black hairs covered them completely. She flexed her fingers, and sharp gray claws extended, then retracted again.

Slowly, Izzy turned her head over her shoulder. Bright-orange fur ran down her back all the way to the fluffy taper of her tail, which swished slowly back and forth.

Her pulse whirred. She had Changed into a fox without even trying. No tricks, no breathing exercises. Not only that, she was *still* a fox. At this point in her tutorials with her friends, she would have looked down, seen that she Changed form, and then promptly lost hold of it. But this time was different. It didn't feel like she was trying to pretend to be something she wasn't.

This wasn't a Likeness. This was her.

Izzy swished her tail up and down a few more times. She padded down the hallway. Still a fox. She hopped up and down on the carpet. Still a fox. Excited, she bounded to the end of the hallway and leaped up, doing a quarter turn in the air. She landed softly on padded paws. This was unbelievable. She was just about to run downstairs and show the others when she heard voices.

With a minor adjustment, Izzy could turn her ears toward the sound. It was like dialing in a signal on an old-fashioned radio.

Not quite.

Not quite.

There.

Izzy's ears scooped the words out of the air like she had big dishes on top of her head. The whispers snapped into sharper focus, and she could make out who they belonged to.

It was Good Peter and Tom Diffley. Izzy padded farther down the hall, closer to Peter's room. His door was shut, but she could make out their words as clearly as if they were standing right next to her.

The first voice, low and anxious, belonged to Peter. "You saw nothing at all? Are you sure?"

"Sure as a tack in your seat," whispered Tom. "The scouts have been up and down the Liadan River on both sides. And I've been up in the *Muscadine* for two days, covering the rim of the Edgewood. I've spotted Ungler tracks, but they're all old ones that I found before."

Peter didn't reply, but Izzy could hear the faint sound of his flute tapping against his palm.

"I think we've finally driven them off," continued Tom. "We always used to see at least one or two a week. But I think they finally scattered away."

"Hmm," mused Peter. "That seems too easy, doesn't it? Morvanna bred almost four dozen Unglers. At best, we've taken care of half that number. Where are the others? They wouldn't just vanish." Peter's voice alternated between loud and soft as he paced the room. "I'm leaving for the Edgewood in an hour. I can check things out for myself on the ground. If you're right, it will be the best thing we could have hoped for."

"It'll make our job easier, that's for sure," said Tom. "You going to check on how she's getting along?"

"I'm going to light a fire under her feet if that's what it will take to get her going. I want everything in place in three more days at the latest. Whether she thinks she's ready or not. You stay here. I need someone keeping an eye on Lufkin and that useless Watch."

Shoes clanged harshly against the stone floor, and Izzy knew she was seconds away from getting caught eavesdropping. She dashed down the hall and slipped into her room before Peter's door clicked open.

Panting, she looked down at her paws. They were hands

again. She hadn't meant to return to her normal form, but it didn't matter. She'd done it. She'd Changed. She had to tell her friends right away.

Downstairs, the dining table had been transformed into mask-making central. Feathers and sequins, wool scraps, dried flowers, and ribbons in every shade lay scattered all over the tabletop.

Izzy gathered Dree, Lug, and Selden in a corner of the dining room to tell them about Changing and everything she'd overheard in Peter's room.

"Well, that's good news about the Unglers, isn't it?" said Lug quietly. "It sounds like they've finally gotten rid of them. We can all breathe a little easier knowing that."

"Yes, but what's Peter planning?" asked Selden. "What are he and Tom in on?"

"Isn't it obvious?" said Dree. "He's getting ready to do an Exchange."

"He did talk about getting someone ready," said Izzy. "A girl."

Dree chewed the tip of her finger. "It must be Hale. She's the oldest. And it's past her turn to go to Earth."

"But why keep that a secret?" asked Selden.

"Maybe for the younger ones' sakes," whispered Dree. "They're going to bawl their eyes out when Hale leaves."

Izzy watched Hale helping Sibi attach a veil of netting to her spider mask. "I have a feeling Hale will be even more upset. She loves them."

"That's the whole reason for having her go," said Dree.

"She's been here too long, and she's making it too comfortable for the little ones. If I had Hale taking care of me, I'd never want to go to Earth."

"This way, she'll have a family of her own," said Lug. "Someone to take care of her for once. It's nice of Peter to let her stay for the Solstice. One last fairy party before she goes."

Selden shut one eye halfway and shook his head. "I don't know. Peter's a lot of things, but since when would you describe him as 'nice'? Something else is going on."

"Aren't we forgetting something?" said Dree. She hooked one arm around Izzy's neck and yanked her close. "Izzy Changed! And she held it for ages without even trying!"

"Right you are, Dree," said Lug, pinching one of Izzy's cheeks. "A monumental accomplishment."

Izzy covered her head, because Selden looked ready to give her a celebratory noogie. "Thanks, thanks! OK, can you let me go now?"

Dree released her. "And what's the first thing you did in your Changed form? Spied on someone." She pointed her finger at Izzy's nose. "Some things never change."

Izzy smiled. "At least I can say I'm not one of those things anymore."

10

A PROPER SPY

Izzy sat at her bedroom window, watching the Solstice Celebration crank into full swing down below. The plaza glowed under the rainbow lights of paper lanterns as dancers jigged to a nine-piece band while other fairies watched from the edges, holding drinks and plates piled high with food. Everyone was decked out in elaborate masks and costumes.

Dree had been right—Peter forbade any of the Changelings to set foot outside the castle until he returned. They'd stayed up listening to the band and watching the dancers past midnight. Now everyone but Izzy was asleep. She'd spent so much time trying to Change into her fox form that evening that she wondered if it had made her temporarily nocturnal.

After eavesdropping on Peter, Izzy had tried and tried to Change into her fox form again but with no success. The others said she was just tired and told her to wait until morning. But Izzy worried. What if she could never manage it again?

She pressed her cheek to the glass and looked across the castle to the window of Peter's study. Normally, she'd be able to see golden candlelight flickering behind the glass, no matter what time it was. Lug said Peter never ate, and Izzy didn't think he went to sleep either.

But tonight, Peter's window was dark. He must not have gotten back from his trip to the Edgewood yet. Izzy tapped one finger on the window, thinking about the stacks of papers on Peter's desk and about that small leather journal he hadn't wanted her to see. What was he hiding from her this time? Dree always teased Izzy for being a spy. Maybe it was time to start living up to the name.

Izzy slipped out of her bedroom. The carpeted hallway muffled the sounds of music and shouting from the Solstice Celebration outside. She started toward Peter's room.

As she crept down the hall on tiptoe, trying to be as quiet as possible, she was struck by the strangest sensation. She had done something like this before. But when?

Izzy continued on, trying to figure out what she was feeling. It was a little like trying to remember the lyrics of a song or a line from a movie. The words were there somewhere, floating in the back of her mind, on the tip of her tongue. Suddenly, she felt a rush, like a memory clicking into place, and she realized what was happening to her.

She was Changing.

Izzy crouched down, and by the time her hands touched

the floor, they had become tiny mouse paws. Without pausing to think about what she'd just done, she scurried down the hallway. Air rushed past the long whiskers in her peripheral vision, tickling her upper lip. She glanced down at her feet. Her four paws tippety-tapped so fast, she couldn't even see them. It looked hilarious, the way animals ran in cartoons.

The sight of it made Izzy giggle. The sound of her mouse laughter was so high-pitched and squeaky that it made her laugh even harder. Her sides started to ache, and she had to slow to a trot. And then—

WHAM!

Something heavy and sharp slammed into Izzy from behind. She curled forward and somersaulted across the floor. Somewhere in midroll, she Changed back to herself.

"Ah!" she yelped. She felt the tight pinch of sharp teeth on her right shoulder. She reached behind her, grabbed something furry, and flung it away from her.

A sleek ball of black fur rolled to its feet and Changed from a stoat into Selden. He rubbed the spot where Izzy had grabbed the back of his neck.

"What'd you throw me so hard for?" he hissed.

Izzy put her fingers to her shoulder blade, surprised there wasn't any blood. "You bit me!"

Selden rolled his eyes. "Oh, come on. That was hardly a bite at all. You're lucky I knew you weren't a real mouse. I could have snapped your head off."

"You knew I wasn't a real mouse?"

"Are you kidding? You were laughing like a maniac."

"Oh." Izzy felt her cheeks blush. "What were you doing out here anyway?"

"Me? Nothing. I was just—hold on." Selden tilted his head to one side. "What are *you* doing out here? And don't tell me you wanted to practice Changing in the middle of the night."

Izzy chewed her bottom lip.

"Why, Isabella Doyle," said Selden slowly, a grin spreading across his face. "Are you getting up to mischief?"

Izzy smiled. "Well? Are you in or what?"

Izzy jabbed the piece of wire that Selden had given her into the keyhole in Peter's door.

"Shoot!" she whispered as the wire kinked on itself.

Selden leaned against the wall beside her. "You know, if you'd Change back into a mouse, you could just crawl through the crack under the door and let us in."

Izzy rolled her eyes as she straightened the wire back out. "I told you. I can't just Change like that. Everything has to feel right. I was doing fine until someone had to tackle me and mess it all up."

Click!

"There!" said Izzy, opening the door with a satisfied sigh. "Wow, that's a lot harder than they make it look in the movies."

She tiptoed after Selden into Peter's room and shut the door quietly behind them. They lit one candle and set it down on the floor so no one could see it from the window. Selden went straight for Peter's desk and started looking through the tallest stack of papers. Clearly, he'd come with the intention of doing some spying of his own.

"What is all this?" said Selden. "Izzy, you've got to take a look."

He pushed a packet of documents into her hands and pointed to the word written across the first page.

"*Hale?*" Izzy whispered.

"Peter must have put all this information together to get ready for her Exchange," said Selden, flipping through the other pages. "I had no idea he did all this."

The next piece of paper in the packet was a hand-drawn map of a town with one house marked in red pen. A trail had been drawn running from the back of the house to the woods, where it disappeared in a cluster of trees.

The packet contained notes about the family that lived in the house, down to what they ate for breakfast and how they treated their pets. And, of course, there were pages and pages of notes about the human child whose place Hale would take. This is what Peter must have meant when he said the Exchange was a lot of work.

Izzy spotted the leather notebook on the corner of the desk. She picked it up and flipped it open.

"This is so weird," she whispered. "All the pages are empty. Why did he want to hide it from me then?"

A quiet growl came from Selden's throat.

Izzy looked up at him. "What's wrong? Is there something else in Hale's file?"

Selden held out a folder full of paper. "This isn't for Hale. Look."

Izzy opened the folder and started reading the first page. It was a detailed description of a family. "…kind mother and father…patient…keep to themselves…" There was a scribbled note at the bottom: "Perfect fit for Selden."

"That's not all," said Selden, his voice crackling with anger. "There's a folder here for Dree too. And Lug. This whole desk is full of information about families for every single Changeling!"

Izzy picked up the folders as Selden handed them to her. "But that means…"

There was a loud metallic click at the door. Izzy and Selden froze as it swung inward.

Peter strode into the room, his face all sharp angles and shadows in the moonlight.

Izzy gulped and shut the notebook. If she could have Changed into a mouse at that moment, she would have been halfway down the hall. "I'm so sorry, Peter. I can explain…"

"*What* are you doing?" His voice trembled like a taut line about to snap.

Selden didn't back away. If anything, he was even angrier than Peter. "What are *you* doing?" He held up the folder with his papers and waved it back and forth. "What's all this stuff about?"

Before Peter could answer, they heard boots in the hall outside.

"Saw you got back," said Tom Diffley, swinging the door open. "So did you talk to—" He froze midstep when he saw Izzy and Selden.

"Talk to who?" asked Izzy.

"To...uh...to..."

Tom looked at Peter for permission to answer. Peter sighed and nodded.

"...to Marian," said Tom.

"Marian!" cried Izzy. "Is everyone in on this secret except us?"

Peter ran his fingers through his hair, his anger giving way to resignation. "Come inside and shut the door, Tom," he said quietly. He looked at Izzy and Selden. "I suppose it's time to finally tell you the truth."

THE PIPER'S PLAN

Izzy sat on the couch in Peter's study between Selden and Tom Diffley. Peter had rung for a servant to bring coffee up for Tom. Izzy didn't see why he needed it. She'd never felt more awake in her life.

Peter paced the carpet steadily. He kept taking a breath to start talking and then shutting his mouth again. Normally, Izzy wished she could know all Peter's secrets, but at the moment, he looked so worried and agitated that she wasn't sure she wanted to hear what he was about to tell them.

Selden, still angry, sat with his arms crossed tight. "I can tell you're trying to figure out how to tell us what's going on without actually telling us anything," he said. "Don't you think it's time to stop keeping us in the dark?"

"It isn't like that," said Peter. "When you've been alive as long as I have, you know a great many things. It makes it tricky to decide where to start telling a story." He stopped pacing and stood in front of them. "Perhaps it's best to work backward and start with what you know. With Morvanna."

The witch's name echoed a little too loudly. Izzy remembered they were sitting in her old bedroom, and it made her shiver.

Peter resumed his pacing. "Morvanna first came to Avhalon because she was looking for Changelings. When I met her, she'd already discovered that Changeling heart was an ingredient in the elixir that would make her young and strong again. I always wondered how she learned that. It's not really the sort of information you find out by accident."

Selden snorted. "Are you kidding? I can't think of anyone more likely than Morvanna to go around cutting children's hearts out just for laughs."

Tom Diffley gulped his coffee.

"So how did she know?" asked Izzy.

"Someone told her." Peter walked to his desk and picked up the slim notebook Izzy had flipped through just moments ago. "After Morvanna's death, I found this among her things. It's her journal."

"But it's blank," said Izzy. There was no point denying she'd already looked through it, since she'd been caught in the act.

Peter took a candle from his desk and brought it with him to the couch. He blew out the flame. A wisp of white smoke streamed up from the wick. Peter held the journal behind the candle. The smoke acted like a flickering lens, revealing dense blocks of words scrawled onto the page.

"I guess that's a pretty good way to keep people from reading your journal," said Selden.

Peter snapped the notebook shut and took a sheaf of papers from one of his desk drawers. "I transcribed everything from the journal here," he said, flipping through the papers in his hands. "This entry is dated one month before Morvanna first arrived in Avhalon."

"*At last, I know the ingredient I have been missing. I should have thought long ago to ask those dear, devilish ladies at the bottom of Lake Umbra...*"

Tom sucked in a plug of coffee and started choking.

Izzy patted him on the back while he coughed. "Lake Umbra? What is that?" she asked.

"Demon's...Lake..." sputtered Tom. "Fen...Whelps..."

"Lake Umbra is one of the oldest bodies of water in Faerie," said Peter. "It lies on the border of the Norlorn Mountains. The spring that feeds it goes all the way down to the heart of the world."

"Water's black as blood," croaked Tom. "Anyone falls in, they never get out. Everyone says the creatures who live there—the Fen Whelps—chew them up, bones and all."

"Only if you make them mad," added Selden. "If they like you, they'll tell you the answer to any question you ask. That's what the old stories say anyway."

Peter nodded. "The Sisters—or Fen Whelps, as the common fairies call them—know everything that has ever happened in Faerie. If it suits their whims, they will answer one question—and only one. But even though the Sisters have been alive longer than I have, they are childish creatures. They find it humorous to play with desperate questioners. They answer in riddles or give answers with double meanings."

Peter returned to the papers in his hand. "This is what they told Morvanna when she went to them: *The key to a witch's greatest desire lies in another's heart. Hunt the Bretabairn, and you will find it.*"

The hairs along Izzy's spine stood on end. "So the Fen Whelps knew Morvanna's greatest desire was to be young and powerful again. They told her exactly what she needed."

Selden rubbed his hand across his chest. "Remind me to send them a thank-you letter."

"Yes, the Fen Whelps did indeed point Morvanna to the missing ingredient in her elixir," said Peter. "But I believe that is not all they were trying to tell her."

Selden and Izzy glanced at each other, then watched Peter as he walked to the open window beside his desk.

Even though the room was a hundred feet from the ground and it wasn't very likely someone would be hanging around outside listening in, Peter pulled and latched the window, shutting out the sounds from the party below. The room instantly felt still and stuffy.

Peter lowered his voice. "When the Fen Whelps said the key to a witch's greatest desire lies in the heart of the Bretabairn,

I think they were talking about a different witch. And a different key."

Tom wrapped both arms around himself. "Another witch?"

Peter nodded. "Most witches eventually make their way to the Norlorn Mountains. It's remote enough to have escaped my purge of spell books but still close enough to Avhalon to have access to the information that passes through here. They are solitary for the most part, keeping secrets from each other and coming together only to boast or compete. But over the last few years, a small group has formed to learn from a masterful witch. His name is Rine."

"Rine." The curious name slipped out of Izzy's mouth before she realized she was whispering it.

"How come we've never heard of him before now?" asked Selden.

"Because he's not like Morvanna," answered Peter. "He doesn't want fame or fortune or to rule over Avhalon or any other city in Faerie. He has been growing his power, slowly and quietly, and now he is ready to try for a much bigger prize. And if he finds what he's looking for, no one will be able to stop him."

"Earth," said Izzy.

Selden and Tom both looked at her, surprised.

"I'm right, aren't I?" said Izzy. "It's like you told me when we were leaving Camp Kitterpines. If a witch could get back to Earth, they'd be very powerful there."

Peter dipped his head. "You are a good listener."

"But he can't get to Earth," added Izzy. "You put a ban on all the witches. If he tries to go down through those tunnels, he'll be crushed between the worlds."

Peter rubbed a hand over his eyes. For someone who didn't need to sleep, he looked very tired. "There are only two ways to get around my ban. This is the first." He tapped the jacket pocket where he kept his flute. "But Rine couldn't use it unless I gave it to him, which he knows I would never do."

"The second?" asked Selden.

"When Faerie and Earth first split, the fairy king, Revelrun, and his human equivalent, Master Green, worried they hadn't made enough roads to keep the worlds connected. They created a magical object called the King's Key. With it, you can travel down any fairy road regardless of whatever enchantment was placed on it. You can also use it to create an entirely new path or seal them all off forever.

"A few centuries and several wars later, it became clear that the King's Key was too powerful," continued Peter. "So the descendants of Master Green and King Revelrun hid it somewhere in the Edgewood. They hid it so well that no one has ever found it. Even I don't know where it is."

"Couldn't Rine go to the Fen Whelps and just ask them where it is?" asked Selden.

Peter huffed a short laugh. "He did. And he wasted his question. I told you, the Fen Whelps like to toy with questioners.

All he learned from them is that the King's Key lies 'resting in the dark,' which doesn't offer much of a clue. If he'd been a little more polite and asked his question in the right way, perhaps they would have told him. For a long time, I thought those tricky Sisters had saved us all. But now I worry that our luck has worn thin. I have tried to keep everything about Morvanna as secret as I can. But secrets spread in Faerie. I remember that Rine was a bright boy. I think he has already put the pieces together about Morvanna, the Fen Whelps, and Changeling hearts."

"You think he's coming for us," said Selden.

Peter's eyes darted to Tom. "Tell them what you've seen."

Tom Diffley looked ready to throw up. Whatever he and Peter had been conspiring about together, it was clear Peter hadn't told him it had to do with another witch. "After Morvanna was killed, the Unglers scattered," said Tom. "We thought that without their master, the beasts were gone for good. But a few weeks ago, I started spotting them from the *Muscadine*, skirting the banks of the rivers around Avhalon or lurking in the Firfara Forest. And then I saw a pair of them, crossing the plain, heading into the Edgewood."

"Edgewood?" said Selden. "But there aren't any Changelings there. We're all here in Avhalon."

"Witches are banned from leaving Faerie," said Peter. "But the Unglers can go to Earth and bring back whatever they catch."

Izzy's mouth had gone dry. She knew that all the roads leading to Earth from Faerie started in the Edgewood.

"I think Rine is controlling the Unglers," said Peter. "He is training them to go to Earth and find Changelings who have already been Exchanged. The beasts wouldn't be able to travel far without drawing notice, but if a Changeling was close by a fairy road—"

"Like at Camp Kitterpines," said Izzy. "So I didn't hallucinate them at camp."

Peter gave a quick nod.

Izzy slid her hands under her knees so Selden wouldn't see them trembling.

"So our hearts are back on a witch's shopping list," said Selden. "That's nice."

"This is nothing to joke about," said Peter, his voice rising. "Morvanna was easily played, but I can't protect you from Rine. He is more powerful than she was. And even more determined to get what he wants."

Selden stood up and walked toward Peter's desk. He pointed to all the papers and the packets with the Changelings' names on them. "Is this how you're going to protect us? By giving us away? I understand why you're doing it for the little ones. They'll be Exchanged anyway. But Lug and Dree? They are going to lose it when they find out you want to take them back to Earth. We had our chance at the Exchange, but no one wanted us. We're not going back. I'd rather stand up to Rine than go through that again."

Selden's voice had risen. Izzy expected Peter to scold him,

but he stayed silent, his eyes moving between Selden and the floor.

"Selden, settle down," said Tom. "You can't fight a bunch of witches all by yourself. Peter's thought this through. He wouldn't do it if he didn't think it was the best thing for you."

"Why does he get to make all the decisions?" Selden turned from Tom back to Peter. "All this time, you've been lying to us. You let us pick our rooms, decorate the castle, make stupid forts. You made us feel like it's a home. And the whole time, you've been planning to split us up and send us off."

"Selden…" said Izzy.

"You don't even know what you're doing!" shouted Selden. "The whole reason we're in danger at all is because you messed up with Rine. You brought the wrong kid to Faerie, and you put him with the wrong family." Selden bit his bottom lip, stopping short the rush of angry words. Then he added, "You're an expert at that, I guess."

"That's enough!" snapped Peter.

Izzy got up and stood between them. "You don't have to Exchange Selden," she said to Peter. "Or Lug and Dree either. They can come live with me. My family will understand. I'll make them. And no one will know. Our house is in the middle of nowhere."

Peter turned his back to Izzy. "You aren't staying in that house."

"Wait. *What?*"

"Your family's house sits right on a fairy road," said Peter. "After seeing how easy it was for the Unglers to find you at that camp, I've decided you'll have to move." Peter picked up a folder they hadn't seen yet. It had Izzy's name on it. "Smudge and I have already started making the arrangements."

Izzy's brain spun, trying to process what Peter was telling her. "Move again? I can't do that!"

Peter's voice was thin and mechanical. "It's already decided. Marian will arrive in Avhalon in three days, and we'll all go to the Edgewood to start the Exchange."

Three days.

Thirty-six hours, and then Izzy would leave Faerie forever, and her friends would be scattered around the world like dandelion seeds. She looked up at Selden. He glared at Peter, his jaw tight. Without a word, he stormed past Izzy and left the room, slamming the door behind him so hard that it made Izzy flinch.

When she opened her eyes, she was surprised to see anything in the room still standing. It seemed to her that the whole world had fallen down.

THE SOLSTICE CELEBRATION

THE SOUNDS OF CRASHING metal and people shouting rattled Izzy awake. She sat up and blinked, disoriented and sweating, waiting for her eyes to adjust to the dark. For a second, she thought she was still sitting on the couch in Peter's study before she remembered she had come back to her own room and collapsed on her bed. She looked at the bed beside her. Dree was still gone.

The last thing Izzy remembered before she fell asleep was Selden shaking Dree awake. "I've got to tell you something," he'd said. "You, me, and Lug have to talk."

Izzy hadn't followed. She didn't want to see how Lug and Dree took the news. As upset as Izzy was over the thought of moving yet again, she knew her friends had it much worse. She felt awful for them and guilty that she didn't have to share their anguish over being placed in yet another home that might not want them.

Izzy went to the window and looked down on the lantern-lit plaza below. The crash she had heard was the band, who'd either fallen or been pushed off the stage by gyrating dancers. The eastern horizon glowed purple in the dark sky. It was almost dawn. The Solstice Celebration showed no sign of slowing down. If anything, things had gotten even more rowdy, with some fairies forming a pyramid and others vaulting off their backs into the fountain. They were having the time of their lives, completely unaware of the hearts breaking in the castle right above them.

This would be the last fairy festival Izzy would ever see. She was suddenly filled with sadness and longing and anger about being forced to leave. She turned from the window and yanked on her boots, pulling a shirt on over her nightgown. Maybe Peter could make her go back to Earth, but he couldn't stop her from watching the sun come up. She left her room and headed downstairs.

The fairy assigned to guard the back kitchen door wore a flop-eared dog mask. He leaned back on a stool, balancing it on two legs, clearly trying to impress a girl in a mask covered in spotted feathers.

Izzy didn't pause. With a brush of her hand over her sleeve, she took on Peter's Likeness midstride.

When the Watchman saw her, he tipped over backward off his stool. The feather-masked girl giggled. "Oh—Good Peter, sir," stammered the guard. "I was just—"

Izzy flipped up her palm. "Don't make excuses. Just get back to work," she snapped in Peter's voice.

Outside, she dropped the Likeness and headed to the plaza. Izzy expected to be swept up in the rowdy celebration, but by the time she got there, the band was packing up, and the dancers had stopped. The revelry had quieted to a rhythmic murmur. Fairies could be serious when they wanted to be, and they were serious about their traditions.

They started to gather thick and solemn around the stone fountain in the plaza. With the crowd so hushed, Izzy could hear the rush of the Liadan River that curled a hundred feet below them at the base of the city walls.

Izzy whispered apologies as she bumped into fairies on both sides. She felt self-conscious in her nightgown, with no mask on. A glittery dragon's head leered down at her and clacked a wooden tongue in its jaws. Fairies wearing capes and long gowns moved in between them, pressing on all sides. She tried to shuffle around them, but they shoved back. Everyone wanted to have the best viewing spot for the unmasking. Three fairies with hooded cloaks pushed ahead of her.

A bird mask with glowing orange feathers passed over her, followed by a wrinkle-nosed bat, a warthog, and a hare. Another fairy had a face like a crocodile, with a jagged-toothed papier-mâché snout. These were nothing like the papier-mâché masks Izzy had made in art class. The materials looked rare and exquisite. They flexed and crinkled, showing emotion. In the dim light, they looked like real faces.

Izzy pressed toward the fountain, but it was hard to make headway. She felt so tired, like she was walking through molasses.

Constable Lufkin, recognizable by his swaggering belly even under a lion's mask and mane that cascaded down his back, climbed onto the rim of the fountain. "Ladies and gentlefolk," he called to the crowd. "The time has come! From now on, the days shall wane. This night marks the end of high season and the descent toward winter and darkness. But for now, together, we celebrate the light!"

He raised both arms to the east, where the sun was just beginning to rise. It should have cast its rays over the city, bathing everything in a pale rosy glow. But the darkness lingered stubbornly. The sun shone white on the horizon, but none of its light seemed to be reaching them. Some of the fairies murmured that this was odd. Many of them were too bleary-eyed to notice.

Lufkin frowned at the sun, which was robbing him of his dramatic moment. "We celebrate the *light*!" he repeated. When the sunlight still didn't wash over him in glorious splendor, he said, "Oh, to heck with it. Everyone can take their masks off now."

An excited murmur rippled through the crowd. Fabric and paper rustled as the fairies unmasked. The plaza fell quiet, and then a woman's scream broke the silence. The crowd surged back. Izzy had to hold onto a stranger's sleeve to keep from falling over. More screams echoed across the plaza as fairies began running.

Looking past them, Izzy saw a cluster of hooded figures wearing the same masks. It took her a moment to realize they weren't wearing masks at all.

The long snouts stretching out from the hoods belonged to Unglers.

The plaza erupted into chaos. Cloaks and capes swirled and fell to the ground as the fairies clawed past each other to get away from the beasts.

Izzy was pushed back from the fountain, carried by the rushing crowd to the east end of the plaza. She pressed herself against the city wall to keep from getting trampled. Fairies fell down all around her, stumbling in a strange, milky blackness that pooled at their feet.

The Unglers ignored the stampeding fairies. With heavy skulls hanging on crooked necks, the beasts' nostrils quivered as they snorted the air.

Tom had run out of the castle and rang an iron bell that hung at the foot of the steps. "Come back!" he shouted at the panicking crowd. "Defend the castle!"

Izzy tried to run, but something was dragging her back. The shadows at her feet clung to her. They were thick and cold and stuck to her legs, pulling her down. She had to get higher, away from them. She tilted her head back and saw the top of the city wall thirty feet above her. The stones in the wall had been stacked clumsily, jutting out of the mortar at odd angles. Using the stones as handholds, Izzy started climbing.

Halfway up the wall, she looked over her shoulder. Near the castle steps, Selden crouched in his wolf form, his hackles raised high. Lug backed against him as a bear while the Unglers circled closer.

Reared up on his hind legs, Lug was taller than the Unglers. But he wasn't a natural fighter. Izzy could hear the fear in his voice as he cried "Stay back!" and swiped his claws at them. Shadows dripped off him slowly, like globs of black honey.

Two of the Unglers charged forward. They vaulted off their spindly hands and wrapped bony gray arms around Selden's neck. He bit and thrashed and shook them off. But he couldn't move as quickly as usual, slowed down by the shadows at his feet. Another Ungler tackled Lug, dragging him down into the dark mist like it was trying to drown him in it.

Izzy pulled herself on top of the wall. She gripped tight to the rough stones so she wouldn't slip off the other side. The wall was about as thick as a diving board, and it extended ahead of her, encircling the city. Izzy could hear the roar of the Liadan River, rushing past the base of the wall hundreds of feet below.

In the air, a silver bird dive-bombed the Unglers that wrestled Selden and Lug. Selden had cut a deep gash in the face of one of the beasts. He stood in front of Lug, baring his teeth at the other Unglers. Tom stood beside him, waving a short spear.

Across the plaza, three more Unglers slunk out from the shadows of a side street. There were too many for the Changelings to fight.

"Dree!" Izzy shouted. She pointed to the gathering Ungler mob. "You've got to go find Peter!"

Dree paused in midair. When she saw the Unglers, she turned and sped through the castle doors.

The Unglers crossed the plaza, snouts to the ground like bloodhounds. Izzy froze, terrified they'd smell her. But the beasts had picked up some other trail. They lifted their heads and started cantering up the castle steps.

Horror rippled through Izzy. The Unglers had smelled the Changelings inside. Hiron, Ollie, Hale, and all the little ones. Peter must be with them, but what if he couldn't protect them?

"Hey, hey!" cried Izzy. She clapped her hands overhead. "Hey! Look over here!"

The Unglers paused, rocking on their back hooves. They swung around and raised their eyeless faces at her. The Unglers lumbered toward Izzy, slowly at first and then in a burst of rickety motion that made her stomach lurch.

Springing off their long back legs, the Unglers leaped onto the wall. Scraping and scrabbling, they pulled themselves to the top. The beast closest to Izzy opened its mouth wide, baring curling brown teeth at her.

Izzy screamed and shrank back from them, nearly falling off the other side. She flipped onto her hands and knees and started crawling along the top of the wall. Behind her, the Unglers' snorts turned into excited shrieks. Izzy pushed herself to her feet. Holding both arms out for balance, she started to run.

The Unglers followed, chasing her along the top of the wall in single file. The beast directly behind her lunged forward, swiping its wormy fingers through her hair.

The wall extended another fifty feet in front of Izzy, then made a sharp right angle as it wound around the plaza. There was nothing beyond the edge of the wall but open air and a straight drop into the river.

Izzy felt for that wispy trail of memory that had floated in the dark of her mind ever since she first read *The Book of the Bretabairn*. Instead of letting the memory drift past, she grasped onto it and held tight, pulling it close. With a rush, the Change took hold of her, just as her foot touched the last stone in the wall.

Izzy heard the Unglers' shrieking behind her, and then the sounds fell away, down and down, as the beasts careened over the edge. Their bony bodies flailed in the air as they bashed against the city wall and hit the river below.

Izzy didn't fall with them, because Izzy was flying.

Shakily, clumsily, but flying. Her blackbird wings sliced through the night. The air flowed smooth and glassy over her sleek feathers, curling into turbulent eddies beneath her, pushing her, lifting her up. Izzy's heart lifted too. She had done it.

She heard Peter's flute ring out from the castle. It was the happiest sound she'd ever heard.

His song swept the shadowy mist away, and the streets flooded with morning light. Peter marched down the castle steps, switching to a high-pitched tune that seemed to drive the remaining Unglers mad. They writhed and then fled, loping down the side streets with Tom and the Watch at their heels. Izzy opened her beak and cawed triumphantly.

But just as the thrill of what she'd done set in, Izzy glanced down at the dark river far below. Her wings wobbled. Time to get back down to the ground before she lost the Change and crashed.

She tilted her wings at a slight angle and circled over the plaza, trying to spiral down for a landing. She could see Selden and Lug. They looked ragged, but they were on their feet, so they must be all right. Dree had Changed into herself and was tending to a bloody scratch on Lug's shoulder.

Now Izzy had to worry about landing. The ground beneath her suddenly looked very hard and unforgiving. She aimed for the fountain, hoping the water would soften the impact when she landed. Fairies who'd tried to get away from the cold shadows had jumped onto the fountain's rim. Izzy sailed over their heads, her eyes on the water.

As she stretched her feet out to land, cold fingers wrapped around her throat and yanked her out of the air.

Izzy immediately lost the Change and became herself again. She gasped, but the breath strangled in her throat. She reached up and clawed at the fingers around her neck, trying to pry them away.

"Look what I've caught," said a low voice near her ear.

Izzy looked up into the face of the man with the crocodile mask. He loosened his grip on her enough that she could gulp down a breath. Then he took off his mask.

He stared at Izzy with bright eyes, the color of green lichen. The same eyes Izzy had seen watching her in the Edgewood. "Hello, Bretabairn," he said. "I've been looking for you."

SHADES AND SHADOWS

THE GREEN-EYED MAN REGARDED Izzy curiously, the way a little child might watch an insect it planned to crush under its shoe. He had the smooth, unlined skin of a young man, though dark shadows clung to the hollow spaces beneath his cheeks and eye sockets. Locks of dark hair were tucked behind his ears, which were perfectly—humanly—round.

"You are a curious creature, aren't you?" he said to Izzy softly. "You seem to be a Changeling, but you aren't a very good one if I can shake the Change right out of you."

Peter hurried down the castle steps and out onto the plaza. "Put her down, Rine," he commanded.

The name sent a shiver through Izzy. Rine. The witch they'd been warned about.

Rine's eyes swung down to meet Peter's. His thin lips forced a smile, and he clenched his teeth tight as he spoke. "Hello, again, Piper. It's been quite a while since we've seen each other.

It's nice of you to recognize me. Then again, I'm sure I'm one of the more memorable ones."

Peter walked steadily forward. With every step, the shadows thinned and swirled out of his way, like water running down an open drain. "Release the girl, and you won't be harmed."

Rine gave Izzy a shake. "She's not a girl. She's a pathetic excuse for a Changeling, but I've been looking for one for so long that she'll have to do."

All the other fairies standing around the fountain had fled except for a woman wearing a bat mask. She took the mask off, releasing ringlets of thick black hair tucked behind round ears. Another witch. She looked younger than Rine and more nervous. While he talked to Peter, she chewed one side of her lower lip, then the other. Rine snapped his fingers, startling her. He gave her some unspoken signal, and she nodded.

Leaning forward, she put her fingers to her mouth and pulled a thread of spit from between her lips. She drew it out with both hands, like a spider spinning silk. Izzy had seen Morvanna do this before. The witch was making a chain. The spittle changed into loops of glittering silver that she coiled between her palm and elbow.

Izzy kicked, but Rine tightened his grip around her neck until she held still. The witch wrapped the chain around and around Izzy, pinning her arms down to her sides. When Izzy was completely bound, Rine let go of her and pushed her into the curly-haired witch's arms.

Izzy gulped air down her bruised throat. She squirmed against the bindings, but it only made the chain squeeze tighter.

"Don't do anything foolish," the curly-haired witch whispered to Izzy. "Be nice and still, and you won't get hurt. Not immediately anyway."

Selden growled and started forward, but Peter put up his hand. "Don't move. Let me take care of this."

"Yes, take care of things," said Rine coldly. "The way you always do, Good Peter. The way you take care of the Exchange, the way you take care of us humans. You are so good at your job. You don't always get it right, but what's one mistake here or there?"

Peter grimaced. "No, I don't always get it right. But I can make it right for you now. What is it you want? Tell me, and I can arrange it."

"You know what I want," said Rine. "But you won't give it to me. You won't lift the bans."

"I can't," said Peter, taking another step forward. "You know that once I set them, no one can lift them. Not even me."

"The King's Key could solve that problem."

Peter kept taking small steps forward, holding his flute pressed tight to his chest. "I don't know where it is. It might be gone forever."

Rine wagged one finger back and forth. "No, not gone, just hidden. And if you don't know where it is, then it sounds like you don't have much to offer me."

Izzy glanced down. Rine's hand twirled toward the shadows that still lingered at the base of the fountain. His fingers twisted and tapped the air. Below him, the shadows spun, forming a short black rod.

"I'll help you find the Key if you let her go," said Peter. "We can look for it together."

Rine's eyes narrowed. "Do you think I'm stupid? You might have fooled Morvanna, but I've got more sense than to listen to your flattering lies. The only thing you care for are those brats." He swept his arm out at Selden and the other Changelings standing nearby. "Well, I care about them too now. They're the reason I'm here."

Peter raised his flute to his chin. A change had come over him. Izzy almost didn't recognize the terrible, imposing figure striding closer. He seemed to have grown taller, and he glared at Rine with eyes blacker than the shadows at their feet.

"I'm warning you," said Peter, his voice echoing across the quiet plaza. "You have taught yourself well, but you know you still can't match me."

Rine didn't waver. He held the rod of shadow in his fist. With a wave of his fingers, the end whittled to a fine point. When he lifted it, it gleamed solid and sharp. He had made a knife.

Rine stepped in front of the witch with the dark curls and put one arm around Izzy's shoulder. "I recently learned that Changeling hearts hold the secret to finding the King's Key," he said calmly. "I could just take this one and see where that gets me."

"Stop!" said Peter, holding the flute to his lips. "I'm warning you…"

Rine drew the shadow blade back. He aimed the tip at Izzy's chest.

Izzy gasped and held her breath.

Peter's flute played one pure, resonating note. A beam of white light streamed from the flute and shot across the plaza toward Rine.

Rine ducked. Izzy shut her eyes. She felt the heat of the light beam race past her left shoulder. It burned so bright and hot that Izzy's vision glowed red behind her eyelids. When she opened them again, black spots pulsed all around her.

Izzy blinked. The witch with the dark ringlets was gone. A flurry of bright sparks floated down in the place where she had been standing just a moment before.

Peter looked stricken. He dropped his arm, nearly letting his flute slip out of his fingers.

Rine wrapped his arms around his stomach and doubled over, trembling. Izzy was sure he'd been wounded. His whole body shook violently, and the knife slipped out of his hand. Izzy saw her chance. She threw herself down from the fountain and rolled away from him.

Peter recovered himself. He raised his flute and played the same piercing note. Another bright beam of light shot out toward Rine. Before the beam struck him, Rine's body burst into thousands of tiny green pieces. A sharp gust of air picked them up and scattered them across the sky. They looked like shiny leaves flicking back and forth as the wind carried them north and out of sight.

The whole city had fallen quiet. Seconds after Rine vanished, the fairies who'd hidden or fallen to the ground cautiously stood up and began talking, relieved to be alive.

Peter sunk to one knee. Dree, Selden, and Lug ran past him to help Izzy. When they got the chain loosened and off her, Dree wrapped her arms around Izzy.

"Are you all right?" Dree asked, looking her over.

"I'm—I'm OK," said Izzy shakily. "I'm OK."

Lug hugged her close. "Thank goodness Peter was here!"

"Come out, come out, dear friends! He's gone!" Lufkin cried out to the timid fairies. "The witches are no match for our Piper! All hail the Piper! Our protector!"

Cheers roared across the plaza. Peter didn't join them. Izzy didn't either. She'd been close enough to Rine to hear him as he vanished.

He had been laughing.

ONE BLACK FEATHER

IZZY WOKE LATE THE next afternoon with all the muscles around her arms and shoulders in tight knots. It took her a moment to realize the soreness must have been from flying the night before.

She lay in her bed, looking up at the ceiling. She had done it. She'd Changed into her blackbird form, the hardest one of all. The realization should have made her happy, but instead, she was haunted by the image of Rine's glowing green eyes. Any time she tried to remember the feeling of Changing, she remembered the feeling of his fingers around her throat instead.

Izzy tried to remind herself that everything was all right. Peter had reassured them that the spell Rine cast to make himself split into thousands of pieces was a costly one. The sun would have to set and rise three times before he would be able to pull himself together again. Izzy knew his appearance in

Avhalon would affect the plan for the big Exchange, but she didn't know how. She needed to find Peter.

She slid out of bed and got dressed. Dree must have already gotten up, because her bed was empty. Izzy walked downstairs, past the clatter and clang of the Changelings in the dining room and out to the main courtyard. All the open spaces on the castle grounds were shaded by the high castle walls, so the air was still cool. Olligan sat on the wall in his human form, legs dangling over the side. Beside him perched three large crows, each one the size of a cat. Izzy smiled as she watched Ollie having a conversation with them.

He held his arms crossed, and his head dipped respectfully. He made short gravelly caws. The crow beside him answered with a single squawk. Olligan spotted Izzy and hopped down from the wall, Changing into a squirrel in midair, then back to himself again halfway across the courtyard.

"Hiya, Izzy. You feeling all right?"

"I'm fine," she answered, waving one hand casually, touching her bruised windpipe with the other. She wasn't sure how much Ollie knew about the night before, and she didn't feel like talking about it now. "Have you seen Peter?"

Ollie shook his head. "Not since last night. But these guys are asking for him too." He pointed at the crows with his thumb. "Strange birds. Not from around here at all. I was trying to be polite, make small talk, you know. Normally, crows are so chatty, you can't get them to shut up." He scratched his head and looked back at the birds. "But those guys weren't interested in talking. It's weird. Look, here comes another one."

A fourth stout crow circled over the courtyard and landed beside the others. It nodded to the first three and then settled down into a watchful silence. Ollie was right. Izzy had never thought about it before, but it was strange to see crows sitting together, not making a peep.

"What do you think they want?" asked Izzy.

Ollie shrugged. "Maybe they're just passing through. I can't imagine they flew here from very far away though. They look like they're a hundred years old."

"Older than that," said a voice behind them.

They turned around. It was Good Peter. He walked into the courtyard, both hands in his pockets, and took a seat on the bottom step next to Izzy.

"Have you seen them before?" Ollie asked, nodding at the crows.

"A few times," answered Peter. "Don't worry. They won't hurt you." He leaned forward, resting his elbows on his knees. Once again, he looked different. The commanding, powerful figure who had saved them the night before was gone. Peter was back to being his regular, dapper self, though Izzy could tell from the faint crease between his eyebrows that something was bothering him. "I'm glad I found you out here, Izzy," he said. "I wanted to talk to you."

Izzy hadn't gotten the scolding she felt she deserved for

leaving the castle the night before. She waited for the lecture she knew she had coming.

"Don't look so worried. You aren't in trouble," said Peter. "I wanted to tell you that I owe you an apology."

Izzy sat down on the step beside him. "An apology? Why?"

"For snapping at you the other day when you came to talk to me in my study."

"Oh, it's not a big deal—"

Peter held up one finger. "Let me finish. It's natural you would want to know about yourself and your past. I shouldn't have gotten angry with you for asking."

Izzy couldn't remember ever hearing Peter apologize for anything. He'd snapped at her before. He'd snapped at all of them. That's just how he was. She looked at Ollie to see if he thought this was as strange as she did, but Ollie had walked back out into the courtyard to watch the crows.

Peter continued. "When I told you that I don't know who your parents were, it's the truth. I don't know where you really came from."

Izzy nodded. "It's OK. I understand."

"But there is something else I didn't tell you," said Peter. "And I think I should tell you now."

Olligan, who wasn't paying attention to their conversation at all, gave a laugh of surprise. "Hey, take a look at this!" he said, pointing to the sky. "Three more crows! They're coming this way too."

Peter squared his shoulders to face Izzy. His relaxed smile was gone. His words came fast and serious. "Izzy, the man who brought you to me when you were a baby wasn't a fairy. He was a human who I had brought here as part of the Exchange."

Izzy leaned back, unsure what that meant. "Who was it?"

"He wouldn't tell me his name. But I remembered him from many years before. He had something wrong with his leg. He walked with a crutch."

Izzy was having a hard time listening, distracted by Olligan and the crows. The three birds Ollie had spotted landed silently on the courtyard wall beside the others.

Peter also glanced at the birds as he continued talking. "The man told me he found you. You were all alone, with no family. He begged me to take you to Earth and made me promise to give you to a good family there."

Izzy felt a spike of sadness at this confirmation. She was an orphan for sure then.

"But why would you do it?" she asked.

Peter looked down and ran his finger around the cuff of his jacket. "I told you before that sometimes I make mistakes. I don't always find the best homes for the children I Exchange. This man told me I owed him the favor." A pained look flashed in Peter's eyes. "So I took you to Earth. I could tell you were a Changeling from the start. Since you were only a baby, I worried you'd Change accidentally and give yourself away. So right before I placed you with the Doyle family, I put a light enchantment on you to subdue your Changeling powers."

"Is that why I have so much trouble Changing?" asked Izzy.

Peter shook his head. "The enchantment was minor. It would have worn off long ago." He shrugged and continued his story. "I didn't think much about you at the time, I was so busy. But later, I thought something was strange about the whole affair. I tried to find the man with the crutch when I returned, but I couldn't. He had vanished. Then I went back to Earth to try to find you, but you were gone too."

"My family moved," explained Izzy. At least she knew that part of the mystery.

"I decided to let it go," said Peter. "It seemed odd but not important. I forgot about you. I forgot about the man with the crutch." He frowned. "But now I think I should have found out more. The man had been upset when he brought you to me. Frantic almost. It should have been a clue. I suppose I have to add it to the long list of my mistakes."

On the courtyard wall behind Peter, two more crows flapped down. Izzy looked around. There were now at least twenty birds sitting on the wall.

Olligan caught her eye and held his hands out at his sides. "Can you believe this? So odd!"

Peter looked at the birds and then turned back to Izzy. "I thought hiding you and the other Changelings would be the best way to protect you, but now I'm not sure it's possible.

Rine has grown more powerful than I thought. He'll find a way to get to you eventually, even on Earth. Something has been on my mind all day today. For some reason, Rine has singled you out, Izzy. Of all the Changelings in the plaza last night, he grabbed you. In the Edgewood, you were the one he was watching. I doubt even he understands why he is drawn to you more than the others. But I think you had better figure it out before he does." Peter put his hand on Izzy's shoulder. It reminded her of the day, nine months ago, that he told her she was a Changeling. But this time, he didn't give any answers, only more questions. "I think the only way to be safe is to find out the truth about yourself. Where did you come from? Who are you, Izzy? Who are you really?"

Peter's words struck Izzy cold. Those were the very questions she wanted answered more than anything else in the world.

"Then we'll find the answers," she said, putting on a smile. "You'll help me. We'll figure it out together."

Peter closed his eyes tight, and when he opened them, they held so much sadness. "I can't," he whispered. "I can't help you anymore."

"What the heck…" said Olligan. "You guys, take a look at this!"

Izzy and Peter both stood up. A hundred crows now sat perched on the courtyard walls. With the same jerky motion, they each twisted their heads over one shoulder and plucked a long flight feather from their wings.

One by one, they flew down to the center of the courtyard and placed their feathers on the ground, then flew back to their perches on the wall. Olligan backed up until he stood beside Izzy.

"I've got to go get Selden," he said, edging up the steps sideways. "He's got to see this!"

The crows had created a tall pile of shimmery black feathers. When the last crow had added its feather to the pile, the whole flock of them began to caw loudly.

"What's going on?" asked Izzy, shouting to be heard over the din.

Peter put his hand on Izzy's shoulder, and together, they walked out into the courtyard.

The pile of feathers shifted. With each caw from the crows, it pulsed, growing taller and taller. In one surge, the feathers swirled upward in a whorl of purple and black. When they settled, they formed a robe that covered the broad shoulders of a tall woman. Her long hair, iridescent like crow feathers, fell in straight sheets around her face. She gazed at Peter with her wide-set eyes. They were black, just like his, just like the birds.

"Hello again, Piper," she said. "It's been a long time."

Peter bowed to her. "It has, Your Honor."

"Do you know why I'm here?"

Izzy looked up at Peter. His face was calm as he nodded, but she could feel his hand tremble where it rested on her shoulder.

"Long ago, you were given a flute of great power." The woman had a deep, scratching voice, and she made strange clicking sounds between the words. "As a check on that power, you swore an oath never to use it to harm a human. You have broken your promise."

Izzy took a step forward. "But he had to! He did it to save my life!"

"Shh," whispered Peter. "It's all right."

Izzy pressed one hand to her heart. She tried to make her voice calm, even though she was afraid. "Please," she said to the woman. "If Peter did something wrong, it was for a good reason. He won't do it again."

The woman stared down at Izzy. She tilted her head one way, then the other. The crows held still and watchful. Izzy held her breath. Without answering Izzy, the woman turned back to Peter and held out her hand. "You must relinquish your gift," she said. "You have lost the right to use it."

"I don't have the flute," said Peter. "It is gone."

Izzy looked up at him, wondering if he was lying. She'd never seen the flute out of arm's reach of him.

The woman tilted her head again, like she was listening for something. After a moment, she nodded. "You tell the truth."

Izzy took a shaky breath. This was devastating. How could Peter protect them without his flute?

The woman kept her hand outstretched toward Peter. "It's time," she said softly.

Peter slipped his hand off Izzy's shoulder and started walking toward the woman.

Izzy's stomach dropped. "Wait!" She ran beside him and grabbed his sleeve. "Where are you going? Peter, what's going on?"

Peter patted her hand and gently removed it from his arm. "It's all right. Just remember what I told you." He glanced back at the castle. "Tell Selden he's in charge now. Tell him I'm proud of him, and I trust him to take care of everyone."

Tears filled Izzy's eyes. "Peter, stop it! Where are you going?"

She followed after him, but when she got close to the black-haired lady, she stopped. The air surrounding the woman was as cold as a winter night. It made Izzy afraid. She backed up until she could feel the warm, safe summer air again.

Peter stood in front of the woman, and she took his hand in hers. Peter was a tall man, but even he had to tilt his face up to meet her eyes.

"I'm ready," he said.

The woman picked up the edges of her feather robe and wrapped it around his shoulders. The crows took off from the wall and flew in circles around them. The air filled with the snap of flapping wings and the blue-black sheen of feathers.

"Peter!" Izzy screamed.

The birds whirled faster and faster, whipping dust into her face. Shielding her eyes with one hand, she stumbled forward. She grasped for the woman's cloak, but it slipped through her fingers.

The other Changelings burst out from the castle and ran down the courtyard steps. When they saw the swirling black, they stopped, confused and frightened.

"Selden!" Izzy cried. "Help me!"

Selden Changed into a wolf and charged across the courtyard. By the time he reached Izzy, the crows were flying so fast that they were a solid blur of black. Izzy grabbed at the place where Peter had stood. Feathers sliced her fingers, and she pulled them back.

The crows swirled higher. They were no longer birds but a vortex of black air that rose into the sky, higher than the castle towers. It tapered like a spindle, left the ground, and disappeared into the clouds.

Izzy lowered her hand from her face. She and Selden sat alone on the dirt in the courtyard.

One single black feather floated down and landed gently in her lap.

APPEARANCES AND VANISHINGS

THE NEXT DAY, LUFKIN held a showy memorial service for Peter that none of the Changelings could stand to attend. Izzy and Dree watched the spectacle from the open window in Selden and Lug's room, which looked directly over the plaza.

"And so as the old wisdom of Faerie states," boomed Lufkin, his voice quivering with fake emotion, "all those born beneath the sun perish beneath the sun. Of course, the Piper was a Neverborn, so I suppose the saying doesn't really apply to him, but the spirit does." He blew his nose into a lace handkerchief with a loud honk.

"Peter would have ridiculed this nonsense up and down," said Dree. "And look at that horrid necktie the constable is wearing. He could have at least shown a little class. I'm tempted to fly down and snatch off his wig."

"But is it so wrong to pay tribute to Peter?" Lug sobbed, his real tears a stark contrast to the ones the constable was squeezing out. Lufkin had probably stuck pepper grains in the corners of his eyes to get them to water. "Shouldn't we be down there to honor him? For—for everything he did for us?"

"I just can't believe it," whispered Selden. "I can't believe he's really gone."

None of them could. At first, they'd all stood in the empty courtyard waiting for him to show back up. But, of course, he didn't come back, and as the hours passed, Izzy became more and more sure he was never coming back again. Just like the black-haired woman had been able to feel that his flute wasn't in Faerie, Izzy could feel that the Piper wasn't there anymore either. She'd never realized how safe she'd felt just knowing Peter was out there somewhere. Even on Earth when she'd felt alone and miserable, she always had the sense that someone was keeping one eye on her. And now that someone was gone. They could all fall off a cliff, into the abyss, and no one would catch them.

"Who was that woman supposed to be anyway?" asked Selden, his sadness giving way to anger. "Some sort of judge? She wouldn't even listen to you, Izzy, when you tried to explain what happened. Where's the justice in that?"

"It's true," said Lug, wiping his eyes on his forearms. "Peter's been around for so long. He's done so many good things. Surely, that would count in his favor. Surely, the judge could let him have one tiny mistake in all those years."

"That tiny mistake was the only one he couldn't make," said Dree. "He knew it too."

"So did Rine," said Izzy. She thought about his quiet, satisfied laugh. "He set that whole thing up: tricking Peter into killing that other witch. He wanted to get Peter out of the way."

"Oh, but at least we've still got the Watch," said Selden with a grim smirk. "With Lufkin and his fairies protecting us, we've got nothing to worry about."

Dree snorted. "Lufkin keeps asking Tom, 'You're sure the witches only want Changelings? No one else?' I'm surprised he hasn't kicked us out of the city with a big sign around our necks. *Come and get 'em, Rine. Just leave the rest of us alone.*"

Lufkin had shifted the Watch from guarding the castle to just guarding the city gates, which they were all too happy to do. The servants had left them as well, stuffing their pockets with silverware on their way out the door. Tom Diffley was the only fairy still sticking by them.

But even though Tom was a brilliant inventor, he couldn't wrap his mind around how to deal with all the Changelings. They were too heavy to carry away in the *Muscadine* at once. Some would have to walk. And it was too dangerous to try a trek to the Edgewood along the open road. Someone might spot them, and word could get to Rine where they were going.

Tom did what he could, keeping an eye out on the surrounding areas from the *Muscadine*. They had less than two days before Rine would regain his strength. After that, they were certain he'd come after them.

They were like planets spinning off their orbits. No one had liked Peter's plan for the massive Exchange, but at least he had a plan. And now that they'd seen Rine face-to-face, they understood why Peter had wanted to get them out of Faerie so badly. The catch was that now they couldn't do it without him. They could probably find their way to Earth on their own, but without Peter's flute, an Exchange was out of the question.

What would a mob of unruly fairy children do on Earth all by themselves? Where would they go? And what would stop Rine from sending Unglers after them anyway?

Dree leaned forward and craned her neck out the window. "What's going on down there?"

The crowd gathered at the memorial had turned to see one of the Watch running up the street into the plaza. He spoke to Lufkin, making panicky motions in the direction of the Liadan River.

"Oh no. What now?" said Lug.

"We'd better go find out," said Selden.

With no one left to protest their leaving the castle, they followed Lufkin's entourage through the winding streets to the eastern end of the city. The tall gates that opened onto the Liadan Bridge were barred shut. Members of the Watch stood on the ramparts high above, looking nervously over the other side.

"What is all the commotion?" demanded Lufkin, sweaty and puffing from the downhill hike.

"We don't like the look of this, sir!" shouted one of the Watch. "This lady out here, she just appeared out of nowhere!"

The fairies murmured worriedly. Some of the crowd went running back to the safety of their homes.

Lufkin twisted his wig back and forth. "Is it—is it another witch?"

"Don't think so," called the Watch. He gripped the tops of his ears. "She looks like a fairy. Pretty old."

"You open that gate this minute," called a gruff voice on the other side. "Or I'll get a switch and tan your britches!"

Izzy's heart lifted to hear the familiar voice.

"It's all right, Mister Lufkin. You can open the gate!" said Izzy. "We know her. She's not a witch."

Not technically anyway, Izzy thought, squeezing through the gates as they opened. She ran across the bridge to the old woman in question, threw her arms around her, and burst into tears.

"There, child, it's all right," whispered Marian as she smoothed down Izzy's hair. "Now let me get a good look at you."

She held Izzy out by the shoulders. Dozens of tiny wrinkles appeared at the corners of her eyes and lips when she smiled. Marian had lost the splotchy tan Izzy remembered. But she still smelled the same—like herbs just clipped from a kitchen garden.

"Oh, Marian, so many terrible things have happened," said Izzy, wiping her cheeks. "I don't even know where to start."

Marian's smile gave way to sadness. "I know, child. I'm sorry about Peter. I came as fast as I could, but I just couldn't get here in time. I would've liked to tell him goodbye."

"But how did you know?"

Behind Izzy, the city gates creaked as Lug rolled them open on their heavy hinges. Lufkin and all the rest of his entourage stayed behind him, still wary of the strange lady.

Marian put one finger to her lips. "He sent a message," she whispered. "Not to me, but I still got it."

She walked midway down the bridge. Izzy followed behind, then stopped, confused.

"What in the…" Izzy whispered, leaning forward.

A round brown eye the size of a lemon floated in the air above her. It blinked. Izzy smelled the sharp sweetness of hay and heard a fluttering whinny.

Marian made a soft shushing noise. Then she reached up and swiped her hands through the air, like she was pushing aside curtains. She stood so her body blocked any view of what she was doing from the fairies back at the gate. A tangle of golden curls appeared out of the air, followed by a tie-dyed T-shirt and a pair of legs covered in bandages and chigger bites.

Izzy rushed forward. "Hen!"

Her little sister wore a triumphant smile as she put her hands on her hips. "I *knew* you weren't in a sidekick institute!"

Hen's arrival brought a burst of much-needed happy energy to the castle. The younger Changelings were thrilled to see her, and any sadness they felt about Peter was temporarily eased by the bubble gum Hen brought in her backpack.

"Check this out," Hen explained to Phlox, spreading out the gum wrapper. "There are jokes on the inside. And tattoos. Just lick and stick."

Phlox licked the thin paper and slapped it onto her forehead.

"Perfect," said Hen.

Izzy was dying to know how her sister had gotten to Faerie all by herself, but she let Hen reunite with all the others first. After Lug picked her up and swung her around and after Park and Rusk had shown off their wooden fortress and after Hen had given out the friendship bracelets she'd woven at camp, Marian shooed everyone else away and pulled both sisters into the kitchen.

While Marian heated the kettle for tea, Izzy explained as clearly as she could what had happened since Peter took her from Camp Kitterpines.

When Izzy finished, Marian drew off her cap and wiped her brow. "I should've got here sooner."

"I don't know if you could have stopped Rine. The only one who could was Peter."

Marian shook her head sadly. "No, I couldn't have stopped him. But I could've carried out my part of the plan faster."

"What is your part of the plan?" asked Izzy. "Please tell me what's going on."

Marian leaned out the doorway like someone could be listening.

"Don't worry," said Izzy. "All the servants left. We're all alone in the castle. Tom's the only one still with us, and he's up in his ship."

"Humph, that doesn't mean nobody's watching you. How do you think Rine found out you were here in the first place? He must have had somebody spying from inside." Marian pulled the curtains over the sink shut. She carried the steaming kettle from the stove to the table and sat down between Izzy and Hen. "Peter didn't tell you anything about what I've been doing?"

Izzy shook her head. "He told me you were living in the country, working."

Hen's eyebrows bobbed up and down. "Oh, she's been working all right. Show her, Marian."

Marian set her teacup down on the table. She held one hand over the cup, letting the steam drift up between her fingers. She stared at the cup with her lips pressed tight. Her mouth twitched, holding in unspoken words.

Then she tilted her head and narrowed her eyes. She clucked her tongue like she was calling a reluctant puppy dog.

Izzy watched the old woman's face wrinkle in concentration. When Izzy looked back at the cup, she gasped.

"It's gone! You made it disappear!"

Marian smiled. "Not gone. Watch." She lifted the kettle and started to pour.

Water streamed out of the kettle and disappeared, vanishing right into the air. Izzy leaned forward. When she looked down from above, she could see the perfect circle of the surface of the tea. But if the cup was in the way, everything inside was invisible.

"That," said Izzy, "is seriously—"

"Amazing."

They turned to find Dree watching them from the kitchen doorway. Marian waved at her to join them. Dree's eyes stayed fixed on the cup as she sat down next to Izzy.

Hen's chair rocked back and forth as she wiggled on her seat. "She can do it to big things too! I rode all the way here from the Edgewood in an invisible wagon!"

"The horses wouldn't sit still for me, so I had to cover them with bed sheets and do the spell on the fabric," said Marian. She lifted the invisible cup to her lips and slurped. "It's an interesting spell. You ask the light to go straight through a thing instead of bouncing off the sides. Took me a long time to get it right. I learned you gotta be real polite when you ask light to do anything."

Reflection, refraction, transmission. Izzy's science class had been studying those exact concepts at the end of the year. She would never have guessed someone could control them. Izzy had always wondered why only humans could do witchcraft and not fairies. After all, she'd seen fairies do some pretty incredible stuff—like Change from one creature into another. But now she was beginning to understand. There was something decidedly unfairy about the magic she'd just witnessed.

"Can you make the cup visible again?" asked Dree.

Marian waved her hand over the table as she nodded down at the teacup. It reappeared, just as before.

"Isn't she awesome?" said Hen.

Marian leaned back in her chair. "Peter's plan was to have me use this spell to transport all the Changelings to the Edgewood in secret. We were going to hide you all in Netherbee Hall while he Exchanged you one at a time."

"Netherbee Hall!" said Izzy. The last time she'd been in the old, crumbling house, she'd been nearly suffocated by enchanted cobwebs.

"I've been living there," said Marian. She winked. "Don't worry. I cleaned it up. And I put this same cloaking spell on the entire house. You'd never find it even if you had a map." She frowned. "'Course, that was before Peter discovered that Rine was controlling the Unglers. My spell can hide Changelings from sight, but it can't help when it comes to those nasty beasts. If only I could've learned this spell sooner!"

Marian cracked her knuckles one after the other. "I found the spell months ago in an old book in one of the rooms at

Netherbee. But it's taken me all this time just to be able to read the thing. Casting spells takes a lot of concentration, and even though I lived with humans most of my life, it still doesn't come natural."

"It's amazing you can do it at all," said Izzy. "We could still use your spell to get out of Avhalon in secret. But then what? The Changelings can't be Exchanged without Peter. And he destroyed his flute."

"Don't you want to hear my story now?" asked Hen.

Izzy squeezed her sister's hand. "Sorry. Yes, I want to hear everything."

Hen reached down and pulled her backpack up onto the table. "By the way, I knew you weren't at a sidekick facility."

"Psychiatric," Izzy corrected.

"Whatever. I knew something funny was going on. There were too many exclamation points in your letters."

"And that's what tipped you off?" asked Izzy.

"That and I was getting cookies in the mail from Mom and Dad every other day. You know Mom. She hates us to have anything with sugar in it."

"Your little sister's a sharp one," said Dree.

Hen smiled and pushed back her shoulders. "I just had this feeling you'd gone looking for Faerie and that you'd found it without me." Hen's chin wrinkled up, but to her credit, she didn't whine about being left behind. They were long past that, and she knew it. "Then I got this package special delivery yesterday morning. When I opened it, I knew something was really wrong."

Hen unzipped her backpack and pulled out a lumpy package wrapped in brown paper. Fifty dollars' worth of stamps covered the wrapping. Whoever sent the package had wanted to make sure it arrived.

Hen reached inside. Dree gasped as Hen pulled out Peter's flute. The instrument gleamed in the dim light of the kitchen.

"I knew Peter wouldn't be apart from this unless things were bad," said Hen, holding the flute on both open palms. "So I packed up and snuck out of camp while my cabin was at the yarn craft station. I went into the woods thinking Peter would be waiting for me, but no one was there."

"So how did you find your way into Faerie?" asked Izzy. "Did you play the flute?"

Hen lifted the flute to her lips, which was a bit of a shock. It seemed wrong to see anyone play it besides Peter. She blew gently, and it made a hoarse whistle.

"That's the best I can do. But it was weird. Just holding it, I could tell where to go. Like I could see things in a different way than I could before. I found this pathway, this underground passage with stone walls."

"That's exactly how Peter brought me here," said Izzy.

"And I just kind of went down the halls, wherever I felt I should go," continued Hen. "I figured I was going the right way, because these lights kept coming on as I was walking."

Marian nodded. "That flute's a very old magical object. It only works for one master, and it has to be given freely from one master to another. It was given to Peter. And now it seems that Peter's given it to you."

"But why me?" asked Hen, looking down at the flute and turning it back and forth.

"He had his reasons," said Marian. "It's something to take seriously."

"Very seriously," said Izzy. She suddenly worried about Hen having something that Peter had misused. She told them a condensed version of what had unfolded with Rine and the witch with the dark curls.

"Don't worry about me," said Hen. "I can't even get this thing to play a note. I don't think I could hurt anyone with it."

"So we have the flute," said Dree. "But we can't use it. And we can't just sit here waiting for Rine to come and pluck us up. We've got to go back into hiding."

"Selden probably doesn't like that plan, does he?" asked Izzy.

"Actually, he's taking Peter's charge pretty seriously," said Dree. "I think he'd do what's best for everyone, even if it's not what he wants."

Izzy cast her eyes down at the table. "Oh. Gotcha."

Dree leaned in closer. "Why?" she said suspiciously. "Please don't tell me *you* want to stay here and get into a witch fight."

"No, of course not," said Izzy. "I don't want to see Rine ever again if I can help it."

"What do *you* think should be done, Izzy?" asked Marian.

Izzy picked at the edge of the table. She'd been thinking of something all morning, but now she was afraid it sounded completely crazy. She took a deep breath and told them what Peter had said to her in the courtyard, about how finding out the truth of who she really was could somehow help all the Changelings.

"It was the last thing he told me before he left," said Izzy. "It's hard to explain, but the way he said it, it sounded important."

"But how could you find out something like that if Peter didn't even know himself?" asked Hen.

"He told us about this lake," said Izzy. "The creatures who live at the bottom of it will answer any question you ask."

"Lake Umbra!" said Dree. "That's at the foot of the Norlorn Mountains." She leaned close to Izzy, wide-eyed, and tapped her forehead. "Also known as the *Witchlands*."

"I know, I know," said Izzy. "I wouldn't even think about it normally. But seeing that spell of Marian's…" She nodded at the now-visible teacup. "If you could do it to Tom's airship—"

"She could! She could! I know it!" Hen bounced so high in her chair that it nearly toppled over.

"We could zip there, ask a question, and get back without anyone seeing us," said Izzy. "And we'd be so high up, we wouldn't have to worry about the Unglers."

Dree crossed her arms over her chest. "Perfect. Selden's finally being reasonable, and now you've gone and lost your mind. Marian, you can't seriously do what she's asking. Can you?"

Marian poured another cup of tea. The steam drifted around her face, mingling with her white hair. "If Peter thought it was important, then it probably is. He wouldn't suggest putting you children in danger unless it was for a very good reason. Besides, there's an old fairy saying that I always thought was very wise." She smiled at Izzy. "Go with your gut."

Izzy shut her eyes. Her gut, her heart, her brain, every part of her was asking the same thing.

Who are you, Izzy? Who are you really?

She opened her eyes and nodded at Marian.

The old woman stood up and pushed her chair in. "Well, we've got to find Tom. Sounds like I have a ship to vanish."

16

TO THE NORLORNS

THE CARAVAN LOADED UP early the next morning, before the sun came up, before Lufkin was awake, and before they could give themselves a chance to change their minds. Horses hidden beneath their invisible blankets stamped and huffed on the bridge. The older Changelings helped Hale load all the younger ones into the invisible coaches Marian brought with her from the Edgewood.

Olligan kicked at an invisible wagon wheel. "Selden, why do I have to go in this dumb wagon full of babies? I'd rather go with you."

Selden ruffled Ollie's curls. "You've got to be the lookout for Marian. That's a really important job. Plus, someone's got to keep Dree from ruining every bit of fun along the way."

Dree raised one eyebrow but didn't return his teasing. She'd been strangely quiet ever since their conversation in the kitchen the day before. But when Izzy asked her about it, she had changed the subject.

"Are you sure you don't want to come with us?" Izzy asked Dree once more. "You wouldn't add any more weight to Tom's ship."

"Marian might need a flyer," said Dree as she handed a very sleepy-looking Yash to Hale through the carriage window. "Besides, Hiron's a much better choice to go with you. If for some reason you get in trouble in the air, you'll want a gigantic eagle on your side."

Izzy nodded, though she would have much rather had Dree along for company than stodgy Hiron.

Dree hugged Izzy tight. "Be really careful. And don't let Selden talk you into doing anything stupid."

"I heard that!" called Selden from the back of the caravan.

"I meant for you to," said Dree. Then she Changed into a butterfly and flitted onto Marian's shoulder.

Never one for sentimental goodbyes, Marian nodded once, then clucked to the horses, and they were off across the bridge. Anyone watching would have seen an old woman walking alone along the City Road, with a white butterfly fluttering along behind.

The *Muscadine* set off, sailing north over the apple orchard as the sun rose. Lug, Selden, Hen, and Izzy rode in the basket with Tom, with Hiron flying ahead. Izzy had been dead set against Hen coming, but her little sister threatened to tie herself to the ship if Izzy tried to leave her behind again. And Tom reasoned that it could help things with the Fen Whelps to show them Peter's flute as proof of how important their question was. "Anything that persuades them not to chew you up is a good idea if you ask me," he'd said.

Izzy watched Selden, curled around one of the *Muscadine's* invisible cables, the wind riffling through his stoat fur. He leaned far out over the rim of the basket, like a figurehead on a sailing ship.

"You realize if anyone looks up at us, they're going to see a floating weasel coasting through the air?" she said.

"Stoat," corrected Selden. "And don't ruin this for me. It's as close as I'll ever come to flying. Besides, I don't think there are many fairies down there to see me. Come take a look."

Izzy glanced at Tom Diffley for permission.

He nodded to her. "It's all right, I fixed the balance problem." He pointed out the sacks of flour he had taken from the kitchen and tied down along the perimeter of the basket. "Makes us heavier, but we can ditch weight later on if we have to."

Izzy joined Selden at the rim of the basket. She had to feel around with her hands before she finally found a cable to hold onto. Marian had cast her vanishing spell over the *Muscadine's* balloons, including all the ropes and rigging. The underside of the basket was cloaked too so they'd be invisible to anyone on the ground looking up. Marian had left the inside of the basket visible, but that was it.

"We're already over the Avhal Mountains," said Selden, pointing below. A gust of air blew Izzy's hair back as she leaned over the side. Dark prickles of pine trees jutted up from the ground below.

"See that forest?" said Selden. "That's the Needled Larsh. The ground underneath is soggy and full of pits of tacky mud. If we didn't have Tom taking us in his ship, it would take months to get across it."

"Gosh, we're going fast, aren't we?" said Izzy.

"That's because I've got a top-notch copilot," called Tom from his seat at the controls. He patted Hen on the shoulder.

Hen gave a short nod. "Just doing my job." She stared intently at a bank of square dials on the panel in front of her and clutched the handles of the steering frame. Izzy smiled as she watched Tom coach her little sister on maneuvers. Hen was in heaven.

"There, you've got it now," said Tom, pumping more air into the invisible balloons above. "At this rate, we'll be into the Norlorns in no time. I'm gonna try to get us to Demon's Dome by dusk. Otherwise, we'll have to land and spend the night somewhere nearby, which I'd rather not do, to tell the truth."

"Demon's Dome?" asked Izzy. "What about Lake Umbra?"

"The lake's right at the base of Demon's Dome," said Selden. "The story goes that a thousand years ago, the fairies who lived in the mountains captured a demon king and buried him alive. They say Lake Umbra is filled with his blood, which is still leeching out of his heart."

"Can we skip over the talk about blood and leeching?" said Tom with a shudder.

"I'm with you," said Lug. "I'm not going near that cursed lake. The only reason I agreed to this is because we're doing a flyover and won't have to land anywhere near it."

Hiron, in his crane form, gracefully winged in alongside the ship. "Izzy, are you ready to get some practice in?"

Izzy's stomach flipped over on itself. "What, *flying* practice? Now?"

Hiron banked his wings one way, then the other. If Izzy didn't know him better, she'd have said he was grinning. "Come on. The conditions are perfect!"

"No way! We're up so high!"

"It's actually easier the higher up you are," said Hiron. "As long as there's air flowing over your wings, it'll lift you up. And if you do fall…"

With one beat of his wings, Hiron Changed into an eagle with a wingspan the length of the ship. "…I'll be there to catch you!"

"Go on," said Selden. "You did a blackbird the night of the Solstice. Surely you can do it again."

"If you don't want to go, can I?" asked Hen. "I want Hiron to fly me all around!"

Izzy looked at the ground, which was very, very far down. She thought back to that night of the Solstice, trying to remember the impossible feeling of soaring over the city on her own wings.

Instead, she remembered Rine's cold voice in her ear. *A pathetic excuse for a Changeling.*

"No," she said, curling her fingers tight around the basket. "Sorry, I'm just not ready."

"Suit yourself," said Hiron, banking away from the ship.

Izzy watched him glide effortlessly on his broad wings. He folded them back and spun in a tight barrel roll, laughing. Now Izzy understood why Hiron was so serious on the ground. He didn't belong on the ground at all—he belonged in the air.

A flock of white-throated ducks coasted in alongside them from the east, their muscular bodies bobbing up and down with every stroke. Izzy always thought of ducks as clumsy barnyard animals, but they were actually impressively powerful flyers. She sighed. She couldn't even keep up with ducks.

Hiron flew back beside the ship, gliding along behind the flock.

"Should you try to talk to them?" Izzy called to Hiron. "Ask for directions or something?"

Hiron shook his head. "I don't even think they'd talk to Olligan if he were here. Ducks can fly for hours without stopping, and they're so proud of themselves. They never give me the time of day."

"Hey, ducks!" shouted Izzy. "Stop being so snobby!"

Hiron laughed. "Yeah, you think you're better than us or something?" As the ducks put more distance between themselves and the ship, Hiron pointed north with his beak. "Look, we're getting close now. You can see the Norlorns from here."

At the horizon, white spires of snow-capped peaks rose up to meet the clouds. Below the mountains, the ground climbed up sheer and steep, as if the entire northern half of Faerie had lifted straight up like the step of a staircase.

The ducks made a sudden sharp turn to the west, flying away from the *Muscadine* at a fast clip.

"Touchy," said Izzy. "Was it something we said?"

Hiron was back to his serious self as he searched the skies around them. "I don't like the way they left so suddenly like that. They must have seen something we didn't. We should keep our eyes open."

Izzy turned around to see Tom and Hen frowning worriedly at the controls. Izzy used the rigging to help pull herself along until she stood behind her sister. Hen's knuckles were white from gripping the steering frame so tightly. "What's wrong?" Izzy asked.

"We're too low," said Hen, who didn't take her eyes off the view of their course. "If we can't get higher fast, we'll run right into those cliffs!"

The *Muscadine* sped toward the rocky uplift. A deep canyon sliced into the cliff, but it seemed much too narrow for the ship to sail through. A sharp spire of slate guarded one side of the canyon. If the ship ran into it, it could rip the bottom out of the basket.

Hen checked the gauges in front of her. "It's no good," she shouted to Tom. "We're not rising fast enough!"

Tom stood up and jumped behind the air pump. "Selden, Izzy, I need a hand here!"

Selden Changed into his boy form. Izzy joined him, cranking up and down on the wooden pump handles. They could hear the hiss of air but could only hope the invisible balloons were inflating fast enough.

"Hen, how are we doing?" called Tom.

"We've gotta get higher!" said Hen.

"All right, Lug…" panted Tom, still pumping air into the balloons. "Time to start earning your keep!"

Lug began heaving the sacks of flour over the side. The basket tilted and rocked as the weight that had held it balanced went overboard.

"Someone is going to see all that stuff dropping out of the sky," said Selden. "We're going to give away our position!"

"Can't be helped," grunted Lug. "We've got to drop weight, and it's either these flour sacks or me!"

"It's working!" said Hen. "We're rising!"

"Are we going to clear that spike?" asked Tom.

"I can't tell. If we do, it's going to be close!"

A sudden, sharp crack reverberated through the air. More cracks followed, like ice cubes snapping in a glass of warm water but a thousand times louder.

"What in the name of Faerie was that?" said Tom.

Izzy ran to the rim of the basket and looked down. The cracking sound had come from the spire of rock. As Izzy watched, a layer of slate separated from the rest of the spire. It calved off in a single thin sheet, scraping shrilly against the stone.

Izzy expected to see the sheet fall down into the canyon below. Instead, the slate slid upward. It folded back on itself, and two enormous wings of stone stretched to the sky.

"You have got to be kidding," whispered Izzy as she watched the rocky spire transform into the largest bird she had ever seen.

A curved beak the length of a cutlass opened wide. The giant bird screeched. The force of the sound nearly knocked Izzy backward.

The bird scrabbled on its massive claws. Every part of it was made of stone—its talons, its belly, its back, even the wafer-thin sheets of slate that covered its body like feathers. It spread its wings and leaped into the air. Clouds of rock dust billowed down as the bird circled over the mouth of the canyon, then climbed high above the ship.

"Hiron!" Izzy called, waving him over. "What is that thing?"

Hiron flew in alongside the *Muscadine*. "Rock Skyr!" he answered. "But I didn't think they nested so far south! You think it saw the ship?"

Slowing its ascent, the stone bird hovered directly over them. It twisted its head, and sunlight glinted off its polished eye. With a sharp screech, it began to dive.

"Definitely seen us!" shouted Izzy.

"Tell Tom to try a landing!" said Hiron. "I'll try to slow it down!"

Hiron, who had seemed so large in his eagle form a moment before, looked small and delicate compared with the monstrous Rock Skyr. He flew at the Skyr, claws bared right at its eye. The beast barely flinched as Hiron slammed against the bird's skull, his wings crumpling around him.

"Hiron!" cried Izzy.

Stunned, Hiron fell, spiraling down out of the air. Just when Izzy thought he would crash, he thrust out his wings and managed to gain control.

The Rock Skyr circled again. It folded its wings back and sped down at the ship, talons bared like a hawk ready to scoop up a mouse.

"Get down!" shouted Tom.

Everyone on board ducked and covered their heads. But as the Skyr neared the basket, its body jerked to a sudden stop in midair. Hen screamed as the basket jolted. The Skyr had collided with one of the ship's invisible balloons.

The beast flailed, snared in the invisible rigging. The basket tilted sharply. Tom and Selden clutched on to the ship's machinery as Hen went sliding toward the rim.

"Hen!" Izzy wrapped one arm around a rope and reached out with the other hand for her sister.

Hen's backpack slid along beside her. "Oh no!" Hen twisted her body, catching the backpack by one strap but missing Izzy's hand entirely. She knocked once against the rim of the basket and tumbled out into the empty air.

"HEN!" screamed Izzy.

For one horrible moment, Izzy stared at the space where her sister had fallen. Then a flash of golden feathers appeared as Hiron soared up, clutching Hen in his talons by the back of her shirt. He dropped her into the basket, and she grabbed onto Izzy's arm.

The basket spun as the Rock Skyr struggled in the invisible ropes. The whole ship began to plummet.

"We've got to cut that thing loose!" shouted Tom.

Selden Changed into a leopard and slashed his claws overhead. "I could get it free, but I can't see what I'm cutting!"

"We need Marian!" said Hen. "She could make everything visible again!"

Izzy looked around frantically. Her eyes landed on a sack of flour Lug hadn't thrown over the side yet. "That's it, Hen! We've got to make the ropes reappear!"

She flagged down Hiron and shouted her plan to him.

"Good idea!" he said. "Lug! Toss me that last sack of flour!"

Lug heaved the sack over the side, and Hiron caught it in his claws. He carried it over the Rock Skyr and tore into the sackcloth with his talons. The bag ripped open, and flour spilled out and settled onto everything beneath, forming powdery outlines of the balloons and all the ropes and rigging.

"There! I can see them now!" Selden leaped from rope to rope, slashing the ones the Rock Skyr was most tangled in. When he cut the last rope, the giant beast burst free of the ship and wheeled away to the west.

The *Muscadine* continued to sink.

Everyone held tight to whatever they could get their hands on as the ship spun uncontrollably. Izzy could hear a high-pitched whine overhead. The Skyr must have punctured one of the balloons before it got away.

"Everyone hold on!" cried Tom. "We're going down!"

The *Muscadine* dropped down into the canyon below. The ship swayed, knocking into one side of the canyon walls and then the other. With a crunching crash, the ship slammed into a grove of gold-leafed trees, rocked forward once, and then fell down into the shallow river at the bottom of the canyon.

Izzy climbed out of the wrecked basket and stumbled in the knee-deep water. She looked around, dazed. "Hen? Everyone? Are you OK?"

"I'm here!" Selden, in his stoat form, jumped down from one of the tree branches and helped Izzy search the wreckage.

It was difficult, because the half-deflated balloons were still mostly invisible, and they covered everything.

Coated in rock dust and flour, Lug emerged from beneath an invisible clump of fabric. He had Hen cradled in his arms.

Izzy ran to her little sister. "Oh my gosh, Hen! Are you hurt?"

"I'm fine." Hen coughed. "But where's Tom? And Hiron?"

Before they could start looking, they heard a shuffle behind them. Izzy spun around. One man, then two, and then two dozen men and women wearing brown and gray hooded capes stepped out from behind the trees.

Selden backed up against Izzy and Changed into a wolf. Before he could even complete the Change, one of the men bounded into the river and aimed a slingshot at Selden's snout.

Izzy now realized she had been mistaken. This wasn't a man at all. He was as tall as a grown man but covered all over in fine, tawny fur. What Izzy had thought was a brown hood was really a pair of ears. They were long and slender, like a hare's, with a jagged scar running down the edge of the left one.

The strange rabbit-like man kept the slingshot trained on Selden while the rest of his companions swiftly closed in around them.

When they were surrounded, the rabbit-man lowered his weapon and shook his head with a good-natured smile. "Of all the creatures to be taking prisoner today, I didn't expect a handful of Bretabairn."

THE FILLIFUT

IZZY GULPED DOWN HER soup even though she was pretty sure the gritty powder swirling in the bottom of her bowl was dirt. She was so hungry that she could've eaten an entire tower of peanut butter sandwiches, which she realized she wasn't very likely to get, not at the bottom of a rabbit warren at the edge of the Norlorn Mountains.

She sat on the packed dirt floor of a spacious, round room with Hen, Selden, and Lug beside her. Overhead, the squiggly ends of plant roots poked down from the ceiling. Two of the rabbit-people, a short-eared man and a woman with light-gray fur, squatted on either side of the entrance, their faces guarded and blank. Whenever Izzy tried to ask them questions, they just puffed air out their wide nostrils. She hadn't seen their leader, the one with the mangled ear, since they were all taken underground.

Hen leaned her head on Izzy's shoulder. "Do you think Tom and Hiron are OK?"

Izzy put her arm around her sister. After the wreck, the rabbit-people had searched what was left of the *Muscadine*. They hadn't found Tom Diffley. Izzy hoped that was because he was hiding from them and not because he was crushed beneath the invisible hull of the ship. There had been no sign of Hiron on the ground or in the sky.

"I'm sure Hiron flew away," Izzy whispered. "He's figuring out a way to help us right now. And you know Tom. He's building something that will get us out of here."

"It better be something that can dig a deep hole," said Selden, patting the dirt wall beside him. "We've got to be thirty feet underground."

"It's too bad Rusk isn't here," said Lug. "He can Change into a mole. He'd have us out in no time." Lug sniffed his empty soup bowl. "Wish I knew how they made this stew. Smells like dandelion root but more lemony. They must have a different variety up here in the mountains."

"I tried to keep track of where they were leading us," whispered Selden, eyeing the guards. "But once we got underground, I got lost from all the twists and turns. Even if we could fight our way out, I don't think we could actually find our way to the surface."

"No one's doing any fighting," said Izzy. She nodded at the slingshots both guards kept at their hips. "We'll have to come up with some other plan. We just need to think."

A soft thumping echoed in the passageway outside. The

guards straightened up and saluted. The leader with the ragged ear appeared and waved at the guards to relax. He whispered something to the male guard. The guard nodded and retreated on all fours down the hallway.

"Hello again, Bretabairn," the leader said cheerfully as he entered the room.

Izzy couldn't stop staring at this strange mixture of man and hare. His face was long and narrow and covered with fur, and his eyes were set more to the sides of his skull than the front. A smile tugged at the corners of his black lips.

He sat back on his haunches and crossed his arms casually. "And hello to you, human child," he said to Hen with a friendly nod.

Hen crossed her arms and glared back at him. "Hello yourself."

The rabbit-man chuckled. "Fair enough. But let's be friendly, can't we? Haven't we treated you well so far?" The guard reappeared and handed his leader a bowl of the same gritty, herby soup. The rabbit-man took a sip and held up the bowl like he was giving a toast. "Did you eat enough? Say the word, and you can have more."

"The word," said Lug, raising his hand. "And you must tell me, is this dandelion root? Because I distinctly taste—"

Selden elbowed him in the stomach. "Don't make small talk with him! He's our jailer!"

The man handed Lug the rest of his soup. "Your friend is

right, I'm afraid. Now is not the time for polite conversation. Though under other circumstances, I'd happily talk recipes with you." His eyes sharpened, and he tilted his head back, looking at them down the length of his slender face. "Which one of you will tell me what a handful of Changelings is doing here at the edge of the Witchlands in a ship under a witch's spell?"

"Why should we tell you anything?" asked Selden. "We don't know anything about you or who you serve."

The rabbit-man narrowed his eyes. "The Fillifut serve no one but ourselves."

"Fillifut?" asked Izzy.

"The quick-footed ones. My name is Fye. As our herd's leader, I have the right to know the reason you are trespassing on our lands."

Izzy glanced at Selden and Lug, but they seemed just as surprised to learn of the existence of this warren of half-rabbit creatures as she was.

Fye tilted his head, regarding them with one eye. "This is some sort of test, isn't it? To see if we will fulfill our bargain with Rine?"

Izzy's stomach dropped. "You have a *bargain* with Rine?"

Selden stood up. "I knew it! They look like rabbits, but they're rats through and through!"

The female guard snarled and reached for her slingshot.

"Stand down, Race!" barked Fye. "You and Clip go up top. I can handle this on my own."

Race nodded to her leader but kept one eye on Selden. Both guards left, their long feet slapping the dirt as they disappeared down the hall.

Fye turned back to Izzy. "If this isn't a test, then that makes you the most foolish children I have ever met." He frowned, all his friendly cheer gone. "I am under oath to bring anyone I suspect of being a Changeling straight to Rine."

Hen's hands balled into fists. "You can't do that! He'll kill them!"

"Why would the witches help you cloak your ship only to kill you?" asked Fye. "And why would you be heading straight into their domain if you are under such a threat? You aren't telling the whole truth."

Hen broke into sobs. Lug pulled her close, and she turned her face into his shoulder.

Izzy stood up with her palms facing out, trying to keep her voice calm. Fye seemed reasonable. If she could just explain things, she could get him to understand. "Did Rine tell you why he wants you to bring him Changelings?"

Fye shook his head. "We don't speak to each other more than is necessary."

Izzy couldn't keep her words from rushing out, pleading and desperate. "I know this must all look very strange. It's complicated. But Hen's telling you the truth. If you hand us over to the witches, they'll kill us. They want our hearts for some sort of potion, and as soon as they find us, they'll cut them out!"

Fye looked appalled. "Cut your hearts out?"

"What did you think they were going to do?" said Selden. "Invite us in for tea and biscuits?"

"Let me try to explain why we're here," said Izzy. "If we can just get to—"

Selden held his arm out in front of her. "Don't explain anything to him. Can't you see he's going to hand us over no matter what? He swore an oath to the witches. That tells you what sort he is. I bet Rine throws him some shiny brass coins for being such a good servant."

The room swirled in a confusion of black and brown fur. Selden Changed into a wolf, but Fye sprang on him first. The rabbit-man pinned him from behind, the cord of his slingshot pulled across his throat. The sounds of the guards' feet pounded in the hallway.

"Everyone, please calm down!" said Lug.

Race and Clip reappeared in the doorway, but Fye waved them away.

Selden, stubborn as always, struggled against him once more before Changing back to himself and falling down on the floor, coughing and gasping.

Fye put his slingshot away. "Don't talk about things you know nothing about," he said to Selden. He started to leave the room, then turned back to Izzy. "Our pact with Rine is only for the Bretabairn." He nodded at Hen. "We can set her free as soon as we deliver the rest of you."

"Please," said Izzy, her voice coming out as a whisper. "You don't understand what you're doing."

Fye looked at her sadly. "I do. And I'm sorry for it."

He turned and left them alone.

LAKE UMBRA

THAT NIGHT, IZZY AND the others whispered among themselves, trying to come up with a plan to escape. But even though they plotted until their voices went hoarse, they kept coming to the same conclusion—there was nothing they could do as long as they were underground. They'd have to wait until they reached the surface. Hen kept mumbling something about needing her backpack, which was lying somewhere among the *Muscadine* wreckage. But even Peter's flute couldn't do them any good, not when Hen still couldn't play more than one note on it. Their best hope was that Hiron and Tom would figure out a way to rescue them from above.

Izzy slept heavily, without dreaming, until morning—at least she assumed it was morning. It was hard to tell time underneath the ground. The female guard, Race, came in with a candle, bringing the scent of fresh air with her down into the earthy burrow.

"Fye has had a message from Rine," she said. "We're to take you to a meeting point outside the borders of our lands, where we'll hand you over."

"How nice to get the opportunity to march to our own death," said Selden, still groggy with sleep. "Why not hand us over here and get it over with? I'm sure Rine is chomping at the chance to zoom in and scoop us up."

Fye came in and leaned against the doorway. "Rine won't set foot on Fillifut lands," he said. "None of the witches will. When their kind first started arriving centuries ago to set up a settlement in the Norlorns, they had to cross through our valley. My ancestors made them sign a treaty before allowing them to pass. As long as the witches touch Fillifut soil, their spells are useless."

"And you really trust them to stick to that?" asked Selden.

"They don't have a choice," said Fye proudly. "The treaty holds, whether they want it to or not."

Selden snorted. "If you're all so powerful, then why are you working for them?"

"Enough talking. It's time to go," said Race, pushing Selden out the door and into the hall. "And remember, no Changing. We've all got eyes on you, and they don't call us the quick-footed for nothing."

They followed Fye through the tunnel, down winding passages lit by stubby candles set into the dirt walls.

They passed by openings that led to other large rooms

where Fillifut families stood in the doorways. Wide-eyed little bunnies who sucked their fingers and clutched at their mothers' skirts gawked at the Changelings as they passed by.

Fye stopped at the entrance to one of the rooms. He put his hands on the doorway and called inside. A speckle-coated Fillifut woman emerged carrying a small bundle of fur in her arms. She passed the baby to him.

"How is she this morning?" Fye whispered, nuzzling the baby's ears.

"She had a better night than last," the woman answered wearily. "She tried to stand up again this morning."

Fye raised his eyebrows.

The woman shook her head sadly. "She couldn't."

That's when Izzy noticed that something was wrong with the little Fillifut's back legs. Her feet were thin and bowed inward, twisted wrong. Izzy knew she was intruding on a private family moment, but she couldn't look away. She was mesmerized by how gentle Fye was with his baby.

"Give her the rest of the tonic," he whispered to the woman. "There's no need to save it for later. When I get back, I'll have buckets of it. She'll be well again." He smiled and kissed the little one gently. Then he kissed the woman on her cheek as he passed the baby back to her.

They were off up the passages again. Fye glanced down and caught Izzy looking at him.

He cleared his throat. "My daughter isn't well," he said softly.

"I'm sorry," said Izzy. "What happened to her?"

"Some years ago, an illness fell on our herd. Well, not all of us," he added bitterly. "Only the children. They're born with twisted feet. It's painful for them. The only thing that makes it better is a tonic the witches make. They brew it for us in return for guarding their borders. This spring, Rine sent us a message that if we bring him Changelings, he will double the amount of tonic he gives us."

So that was why the Fillifut had to turn them in. Izzy watched Fye's troubled face. He was just as trapped as they were.

They exited the warren through a tangle of tree roots and into a grove of slender trees with pearly white trunks. The sun had just begun to rise, but after so much time below ground, the dim light was blinding. The Fillifut seemed to expect this and lingered near the entrance to let their prisoners' eyes adjust.

A buttery, garlic smell wafted through the air. Several wood fires burned nearby with big kettles swinging over them.

"Oh, bless us all," groaned Lug, looking longingly at the cooking fires.

"I could hear your stomach growling all down the hallway," said Selden.

"Sit, sit, Bretabairn," said Fye, motioning to some long wooden tables near the cook fires. "You've got to fill your bellies if you're going to make the trek ahead of us."

He spoke to the Fillifut manning the fires. They handed

out wooden plates piled high with bright-green herbs drizzled in a honey-colored sauce.

Lug rubbed his hands together. "I'm trying awfully hard not to like this Fye fellow, but he doesn't make it easy."

Izzy knew what he meant. Fye waited until all the other guards had their plates before he took one for himself. He reminded Izzy of her dad a little, the way he knew everyone's name and something about them. And he had a tender spot for the children. He walked over to the small table where they sat having their breakfast. He told a joke that sent them into a fit of giggles.

Izzy followed their lead, scooping up the herbs and sweet sauce with her fingers and slurping it down like noodles.

Beside her, Lug munched his food slowly, like he was savoring each bite. "Fye, sir, what is this that we're eating?"

"Bell clover."

"Bell clover? Really?" said Lug, his eyes wide with interest. "We have it in the Edgewood. But it's different. This looks the same, but the taste is…I don't know how to describe it. A little sharper, I suppose."

Izzy cracked a smile in spite of herself. Leave it to Lug to admire the foliage even in the midst of a crisis.

"It's quite a tough herb," said Fye. "Grows the whole year round, even under the snow."

"Really?" said Lug, sniffing a sprig of the plant. "That's incredible for any kind of clover. Must be some strange hybrid."

"In my father's time, the Fillifut had to retreat south every winter," explained Fye. "But a few years ago, when the bell clover began growing in our valley, we could stay all year. It's helped to strengthen us."

"Oh fantastic," said Selden, pushing his empty plate away. "You'll have to point it out to me if we pass some so I can crush it under my boot."

Fye laughed. "You've got a soldier's sense of humor, Bretabairn."

One of the Fillifut mothers came over to shoo the children back underground. Hen nudged Izzy's arm. "Look," she whispered.

Instead of hopping straight off, they reached under the table to grab crutches and canes. Their feet were wrapped tight in bandages.

Fye whistled. It was time to go. The Fillifut formed a line with Izzy and the others sandwiched between. Izzy could tell Selden was sizing them up.

Race fell in line behind him. She leaned forward and tapped him on the shoulder. "Before you get any ideas, know that there's a pair of Fillifut eyes on you at all times, even if you can't see them."

Izzy looked out into the surrounding trees. Perfectly camouflaged behind the trunks were dozens more Fillifut soldiers. Fye wasn't taking any chances with such valuable prisoners.

They started out hiking along the canyon river, through the stands of lovely gold-leafed trees. The canyon widened and became less steep and then opened out onto a green valley studded with rolling hills.

Fye and his troops loped more easily over the open ground. The entire wide valley belonged to the Fillifut, and their group swelled larger and larger as more of their kind leaped out of burrows to join them. Their troop now had over fifty rabbit soldiers. With a sinking feeling, Izzy realized their likelihood of escaping was even worse now than it had been down in the burrow.

Even if she could have Changed into a blackbird and managed to fly away without a slingshot bringing her down, Selden, Lug, and Hen were earthbound. The Fillifut kept Selden separated, so she couldn't even talk to him about an escape plan. The only way they were getting out of the valley was if Tom and Hiron could make a miracle happen. Izzy kept her eyes trained on the sky, but so far, she hadn't seen or heard any sign of them.

As they neared the edge of the Fillifut lands, the bell clover grew thicker, blanketing the ground in a solid carpet of green. The Fillifut would reach down every so often and swipe up a big handful of the herbs and stuff it into their mouths.

Lug plucked the clover as well. He held it up to his nostrils and sniffed, then held it out to let the sunlight filter through its leaves.

"Absolutely intriguing," he said. "It grows so vigorously."

"Someone hurry him along!" called a soldier. "We can't keep stopping to smell every blade of grass in the valley."

Clip, the short-eared guard assigned to Izzy and Hen, chuckled. "Can you imagine if the wildflowers were blooming? We'd be old hares by the time we reached Demon's Dome!"

Izzy stopped in her tracks. She exchanged a glance with her sister.

"Demon's Dome?" asked Hen casually. "That's a weird name."

"Cheerful name for a cheerful spot," said Clip.

He pointed straight ahead, to the mountain that had just come into view. The top was rounded, like a bald head. Two rocky peaks behind it gave the illusion that the mountain had horns.

"The Dome marks the threshold into the Witchlands," said Clip. "We're taking your friends to the other side for the handover."

"How much farther?" said Hen.

Clip looked west, where the sun had begun tracking toward the tops of the mountains. "If your big friend hadn't slowed us down so much, we could have made it there by nightfall. But we'll have to camp near the base and make the last push in the morning."

Izzy kept her head down. She didn't want the guard to see that she'd started sweating.

Demon's Dome.

Lake Umbra was right there, nestled somewhere at its base. They were now within walking distance of the whole reason for risking their lives to come. Izzy had to get there. But she had no idea how she'd get out from under the sharp Fillifut eyes.

Fye halted the company among a cluster of hills. Demon's Dome loomed to the north. There were no warrens here and no trees to provide cover. The Fillifut seemed nervous, ears twitching constantly, eyes on the border. Whatever treaty they had with the witches, it obviously wasn't built on trust.

Fye set up a perimeter guard and assigned three Fillifut to each Changeling and five to watch over Selden. The friends were kept far apart. Hen pouted and cried about nightmares until Clip broke down and let her sleep next to Izzy.

Hen rolled closer to Izzy. "Did you hear what he said?" she whispered. "Demon's Dome! Lake Umbra has to be close."

"I know," said Izzy. "We've got to figure out how to ditch Clip."

Hen wrinkled her nose. "If I just had my backpack!"

"Will you quit talking about that stupid backpack already?"

"No talking!" barked Clip.

Izzy waited until he looked away. "I just had an idea." She whispered it to Hen.

Her sister grinned. "Just tell me when."

Izzy lay on a pillow of bell clover, watching thin clouds blow slowly across the stars. Hen dozed off beside her, but Izzy stayed awake, listening for the right moment.

The Fillifut were scared. Izzy knew what that felt like.

And she also knew that being scared makes you jittery and awake—at first. But after hours of being tense with fear, you get tired. And when you're tired, you make stupid mistakes. She just had to wait it out.

It took all night, but finally, when the sky over the eastern horizon had just begun to glow a watery blue, she sat up and poked Hen in the ribs.

Camp was silent. Two of the guards assigned to her lay sleeping in the grass. Clip kept watch at the top of the hill. His eyes would close, then jolt back open.

Izzy and Hen trudged sleepily toward him.

"I have to go to the bathroom," said Hen.

Clip yawned. "So go."

Hen shook her head. "Not here. Someone will see." She hopped from one foot to the other. It was so convincing that Izzy wondered if she really did have to go. "Please?" Hen whined. "I really have to go. I really, really, really have—"

"All right!" snapped Clip. "This way."

"I'll go help her," said Izzy. "Last time she went outside, she peed on her feet."

Clip rolled his eyes. He led them down the other side of the hill and through the perimeter guard, muttering something about being on diaper duty as they passed. The girls followed him over the top of another hill. At the bottom on the other side grew clumps of twiggy grass, high as Izzy's shoulders. The guard pointed to the grass.

"That's as much privacy as you're going to get. I'll wait at the top of the hill. I'm counting to twenty, and then I'm coming back. Got it?"

"We got it," said Izzy. She walked Hen down behind the reeds.

"He's not looking," whispered Hen, craning to see over the plants. "Now's your chance!"

Izzy crouched down in the reeds. The ground here was muddy and damp. She tried and failed to Change into her fox form. But even without her keen fox ears, she heard the croak of a frog. Water was close by.

Twenty seconds passed. True to his word, Clip called out, "All right, time's up. Let's go already."

"Here he comes," Hen hissed.

"OK, you just stay low."

Izzy stood up. She smoothed back long gray ears and shouted in her best Race impression, "You idiot! You let them get away!"

Clip gaped at the Likeness of Race. He looked all around for the little girls who had been there just a moment ago. "I—they—they were just here!"

Izzy hopped farther into the reeds. "I saw them head this way. I'll follow them. You go get reinforcements! Go!"

Clip turned and bolted back uphill toward camp. Izzy ran through the grass in Race's Likeness for a dozen yards before letting it drop.

"Hen, let's go!"

"Right behind you!"

They only had a few minutes before Clip would snap out of his sleepy stupor and realize his mistake. But Izzy didn't need much time. They were close now. Up ahead, through the reeds, a thin mist rose off the surface of a lake the color of ink.

"You think this is it?" asked Hen.

Lake Umbra was smaller than Izzy thought it would be. Through the mist, she could make out the opposite shore.

Izzy walked down to the water's edge, her boots crunching in the wet sand. It was strangely quiet. No birds, no insects, not even a breath of wind to rustle the reeds.

"Hello?" Izzy whispered loudly. "Is anyone there?" She stood for a moment, listening to herself breathing. "Please! If you're there, we need your help!"

The girls waited, watching the still water. "Are you sure this is it?" whispered Hen. She turned to look behind her. "They're going to find us if we don't—"

"Shh!" Izzy grabbed her sister's arm. "Look!"

Perfect circles of ripples flowed toward them from the center of the lake. Out in the deep, a blurry white sphere moved beneath the blackness. Floating just below the surface, it split into two as it drifted toward them. The white shapes bobbed closer and closer until they were only a few yards away. The round faces of two girls rose slowly up out of the water.

Izzy and Hen gasped and stumbled in the muck. The Fen

Whelps' chins rested just above the waterline. Their skin was mottled and so white, it was almost blue. One of the girls had a splash of gray freckles across her cheeks. They stared, unblinking, with black eyes set wide apart like a seal's. They immediately made Izzy think of Good Peter. *Neverborns*, she thought.

"Look, Sister," said the first Fen Whelp breathily. Her voice was like the whisper of wind over water. "Visitors."

"A human child and a Bretabairn," said the second Whelp. "We haven't seen either of those in a good while."

Izzy swallowed, fighting the urge to back away from them. "Please, we've come here to ask you a question."

The Whelps both sagged, frowning. The freckled one dug something out of the corner of her eye and flicked it into the reeds. "Questions, questions," she said. "That's all anyone ever comes here for."

"And they're always such boring ones," agreed her sister. "What's the meaning of life? Does so-and-so really love me?" She looked at Izzy. "I suppose you've come to ask us one of those?"

Hen tugged on Izzy's sleeve and whispered. "The flute! I was supposed to bring it to show them. But it's on the *Muscadine*!"

"You lost the Piper's flute already?" said the freckled Whelp with a cluck of her tongue. "Such a shame what happened to him. I always liked him."

The other Whelp pouted sadly. "He used to come visit us all the time. Never asked us any questions. Had lovely manners."

"Good clothes too," said her sister.

Izzy could hear the shouts of Fillifut and the whack of bodies running through reeds. "Please. We're in a hurry."

"Speaking of manners," said the freckled Fen Whelp.

Her sister leaned forward, sizing Izzy up. "If Peter sent you, then he must have told you that we don't answer questions up top."

"You mean we have to go under?" asked Hen.

The Whelp smiled, her thin lips exposing rows of small gray teeth. "That's not your question, is it?"

"No, it's not!" Izzy looked behind her. The Fillifut were drawing closer. "OK. What do we do? Wait!" It was so hard to remember not to waste a question! "What I meant to say is, please tell us what to do next."

The Fen Whelps shared a satisfied smile between them.

Groaning, they rose up to their full height, ribbons of black water rolling off their skin. Izzy's legs felt weak beneath her. The Whelps had bodies like walruses, but they were at least twice the size. Thick folds of blubbery white skin cascaded down from their shoulders. They pumped their tails, heaving themselves into the shallows toward her.

The Whelp with the freckles leaned forward and held out her thick flipper to Hen. "Ready?" she whispered.

Hen reached for the flipper with one hand and pinched her nose shut with the other. "Come on, Izzy."

Izzy took a deep breath and forced herself to walk. She inhaled sharply as her boots filled with the frigid lake water.

The other Whelp grinned down at her. Izzy reached out and took hold of the rubbery flipper.

With a snarl, the Whelp pulled her under.

A TALE OF BETRAYAL
AND HEARTACHE

THE COLD WATER WRAPPED around Izzy as the Whelp pulled her swiftly down, farther and farther from the light rippling on the surface above.

Izzy's chest burned. She writhed in the Whelp's grip, trying to tell the creature she needed air. She was about to die! The Whelp pulled her faster. Izzy's feet touched something solid. The Whelp reached down and scooped a plug of black silt up from the bottom. She shoved it into Izzy's mouth.

Izzy choked on the slime, gagging as it slid down her throat. She sucked in a breath, expecting to feel water fill her lungs. Instead, it felt like taking a gulp of cold air on a winter day. She breathed in and out, cautiously at first, then more easily when she realized she wouldn't drown.

Hen bobbed on the sand beside her, like an astronaut bouncing on the moon. "This is the coolest thing ever!"

Hen's words came out clearly, not in the gurgling voice Izzy expected. "You mean the weirdest thing ever," said Izzy, pushing away a strand of hair that kept floating in front of her face.

The Whelps had swum a few yards away. They reclined on the sand, flicking their tails, looking bored.

"Well, here we are," said the Whelp with the gray freckles, resting her chin on her flipper. "I'd offer you something to eat. But I doubt we have the same tastes in snacks." She licked her sharp teeth with a thick gray tongue.

Her sister picked a wooden doll up off the sand and twirled it around. The Whelps gave Izzy the creeps. She remembered what Tom said about them, how they chewed up people they didn't like, bones and all.

Hen didn't seem afraid of them. She bobbed over to the one with the doll. "Can I see her? Did you make her? I mean—" Hen caught herself. "I *wonder* if you made her."

The Whelp handed the toy to Hen. "Yes, we make all of them." She nodded behind her to a pile of wooden bodies with jointed limbs.

"Oh wow," said Hen. "That's cool. I have dolls at home, but I never made one before."

"They aren't dolls," snapped the freckled Whelp.

The creature swam over and lifted one of the figurines out of the pile. She tugged on strings tied to its limbs, and it danced on the bottom.

"Puppets!" cried Hen. "Me and Izzy love puppets!"

"You do?" the Whelps asked in unison.

"Yeah, at home, we do puppet shows for Mom and Dad all the time," said Hen. "Izzy comes up with the stories, and I act them out. Izzy knows every story there ever was."

The Whelps exchanged a look. "Not *every* story."

The freckled one smoothed Hen's floating curls off her face. "I bet we know one she doesn't."

The other Whelp scooped up an armful of marionettes. "We never, ever get an audience! Any visitors we get just ask their questions and leave."

The freckled Whelp swam close to Izzy. "Have you thought of your question yet?" she said in her ear.

Izzy's pulse quickened, but her brain felt waterlogged. She should have had this part planned out beforehand. She had to ask the question in the right way. If she asked, "Who am I?" or "Where am I from?" the Whelps could answer her with one or two words, and that would be the end of it. She shut her eyes. How had Peter phrased it that day in Avhalon?

"I think there is some story that connects me to Rine and the King's Key," she started.

The Whelps grew still and leaned forward a little.

Encouraged, Izzy continued. "And I know Peter plays some role…"

The Whelps grinned at each other.

"I wish I could know all about him, about me, the witches, and how we all fit together."

"A question," said the Fen Whelps. "It must be a question."

196

Izzy took a deep breath. "All right. I think I've got it. My question is, what part do I play in the story of Earth and Faerie?"

The Whelps broke into giggles. They clapped their flippers together like excited children.

They took Izzy and Hen by the hands and swam them to a gravelly patch of the lakebed.

The freckled one ran her flipper under Hen's chin. "Your sister has asked a very good question! The perfect question. To answer it, we'll have to tell you a story."

Hen squeezed Izzy's arm as they settled down on the gravel. "Good job!"

"I guess," said Izzy. "At least they don't seem like they're about to eat us."

The light shone down from the surface onto a wooden platform built onto the lakebed. It had been set up like a miniature stage, with fabric curtains waving gently at the back. The Whelps swam behind the curtain, whispering to each other as fabric rustled and wood clacked against wood.

The freckled Whelp rose up, grinning. She cleared her throat and announced, "Ladies and gentlemen, welcome one and all! We now present for you…"

"Bada-bum-bum!" said the other.

"…a performance we call *A Tale of Betrayal and Heartache*!"

The light focused on the stage, and the Whelps receded into darkness. A marionette floated down into the spotlight.

Izzy could barely see the silhouettes of the Whelps controlling the strings above.

"Of all the weird things I've seen in Faerie, this is definitely the weirdest," she whispered to Hen. "A puppet show at the bottom of a lake!"

"Shh! It's starting!"

The marionette strolled to the lip of the stage. A blue suit had been sewn onto him, and he held a little tin rod in one hand. He bowed to the audience and raised the metal rod to his face.

"That's got to be Peter!" said Hen. "That's his flute!"

This was a different kind of magic than anything Izzy had seen before. The strange light and the undulating fabric made the Peter marionette seem alive. He sauntered across the stage, flute to his lips. Even though his features were just painted on, the Fen Whelps had captured him perfectly. It made Izzy realize how much she missed him. The curtains parted, revealing a painted forest backdrop that Izzy assumed must be the Edgewood.

Two smaller marionettes followed behind him. They were both boys, both with round ears. These were human children Peter had lured into Faerie as part of the Exchange. They didn't look alike. One had straight dark hair and olive skin. He had a wooden crutch attached to his arm, and it swung out in front of him with every step.

The other boy had thick brown curls. He turned his head

all around, looking in wonder at the painted trees of the Edgewood. The Fen Whelps had used green glass beads for his eyes. They caught the light and sparkled.

"Who's that?" asked Hen.

Izzy sat up straighter. "I think it's supposed to be Rine when he was a boy."

"And who's his friend?"

A swishing whisper came from backstage. *Shush-a-shush-a-sash-a-sash-a.*

"Sasha," murmured Hen. She said it louder. "Sasha? Yeah, I think that's his name—Sasha."

The Good Peter puppet stopped center stage. The boys peeked out timidly from behind him. Two more marionettes, a fairy man and woman, entered the scene. Stiff smiles had been painted across their faces. Peter put one hand on each boy's shoulder and guided them to follow the fairy couple, who hugged them close.

"What's going on?" asked Hen.

"I think Peter is bringing those boys to live with that fairy couple," said Izzy. "They're adopting Rine and Sasha."

The Peter marionette exited the stage. The fairy couple's faces changed. They scowled at the two boys, who cowered under them.

"I don't like them," whispered Hen. "They look mean."

Rine and Sasha sat at the lip of the stage, scrubbing at the wood with tiny rags while the fairies loomed over them, wagging their wooden fingers. At one point, the woman kicked Sasha's crutch out from under him, and he clattered against the stage.

Hen gasped. "Hey! They can't do that to him!"

"Peter told me that sometimes the Exchange goes wrong," whispered Izzy. "He said that fairies aren't always nice to the human kids they take in."

The light flared in Rine's glass eyes, but he couldn't fight back. The stage lights dimmed.

"Was that the end of the show?" asked Hen.

"I think it was just the first act," said Izzy.

The lights came up again, and the boy marionettes had been replaced with older versions of themselves. The same green glass eyes for Rine, the same crutch tucked under Sasha's arm. In this scene, the friends were on the run.

Or rather, one of the Fen Whelps held the puppets dangling at center stage while the other turned a crank that made the painted backdrop scroll quickly behind them. When it stopped, it showed tall mountains topped with snow. A stone cottage stood on one of the slopes. The friends smiled. They hugged each other. And even though Izzy knew she was watching Rine, her enemy, she was glad the boys had escaped their cruel fairy family.

The next act of the play showed Rine and Sasha hard at work. They were learning how to be witches.

Sasha sat at a desk piled high with a stack of books. He

pored over them while the stage lighting went from bright to dim, again and again, to show the passage of days. Sasha obsessed over one book in particular. Izzy scooted closer to the edge of the stage to see. Her heart thumped when she realized what it was. The leather cover had a scrolling *B* on the front, just like *The Book of the Bretabairn*.

While Sasha stayed inside with his books, Rine hiked all over the stage, lifting up rocks and looking underneath, plucking plants and grinding them up. When the two friends came together, they showed each other the magic they'd learned that day. Rine had been working on something special—something he was eager to show his friend.

In the next scene, Rine and Sasha stood in the Edgewood again, near the village where they had first been adopted. The Rine marionette approached the village, arms held out.

Hen sat up on her heels. "What's he about to do?"

Izzy shivered, remembering what Peter had told her the day he brought her back to Faerie. *Some humans have quite a capacity for vengefulness.* "I think he's about to get revenge," she whispered.

The stage lighting shifted to red. One of the Fen Whelps rippled yellow and orange ribbons among the village buildings. Rine had used his spells to set the entire village on fire. He watched it burn, his green eyes glowing with the light from the flames. Sasha tried to stop him, but Rine shook him off.

Rine turned his back on the burning village and walked off

stage without looking back. Sasha watched him leave, shielding his eyes from the blaze.

Hen rose up on her knees and pointed to the burning village. "Look, look! There's something in there!"

Izzy leaned forward so she could see. A small object lay tucked in between the buildings. Sasha crept toward the fire. He plucked the tiny bundle up out of the flames and held it in the crook of his arm. The Whelps added sound effects: a gurgle and coo.

"Aw," said Hen. "Look, Izzy. It's a baby."

Izzy held very still. The bundle was just a stage prop, a smooth stone wrapped in a scrap of fabric. But Izzy knew they had come to the point in the story where she made her entrance.

That little bundle was her. And all the rest of her birth family and her village were burning up, smothered in the red and yellow ribbons of fire.

The lights blacked out. Time for the next act.

Back in their mountain cottage, a spotlight shone on Sasha's desk, center stage. The other lights remained low. It was nighttime, and he was alone. He held the baby, bouncing it on his good knee, turning the pages of *The Book of the Bretabairn* with the other hand. In one swift motion, he ripped out a page. He sat looking at it for a long time. Then he folded it into a small square.

Sasha placed the square of paper on the baby's chest. He

shut his eyes and swayed gently, like he was rocking her to sleep. A golden light began to glow on the baby where the square of paper lay. The baby cooed, comfortable in Sasha's arms, while he kept repeating the spell over and over.

Izzy placed her hand over her own chest. She felt a warm prickling sensation in her heart as she watched the light grow brighter and brighter and then blaze like a firecracker before going out completely.

Hen reached over and took Izzy's hand. "Are you OK? You look like you're going to be sick."

Izzy nodded but couldn't answer. She felt hot and cold at the same time, and her pulse thrummed in her temples.

Onstage, Sasha peered down at the baby, looking worried, but she was fine. She even laughed when he tickled her. The page from *The Book of the Bretabairn* was gone. Sasha had hidden it inside the baby's heart.

In the next act, Sasha and Good Peter appeared onstage together. Sasha pressed the baby into Peter's arms. Even though the puppets didn't speak, Izzy knew this part of the story. Sasha was asking Peter to hide the baby somewhere Rine could never go. He was begging Peter to take her to Earth.

Peter tilted his face at Sasha, as if to ask why, but Sasha shook his head. He wouldn't explain. He looked over both shoulders, like he worried someone would be listening. Finally, Peter shrugged and nodded. He would take the baby.

Sasha bowed to him. He turned and exited stage right,

leaning heavier on his crutch than before. Peter left the stage in the opposite direction with the baby.

One final act remained. The lights dimmed. Props scraped against the stage as the Fen Whelps set the last scene. When the lights came up, Sasha lay in bed, his crutch leaning against the headboard. Rine kneeled beside him, waving his arms over the bedcovers, working spell after spell. Sasha held up his hand to stop him.

"Oh no," whispered Hen. Izzy squeezed her hand.

There was nothing else to be done. Rine hadn't learned the spell to stop death. Maybe that spell didn't exist.

The lights went down. When they came up again, Rine stood looking down on a gray headstone, holding Sasha's crutch. He bent down to lay the crutch over the grave, but at the last minute, he flung it off the lip of the stage. It landed in the sand near Izzy's feet.

Rine's wooden jaw dropped open, and he let out a horrible, heartbreaking cry. He sank to his knees, head hanging down in his lap. The marionette was so still that Izzy thought the play was over. But then Rine looked up into the audience, straight at Izzy and Hen.

His eyes flickered angrily. The light in them grew brighter and brighter until the whole marionette glowed like a torch, tinting the stage and the sand green. Rine flamed white hot. Izzy shielded her face. There was a loud crack, like an explosion, and then everything went dark.

Izzy opened her eyes. Trails of bright-green sparks floated down from the stage and fizzled in the sand.

The Fen Whelps floated out from behind the curtain and swam in front of the stage. They linked flippers and bowed deeply.

Hen wiped the corners of her eyes. She stood up and applauded.

"There you have it," said the freckled Whelp.

"I do believe that was the best performance we have ever given," said the other.

Izzy still held her hand over her heart. She felt numb, like her mouth wouldn't form words. Her lungs had started to burn.

Izzy looked at Hen, who had a strained look on her face.

"Oh, we should tell you," said the freckled Whelp casually. "Once your question is answered, you must get back to the surface."

The other Whelp yawned and stretched. "Else you'll drown."

Izzy gasped, sucking down a cold mouthful of water. She grabbed Hen's hand and kicked off the lake bottom. They climbed and clawed their way to the surface. Izzy shut her eyes tight, her chest about to collapse. Her energy had just run out when a pair of furry arms shot down from the surface and grabbed the back of her shirt.

The arms pulled her up out of the lake and hauled her to the shore, where she promptly threw up a stomach full of black water.

TWISTROOT

Two Fillifut soldiers hauled Izzy out of the water and dragged her through the murky shallows to shore. Izzy knelt in the mud and doubled over, gasping for breath. Her stomach convulsed, and she threw up another plug of water.

Behind her, Race held Hen's hand, leading her out of the lake. Hen's curls and clothes were plastered against her skin, and her teeth chattered, but she smiled excitedly.

"Selden!" she cried. "Wait till you hear what we just did!"

Selden stood on the shore, surrounded by Fillifut guards. He nodded at Hen, then tried to get Izzy's attention. "Did they answer you?"

"Quiet!" barked the guard at his side.

Izzy nodded at him and then stared down at the mud again, trying to make sense of everything she had just learned.

The key to Rine's greatest desire wasn't just inside in any Changeling heart. It was in Izzy's.

The page from *The Book of the Bretabairn* must have been the instructions for finding the King's Key. Sasha had hidden it inside Izzy, because he wanted to keep it away from Rine. He wanted to protect Earth from his friend's terrible power.

"Come on, on your feet," said Race, pulling Izzy up by the arm. "That was a pretty stupid trick, trying to swim across Lake Umbra. It's a good thing the witches won't care if you're sopping wet as long as you're alive."

The Fillifut marched them up the hill, back to camp, where Fye waited with the rest of his soldiers.

He shook his head at Hen and Izzy, more impressed than angry. "You're slippery little fish, I'll give you that." He knelt down so he could look Izzy in the eye. "If you were trying to run away, you didn't choose a very good route." He lowered his voice and said, "So maybe you weren't trying to run away then."

Izzy returned his stare but didn't answer. Hen stuck her tongue out at him.

The corner of Fye's mouth lifted as he touched the jagged edge of his left ear. "I hope the Sisters were more helpful to you than they were to me. Luckily, they just took a nibble."

"Fye, sir!" called a voice from over the hill. A Fillifut soldier ran up the slope and waved one arm overhead. "Our scouts have seen the witches' signal flag. They're on the north face of Demon's Dome!"

Fye's face turned serious, and he stood up. "Take the prisoners, and let's go," he said to Race.

Lug hurried toward them from the other end of camp with three Fillifut at his heels. "Wait! Please!" He held out a thick tangle of dirty plants. "Mister Fye," puffed Lug. "I have something important to share… I've determined what's so strange about this clover!"

The Fillifut soldiers groaned and rolled their eyes. Fye looked annoyed. "Grab him, and let's get going."

Lug stood up to his full height, eye level with the tips of the soldiers' ears. "You must listen to me!" he boomed.

Everyone stopped. Some Fillifut drew their slingshots.

Lug held out the soil-crusted plants to Fye. "I thought this tasted strange. The leaves look like bell clover, but when you pull it out of the ground, you can see that it isn't." The roots of the herb hung down from his fingers, three times the length of the plant itself, and curled like a corkscrew. "This clover has been crossed with another plant. Twistroot. Basket makers use it. They crush up the stems to make a kind of paint. They soak a straight piece of wood in it that they want to bend or twist to use as a handle. It's quite useful but highly poisonous to eat."

Race snorted out a laugh. "We eat that clover three times a day all through the year. You can see how fit we are. Seems like you don't know your plants, Changeling."

"Lug knows more about plants that anybody," said Hen.

"That's right," added Selden. "He knows every plant that grows in the Edgewood. He makes us medicines when we get sick."

Lug pushed the clover into Fye's paw. "Maybe the concentration in the leaves isn't enough to affect you. But for someone smaller…"

Izzy gasped. "Like a child?"

Lug's lips were pulled tight. "If a child ate this, it would make them sick. Very sick."

Fye hadn't said a word. He ground his teeth as he rubbed a clover leaf between his fingers.

"Fye, you said this clover changed," said Lug. "When did it start spreading through your valley, growing all year round?"

"About four years ago," said Fye flatly.

Clip, who'd hung back from the other soldiers, now stepped forward. "You made the bargain with Rine four years ago, sir."

Izzy touched the sleeve of Fye's tunic. "The Fen Whelps told us all about Rine. He tried to heal his friend who had a hurt leg. He would know about these sorts of plants."

The Fillifut lookout jogged up to them. "Sir, the witches have rounded Demon's Dome. They say they're done waiting and are coming to fetch the prisoners themselves."

"They can't do that!" said Race. "We're still in our valley. They aren't allowed to set foot here."

"They haven't set foot anywhere," said the lookout. "You need to see this for yourselves," he added.

Worried whispers rippled among the troops.

Fye took Lug aside. "The antidote the witches have been giving us—can it truly remedy the effects of this twistroot?"

"As long as you stop eating the herb," said Lug, nodding. "The tonic is simple to make. It's a tea of possumhaw bark. Possumhaw grows almost everywhere here. There's a cluster of it back where we camped." Lug pressed Fye's paw between his big hands. "It would take me less than five minutes to show you."

"We can't trust him, can we?" said Race. "He's our prisoner. He's trying to bargain for his life!"

"Ask any basket maker," said Lug calmly. "They'll tell you the same."

Fye whistled and called one of his soldiers. "Farrow! Go with him to the possumhaw and learn his recipe quick as you can."

The soldier nodded, and he and Lug sped down the hill together.

Fye drew his slingshot off his back and checked his shot bag. "Race, I want your troop to stay with me. Circle around the prisoners. Clip, you and Trillo take your troops behind the hill and wait for my signal."

Race hesitated. "Sir, this is ambush formation. What about our deal with the witches?"

Fye loaded a stone into his slingshot. "Don't you see? Rine has kept us enthralled to him all these years with the promise of that antidote. The antidote to a poison *he* pushed upon us. Anyway," said Fye, smirking, "our treaty forbids them from entering our valley. So they broke it first."

Fye took his place at the front of his soldiers, with Hen, Izzy, and Selden behind him.

"What's going to happen?" Izzy asked him.

Fye turned around. He glanced down at the ground, then looked at Izzy and Selden. "Bretabairn, it seems that I've made a serious mistake. I want to make it right, but I'll need your help to do it."

"They're here!" shouted the lookout. "Rine and four others. Two hundred yards out!"

Fye put one paw on Izzy's shoulder and one on Selden's. "That trick you played on my guards—looking like a Fillifut soldier—could you both do that again right now?"

Izzy and Selden looked at each other and nodded. They passed their hands over their heads and drew them up, forming long, slender ears. Izzy took on Clip's Likeness. Selden did a passable version of Farrow.

Fye smiled, impressed. "Good." He turned to Hen. "You'll need to play a part as well. I don't think I need to ask if you can be brave."

Hen planted her feet and stuck her chin out.

"That's what I thought," said Fye. "Now pull your hair over those human ears and stay close to me."

Izzy put her paws on her hips to keep them from shaking. She wished she were as brave as her little sister. If Fye was going to do what she thought he was going to do, she'd need all the bravery she could muster to hold onto her Likeness.

Moments later, Rine floated silently over the top of the hill with four witches standing close behind. When the lookout said they didn't set foot on Fillifut soil, he was technically right. At first, Izzy thought they were flying. When they came into full view, she realized they rode on a bright-green wave of bell clover.

A witch with dark-red lips and black hair braided in hundreds of tiny rows stood to Rine's left, holding both hands out. With a subtle flick of her fingers, the clover sprouted new shoots, flowing like a wave as it grew. The five witches rode on top, standing on a dense pad of leaves.

The other three who stood behind Rine, sneering down at the Fillifut, looked young, not much older than Izzy's counselors at Camp Kitterpines. A nervous-looking boy with a mop of blond hair kept his eyes on Rine, watching his every move. The other two witches wore dark-blue robes and carried long wooden staffs.

The witch with the braids flipped her hand over, and the carpet of clover lowered down in front of Fye. Izzy's pulse quickened to see Rine so close. He had the same fierce green eyes as the Fen Whelps' marionette, but he was older and paler than the version from the Fen Whelps' play. Even in the growing light of morning, the shadows seemed to cling to his skin and dark robes.

Izzy focused on breathing steadily, concentrating on the Likeness of Clip while Rine cast his sharp eyes down at the soldiers.

Skipping over any greeting, he spoke directly to Fye. "Your messengers reported that you captured three Changelings." Rine nodded at Hen. "Where are the rest?"

Fye squeezed Hen's shoulder. "Messages get distorted in the mountains," he said cordially. "We have only this one girl."

Rine looked around at the camp. "Very well. You may bring her forward."

Fye smiled and folded his arms. "May we? How gracious of you to give us permission on our own land. This is *our* land, isn't it?"

Rine eyed Fye warily. "Yes, it is. And we haven't violated the terms of our treaty, as you can see." He nodded to the witch with the braids. "I've instructed Hyan to make sure we stick to our agreement." He turned and addressed the blond, doughy-faced witch. "Delin, give our friends the reward for their service. That way, he can see that we honor our promises."

Delin nodded and tossed a flask down to Fye.

Fye caught the bottle with one hand. He opened it and took a sniff before tipping it upside down, letting the liquid inside glug out onto the ground.

Rine's nostrils flared as the witches whispered among themselves.

"So kind of you to bring this," said Fye, dropping the flask at his feet. "But we don't have a need for it any longer. We've learned to make it ourselves. Luckily for us, we ran into some basket makers."

The other witches exchanged worried looks, but Rine didn't break his stare with Fye. "I don't care what you do," he snarled. "We've delivered on our part of the bargain. Now it's your turn." He pointed down at Hen. "Give that girl to me. Now."

"You don't give orders to our leader," said Race.

Rine's eyes flickered. "Is that so?" He raised his hands, ready to cast a spell.

Everything happened so quickly that if Izzy had blinked, she'd have missed it all.

Fye whistled once and the air blurred gray and brown as Race and her troop fired their slingshots. They knocked the blue-robed witches standing behind Rine off the clover and onto the ground.

Race's troop continued its fire, giving cover to Clip's soldiers as they rushed over the hill and pinned the fallen witches to the ground. The witches tried to fight back, but on the ground, they were powerless.

Hyan raised her arms, and the bell clover swelled into a thick tower. Clover leaves rained down as the new growth carried Rine, Hyan, and Delin high into the air.

"Scatter!" Fye commanded his soldiers. He turned to Izzy, Selden, and Hen. "Run. Back through our valley, to the canyon. Go!"

Izzy dropped the Likeness, grabbed Hen's hand, and ran. They wove through the soldiers, trying not to get trampled. Fillifut bounded in every direction, lobbing round after round of shot at the witches. But Hyan's pillar of bell clover had grown so high that they were out of range.

Izzy looked over her shoulder. "Where's Selden? Hen, do you see him?"

"There!" Hen pointed behind them. "He's still there with Fye!"

Selden, in his leopard form, rushed the base of the clover tower, slashing it with his claws. The tower rocked and shuddered, making the witches on top stumble. Hyan leaned down and aimed her hands directly at the tower's base. Shoots of new growth sprouted, replacing the clover as fast as Selden could cut it away.

Rine pushed back the sleeves of his robe. He swept his fingers up, collecting the shadows cast by the clover tower. They swirled around the tower's base and flowed to his fingertips. Like a potter forming clay, Rine worked the shadows in his hands. He shaped them with his fingers, drawing them out into long, wispy strands.

Rine breathed on the shadow strands, and they stiffened, their sharpened tips glinting like metal in the sunlight. He had made arrows.

He passed them to Delin, who hurled them down at the Fillifut. The soldiers leaped out of the way easily. But when the arrows hit the ground, they turned into tacky puddles. The shadows clung to the Fillifut, slowing them down. Some of the soldiers fell, struggling to drag themselves up again.

"How are we going to get Selden out of there?" said Izzy.

"Izzy! Hen!" A voice called out to them from faraway.

"That's Lug!" said Hen. "Lug, where are you?"

"Up here!"

Izzy and Hen looked up. The upper half of Lug's body floated in the air a hundred feet over their heads. He vanished from sight and then reappeared. He flung his arms out, and a rope ladder tumbled down toward them.

"Tom and the *Muscadine*!" said Hen. "And look up there!"

The tiny silhouette of an eagle circled high over Lug's head.

Izzy grabbed the end of the ladder and held it out for Hen. "You go first."

"I hope Tom saved my backpack!" said Hen as she started up.

Izzy held the bottom of the ladder steady while Hen climbed hand over hand toward Lug's open arms. "Go, go, go," Izzy whispered, looking nervously behind her.

If Rine saw them climbing a ladder to nowhere, they'd be picked off easily. But the Fillifut were keeping him busy. Rine's eyes were trained on the ground below him. He'd made enough arrows that Delin had plenty of ammunition to hurl down onto the Fillifut. Only Fye and Race had the strength to fire their slingshots anywhere close to the witches. They gave Selden cover while he continued to cut away at the bell clover. Their only chance was to knock Rine and the others off the tower onto the ground.

Izzy shaded her eyes against the bright sunlight. She saw Rine's fingers working to form something else from the shadows, but she couldn't tell what it was. His hands moved quickly, and the whole time, he didn't take his eyes off Selden.

"I've got Hen!" Lug called down from the ship. He gave Izzy the thumbs-up as Hen's legs flipped over the invisible lip of the basket.

The rope ladder swung as Izzy started up. Lug began hauling it in as she climbed the slippery rungs. A gust of air rushed over her as Hiron swooped in and hovered beside her.

"Izzy! I keep trying to get close to the witches, but that one with the arrows has his eye on me!"

"No, don't get close to them," said Izzy. "They're too dangerous!"

"But what about Selden?"

"We've got to figure out a way to knock the witches off that tower." Izzy looked up at the ship. "I think I've got an idea!"

As soon as Lug pulled her over the side, she hurried to Tom. "How close can you fly us to Selden without the witches seeing us?"

Tom gripped the steering frame and checked his gauges. "Pretty close, but I'll have to stay higher than them, or they'll spot us. We've got one whole balloon gone, so it's gonna be tricky."

"Get as close as you can," said Izzy. "And is there anything on board that Marian made invisible that's not lashed down? Something heavy?"

Tom looked over each shoulder. "I pulled off the rigging from the deflated balloon and wound it in a coil. It's around here somewhere, but I don't know how you'll find it. It's invisible!"

"I'll look," said Lug. "Help me, Hen!"

"Not now!" Hen crawled along the floor of the basket, lifting up cargo and looking underneath. "I have to find my backpack!"

"Izzy!" shouted Hiron as he flew in close to the ship. "The witches have Selden!"

Izzy ran to the side of the ship. Now she understood what Rine had been making. He had caught Selden in a net of shadows. Selden Changed from one form to another, but the net stuck to his fur, trapping his limbs against his body. Fye tried to pull it off him, but the shadows flowed like sap, gumming up his paws.

Rine held tight to the end of a tether attached to Selden's net. He swirled his fingers, and the tether shortened, lifting Selden off the ground. Rine began to reel him in.

"Oh no! We have to hurry!" said Izzy.

"I found the ropes!" Lug stood up, cradling an invisible weight in his arms.

"I found my backpack!" shouted Hen. She waved it triumphantly over her head. "Now I just hope they didn't fall out..."

Izzy waved to Hiron. "Can you take that rope from Lug

and carry it over the witches? If you drop it onto them, they won't be able to see it coming."

Hiron nodded.

He flew in close to the ship. Lug leaned over the side and tossed his invisible burden into the air. Izzy couldn't see the rope, but she knew Hiron caught it, because his body lurched down. He pumped his wings, carrying the rope high overhead.

Rine had now pulled Selden halfway up the tower. Hyan angled her hands. The tower leaned as the bell clover began flowing north. They were retreating, and they were taking Selden with them.

Fye ordered his troops to circle around the base of the witches' tower. With their powerful hind legs, the Fillifut scratched and kicked at the clover, sending shredded leaves and roots flying. They could have brought the whole thing down if they didn't have to keep dodging the shadow arrows Delin hurled at them.

"Come on, Hiron, come on," whispered Izzy as she watched him circle higher and higher.

Hiron folded his wings behind him and dove down at the witches. When he was twenty feet above their heads, Delin looked up and saw him.

"Now!" Izzy yelled.

Hiron's talons unclenched. There was a pause as Delin aimed one of his shadow arrows at Hiron's chest. As he threw it, his body jolted backward. He lost his balance and fell. Hyan reacted quickly, sending a spurt of clover out to catch him, but it only slowed his fall. Delin hit the ground hard. The Fillifut swarmed over him, keeping him pinned to the ground.

Izzy started to cheer, but then she saw Hiron holding his right wing stiff while the other wing beat double time. The arrow must have hit him after all.

Hiron struggled to make his way back to the ship. He Changed into himself and collapsed in a corner of the basket, holding his right elbow. Lug rushed over to help him.

Tom had managed to get the ship closer to Rine. The *Muscadine* now hovered just a few yards above the witches.

Rine wore a cold snarl on his lips. He had pulled Selden on top of the clover tower. Izzy could barely make out Selden in his boy form beneath the dark bindings that covered his whole body.

"Hyan, take us away from here," Rine commanded.

Hyan grimaced, concentrating. Her arm muscles strained as she waved her hands to the north. The bell clover began flowing faster.

Hen joined Izzy at the side of the basket. Suddenly, she jumped up and leaned over the side. "Hey, witch lady!" she shouted. "Check this out!"

Hyan looked up, confused. Hen reared her arm back and chucked a small ball at Hyan's chest. A high-pitched whine followed the ball through the air as it fizzed and smoked. It spun wildly, sending off sprays of white sparks.

Now Izzy knew why her sister wanted her backpack so badly. Hen had smuggled fireworks into camp after all, and she'd brought them with her to Faerie. The ball she lobbed at Hyan was called a Zippy Zinger.

Hyan shielded her face as the sparking ball hit her square in the chest. She tumbled off the tower of clover, down to the mob of Fillifut waiting on the ground.

The tower of clover swayed. Without Hyan to keep it growing, the Fillifut's claws would bring it down any moment.

Rine's eyes flared with anger. With one flourish of his hand, he formed a dagger of shadows. "It seems like I'll have to make a rushed exit," he said to Selden. "I can't take you with me, but I could at least take what I came for."

Rine waved his other hand over Selden, and the shadow net fell away. Selden lay on top of the pad of clover, panting.

Izzy knew she only had seconds to act. She climbed up onto the rim of the basket. She took a deep breath and leaped onto the clover tower, landing on her hands and knees behind Rine.

She got to her feet. "Rine, stop!" she said.

Rine spun around. When he saw her, the anger in his eyes changed to shock. "S-Sasha?" he whispered.

Izzy held perfectly still, wearing the Likeness of Rine's old friend.

"Sasha?" Rine's words caught against each other. "Is that really you?"

Izzy focused on holding the Likeness, watching Selden from the corner of her eye. She wondered if he had enough strength to do what needed to be done. The shock was fading from Rine's face. The witch's eyes narrowed as he started to realize what he was really looking at.

Slowly, Selden drew his knees up to his chest. With one quick sweep of his legs, he kicked Rine off the tower.

Izzy let go of Sasha's Likeness and leaned over to watch Rine fall. Moments before he hit the ground, his body convulsed and separated into thousands of bright-green shards. The pieces scattered and floated north on the wind.

Lug leaned down out of the *Muscadine* and pulled Selden on board. Izzy climbed in after him.

"Are you OK?" asked Izzy, kneeling over him.

Selden nodded as Lug wrapped a scrap of deflated balloon around his shoulders. "I'll be fine." He looked up at Izzy. "Thanks. That was a good trick."

Izzy exhaled and collapsed onto the floor of the basket. She felt completely spent. "How about Hiron?" she asked.

Lug dabbed a bloodstained rag on Hiron's wound. "No flying for a while, I'm afraid. But Hiron's a lucky soul." He slapped Hiron on the back, making him wince. "The arrow only grazed him and didn't stick in."

"Uh-oh," said Hen. "Izzy, come here and look!"

Izzy hurried to join her sister at the rim of the basket. Fye stood below them, aiming his slingshot straight at the

Muscadine. Hen ducked down, but Izzy stayed and held her hands overhead. She wanted Fye to be able to see what he was aiming for.

The slingshot twanged, and a small object sailed in a perfect arc, landing gently in the center of the *Muscadine*'s basket. Izzy picked it up. It was a small rock with a piece of paper wrapped around it and held on with twine. Izzy untied the note.

Hope we made it right by you, Bretabairn.

Izzy leaned over the side of the basket. She held both thumbs up, which she hoped was the universal symbol for "*Yes—and thank you.*"

"Next stop, Netherbee Hall," called Tom.

Izzy frowned and rubbed her hand over her heart. "Not yet," she said. "There's something we need to get first."

CHECKING OUT

"Hey, Izzy," Selden whispered.

"Shh."

"Hey, we need to talk."

Izzy leaned out past the corner of the bakery, across the street from the library in Avhalon. The lane was empty for now, and she and Selden wore Likenesses of baker's apprentices, but she still didn't want anyone to see them or ask questions.

"If I thought you were going to make so much noise, I would have told you to stay back at the *Muscadine* with the others," she said.

Selden scowled. "Hey, I'm the one who's supposed to be in charge. You can't just go ordering Tom to bring us back to Avhalon without even talking to me about it."

"Like I told you, we're just making a quick stop," said Izzy. "Hen will be in and out, and then we'll be back in the air before anyone even knows we landed."

"I still don't understand why we have to get the whole *Book of the Bretabairn*," said Selden. "If that crazy puppet show you saw was the telling the truth, then that witch—"

"Sasha."

"Fine, Sasha—took what was important out of the book."

Izzy frowned and rubbed her shirt collar between her fingertips. Maybe Selden was right and they were taking a foolish risk to come back to Avhalon. But she couldn't stop thinking about that electric buzz she felt when she'd held the book. It meant something. She was sure of it.

"If we don't get the book now before we meet the others at Netherbee Hall, it'll be impossible to come back later," she said. "And we might need it to find the King's Key."

Selden's mouth flew open. "Find the Ki—"

"Shh!" said Izzy. "Here comes Hen!"

Hen walked toward the library, looking over each shoulder as she approached the double doors.

"Come on," said Selden, standing up and walking into the street. "We better get closer so we can keep an eye on her once she goes inside."

Izzy put her hands in her apron pockets, trying to act natural. They crossed the street quickly and slid up against the side of the library, ducking under a window at the center of the building. Selden looked around to make sure no one was watching. Then he stood on his toes and pressed his palms against the windowpane. It opened with a soft squeak. They crouched down, eye level with the inch-wide crack, and dropped their Likenesses.

"You really think your sister is up for this?" asked Selden. "What if she gives us away to Nettle?"

Izzy shook her head. "Everyone thinks Hen is so cute and sweet, but that girl is the world's greatest liar. She had my parents totally convinced she wasn't bringing fireworks to camp!"

Inside, Hen walked casually up to the circulation desk.

"Ah, bonjour, mademoiselle, good morning and welcome." Dr. Nettle's voice carried from a far corner of the library, followed by the clicking of his hooves across the parquet floor.

"What, pray tell, may I do for you this fine morning, hmm?" he asked. "Would you care to peruse our periodicals? Ruminate in the reference section?"

"Thank you," said Hen. "I'll just look around for a minute if you don't mind."

"Please do. I am here to serve as your guide to the kingdom of bibliodom."

Hen walked slowly from the circulation desk toward the stairs. Izzy had told her exactly where to find *The Book of the Bretabairn*. She hoped no one had moved it since she and the others had looked at it last.

"You have a really nice collection here," said Hen in her sweetest voice, the one she used to get double helpings of pumpkin pie at Thanksgiving.

"See, I told you," Izzy whispered to Selden.

"I don't suppose you have ever been in a library?" Dr. Nettle asked Hen hopefully.

"Oh, I have. I've been in libraries all over. But never one as nice as this." Hen whistled. "It's pretty impressive if you ask me."

Dr. Nettle rubbed his bearded chin with pride. "Thank you, my dear. It is nice to be appreciated. Please, make yourself at home."

Hen nodded at him and began making her way upstairs. Izzy hoped her sister would be able to find the book from her directions.

Selden jabbed Izzy in the ribs. "Hey, we need to talk about this! You never said anything about finding the King's Key. Now we know that Rine's greatest desire isn't just in any Changeling's heart. It's in—"

"Mine," said Izzy.

"Right. And now that we know that, we have to protect you from him. We should be practicing your bird form, so you can fly and—"

Izzy shook her head. She'd given up on Changing. "We don't have time for that."

"Then we definitely don't have time to go looking for that Key!" said Selden. "It could be anywhere. We should get you back to Earth."

"Rine would just send the Unglers after me," said Izzy. "I

might be safe for a little while, but they'd find me eventually. They found me before. But if we could find the Key, I could take it to Earth and hide it. Drop it into the ocean or something like that. Then there would be no point in coming after me or any of the Changelings anymore."

Selden stared at her, considering all she said. He nodded slowly. "Rine wouldn't be able to cross over to Earth and get it, not even with the Unglers' help."

"Exactly!" said Izzy.

"I don't know," said Selden. "I have to think about what Peter would want me to do. Now that he's not here, it's up to me to keep us all safe."

"But that's the whole point," said Izzy. "As long as Rine is looking for the Key, none of us are safe. He wants it so badly. If we want to stop him, we have to take away the possibility that he can get to it." Izzy slumped against the bricks of the library. "You probably think this plan sounds totally crazy."

Selden half smiled. "You know you're in trouble when *I'm* the one calling your plan crazy. Hey, look!" He grabbed Izzy's shoulder and turned her toward the window. "Your sister found the book!"

Hen bounced down the stairs with *The Book of the Bretabairn* tucked under one arm. With a thump, she set it on the circulation desk. "This one looks good to me," she said.

Dr. Nettle bobbed his chin. "It's not as literary as some of our other—"

"Where'd you get it?" Hen interrupted.

"Oh, that book has been here at least as long as I have," said Dr. Nettle with a wheezy cough. "About ten or so years ago, a young man borrowed it and then disappeared. I thought we'd never get it back, but miraculously, I found it returned on the front stoop in perfect condition."

"Not quite perfect," whispered Izzy, thinking of the page Sasha ripped out.

"That incident is what made me institute our membership policy," said Dr. Nettle. "Only members may borrow materials. So tell me, dear, are you a—"

"Yup," said Hen. "Here's my card." Hen took a rectangle of plastic out of her shirt pocket and handed it to the old goat.

Dr. Nettle held the card ludicrously close to his face and flipped it back and forth. "I, well, I'm not sure this is valid…"

Selden leaned closer to Izzy and whispered, "Uh-oh. This isn't good."

"Shh," said Izzy. "Just wait." She crossed her fingers and hoped she was right about old Nettle's ability to read.

"Huh, that's funny," said Hen. "I just renewed it last week. Here, let me see." Hen reached across the desk and took the card back. "Oh yes, see here? It says 'Library Card. Good for Checking Out One Book.' And you can see I've still got five books left until I have to get a new one."

"Hmm, well, I haven't seen this type of card before," said Dr. Nettle, rubbing the fur between his horns. He coughed and then lowered his voice. "The truth is, my dear lady, no one has ever come in with a library card before."

"Oh, well, don't worry about that. There's a first time for everything. I'll show you how to use it, and next time someone comes in, you'll know what to do." Hen leaned close and shielded the side of her mouth with one hand. "And don't worry. I won't tell anyone you didn't know how to do it."

Dr. Nettle sighed gratefully. "That would be lovely. I have a very important reputation in this town to uphold."

Hen pointed to the bottom of the card. "See those symbols? Each one of them is a torch of wisdom. And when you check a book out to someone, you punch a little hole through one of the torches. Easy, right?"

"Ah, that is easy!" Dr. Nettle took the card and placed it between his teeth. He chomped, sending a fleck of plastic across the desk. "There. Now you are all checked out. That book will be due back in...well..."

"Two weeks is pretty usual," said Hen, taking the card and sliding *The Book of the Bretabairn* off the desk. "But I don't know what your policy is."

"Yes, that is our policy as well," said Dr. Nettle. "Thank you for your business, my dear. See you very soon. Au revoir."

Hen tucked the book under her armpit and headed for the front of the building. When she reached the door, Dr. Nettle called out. "Wait! Young lady!"

Izzy and Selden both held their breath as Hen turned around slowly.

Dr. Nettle clackety-clacked across the wooden floor toward her. "You almost forgot this." He held Peter's flute out to her with a flourish.

"Oh!" said Hen, blushing bright pink. "Thank you. Bye now. Bonbon voyage." The bells on the door handle jingled as the door swung shut behind her.

Hen clutched the book to her chest and hurried down the street with Izzy and Selden close behind. None of them said a word to each other until they were through the gates and out on a grassy field in the center of the orchard, where Tom had hidden the *Muscadine* among the apple trees.

Izzy and Selden both climbed into the *Muscadine* after Hen. While Tom and Lug got the air pumps whirring back to life, Izzy hugged her sister.

"You were great!" said Izzy. "You deserve an award or something for pulling that off."

Hen grinned and wrinkled her nose. "Thanks, but I can't believe I almost left the flute behind! I was just so nervous." She took the "library" card out of her pocket and held it out to Izzy. "I can't believe he actually fell for that."

Izzy flipped the card back and forth. The bubble letters

across the front read, "Momo's Frozen Yogurt Punch Card. Buy 10, Get 1 Free Kidz Cup."

Izzy smiled. The "torch of wisdom" symbol Dr. Nettle had chomped was an icon of a swirly soft-serve cone.

Tom settled into his seat behind the controls. "All right. Off to Netherbee Hall now?"

"Yes—and we need to hurry," said Selden. He looked at Izzy and smiled. "If we're going to find what we're looking for, we'll need all the time we can get."

REJOICE IN THE MAKING

"Sit still!" hissed Marian.

"I *am* sitting still," whispered Izzy out of the corner of her mouth.

Marian exhaled. She shook out her hands, then held them palms up in front of Izzy. She glanced down at the paper on the table beside her and began working through the spell again.

Izzy pressed her legs into the seat of her chair to keep herself from fidgeting. *We're lucky this is me and not Hen*, she thought. Hen wouldn't have sat still for thirty seconds, let alone an hour, which was how long Izzy and Marian had been shut away, working on getting the page out of Izzy's heart.

Izzy allowed her eyes to drift around the room. They were in Marian's study on the second floor of Netherbee Hall. Bouquets of dried herbs and flowers hung from the ceiling. Potted plants crowded for space on the floor. What shelf space wasn't taken up with jars of powder or spices held stacks of books. The spell Marian was using had come from one of those volumes.

Peter had given Marian every spell book he had collected over the years. Most of them were full of farmcraft—spells to grow bigger pumpkins or keep the blight off tomatoes. But a few of the books held deeper, more powerful spells. Even then, they'd been written by human farmers. The invisibility spell was originally written to protect a peach crop from being seen by hungry birds. These powerful spells were longer—multiple pages written in tiny print—and more complicated. Painstaking instructions directed the spell caster on how to hold and move their hands.

Marian's fingers wove through the air in front of Izzy like she was braiding with invisible threads.

A prickle of heat began to bloom in Izzy's rib cage. It was a faint, flickery feeling, like an itch between her lungs. She had to fight the urge to cough. The wrinkles in Marian's forehead deepened, and the fluttering sped up. Izzy shut her eyes and held her breath. Suddenly, the sensation ceased.

Marian threw her arms down with a huff. "No good. I can't do it."

Izzy slumped in her chair, the tickle in her chest fading away. "We were really close that time. I could feel it. If you just go a little longer."

Marian ran her fingers across her forehead. Strands of white hair parted and then fell back into place. "Izzy, I don't think you know what you're asking me to do. This spell. It's harder than anything I've tried before."

A voice behind them said, "Harder than making something invisible?"

Izzy turned to see Dree leaning against the doorway to Marian's room. Izzy didn't realize she'd been watching them.

Marian stood up and pushed her chair back. She picked up one of the books off the stack on the table beside her and flicked her thumb across the tattered pages. "It took me months just to learn the hand motions of the invisibility spell, another month to memorize the words. Even longer to put it all together. You're asking me to do the same thing in a couple of days."

"You're doing good so far," said Izzy, trying to sound encouraging. "Are you sure you're saying all the words right?"

"That's the problem," grumbled Marian. "You don't *say* the words in a spell. You think them. The words have to be the only thing in your mind when you cast them. You can't let any other thoughts creep in and get in the way."

"Thoughts like damaging someone's heart, for instance?" said Dree.

Marian glanced at Izzy and frowned. "The invisibility spell doesn't have consequences. If I get it wrong, the light doesn't listen to me, and it does its own thing. But this spell." She pointed at the paper lying next to Izzy. "I've got to get it perfect. If I mess up even one word…"

Izzy swallowed and rubbed her hand over her shirt. "I guess it's not like you can practice either."

"No," said Marian. "I get one chance, and that's it."

Izzy stood up and shook out her stiff arms and legs. She could tell Marian was exhausted. "Let's take a break," she said with a smile. She walked to the door casually, as if they weren't desperately crunched for time. "I'm going downstairs to see how the others are coming along with the book."

Marian nodded and picked up the spell again. Izzy expected Dree to follow her out of the room, but instead, she took Izzy's empty chair. Good. Maybe Dree could talk to Marian and make her feel more confident.

Izzy crossed the hall and started down the staircase. Even though it was early afternoon, the house was dark. Thin strips of bright sunshine fell across the floor where they had snuck in between cracks in the heavy curtains. Marian had cast her cloaking spell on the whole house, even the windows, so there was no danger of being seen through the glass. The heavy drapes were there to muffle the sound of the nineteen children hiding inside and to mask their scent as much as possible from the Unglers.

Keeping the house so dark lent the place a creepy feeling. The last time Izzy had been in Netherbee Hall, spiderless cobwebs had overrun the building and trapped Marian inside, nearly suffocating her. Izzy herself had barely escaped. Marian had cleaned up and made repairs since then, but the house still felt cold and secretive, even more so with the warm summer sunshine banished.

Izzy stopped for a moment in the entry hall, in front of a large painting that hung below the stairs. She had been drawn to this painting the first time she saw it. Even now, flustered and in a hurry, she had to stop for a moment to look. It showed a scene she had come to know well: King Revelrun and Master Green shaking hands, with a circle of Changeling children dancing at their feet and more crowded around watching. The Changelings had been painted with animal bodies and children's faces.

The way the paint had faded over time—with the reds, greens, and blues darkening almost to black—made the children's smiling faces stand out, as if the painter had mixed shimmering gold and bronze into his brush so they would catch the light.

"Where do you guys think it is?" Izzy whispered to the two men in the painting. She waited a moment, then sighed. "Fine. We'll just have to find it without you."

Izzy turned and went into the sitting room. Hiron and Hale knelt on the floor with *The Book of the Bretabairn* open in front of them. Lug stood behind, his wide face twisted in concentration. The floor all around was scattered in papers.

Hen sat on a chair in the corner, her chin resting on the tip of Peter's flute. Izzy raised her eyebrows at Hen hopefully, but her sister wrinkled her nose and shook her head. Not a great sign.

"How's it going?" Izzy asked, kneeling down on the other side of the book.

Lug looked up and smiled. "Well, we aren't any closer to finding out the truth, but we aren't any farther away either. So that's promising."

"What he means," Hiron said, "is that we haven't made any progress at all." He sat up and winced as he adjusted the sling that held his injured arm. He was healing, thanks to Marian and Lug tending his wounds, but he wouldn't be flying for weeks. Being grounded had made him cranky.

Hale sat back on her heels and stretched her arms over her head. "We've gone through the book over and over, but we haven't found anything that looks like a clue. None of the poems mention the King's Key—or any key for that matter."

"Did you try the titles?" asked Izzy.

"We wrote each one of them on a separate page like you suggested," said Hiron, pointing to the papers on the floor. "But they don't make any sense. When you string them all together, it's just a scramble of random phrases. And there are two hundred and forty-six poems in the book. If the solution is to shuffle the titles to get them in order, it will take us years."

They didn't have years. They had two days. After that, Rine would get his strength back and come looking for them.

"Izzy, we did find something interesting," said Lug. "Show her, Hale."

Hale flipped toward the back of the book. She ran her

finger across the ragged seam in the middle. "This must be where Sasha tore out the poem he hid."

Izzy felt along the paper's torn edge. The image of the Sasha puppet ripping out the page flashed in her memory and gave her a chill, like she was still sitting at the bottom of Lake Umbra.

Hiron took off his glasses and cleaned them on the hem of his shirt. "You know what I just realized, Izzy? I don't think we found your poem in the book."

"You didn't. Because it isn't there." Izzy had scoured the pages of the book during their trip from Avhalon to the Edgewood. She'd had a feeling before she even started that her poem wouldn't be inside.

Hiron hooked his glasses back onto his ears. "So that means Sasha hid your own poem inside your heart. How did he know which one was yours?"

"I don't know," said Izzy with a sigh. "Lucky coincidence, I guess."

Lug smiled and reached over to pat Izzy's arm. "Sometimes, the world has a way of being rather surprising."

Hale shut the book and rubbed the back of her neck. "I don't think we're going to find anything to help us in there. Sasha must have chosen that page to hide because it held all the clues to finding the King's Key. The location of the hiding place could have been scribbled on the back or something like that."

Izzy picked up the book and held it on her lap. Her

fingertips still held a faint buzz whenever she touched it. That had to mean something. But Hale was right. They were running out of time to find out what that something was.

Three pure and perfect notes rang out from the corner of the room. Izzy jerked her head up and looked at her sister. Hen's eyes were wide.

"Holy moly," said Hen, a grin spreading across her face. "Did you guys hear that?"

Lug clapped his hands. "Well done! That actually didn't sound like a dying cat for once."

Hen put her lips to the flute and played the same notes. They didn't ring quite as loud or true as the first time, but at least they sounded like something a flute should play.

"Hale! Oy, Hale!" Olligan stumbled into the room with Yash and Sibi hanging off each of his arms like barnacles. "Hale, you've got to help me out. I can't handle watching them anymore! They won't give me a moment's peace. Mote and Mite keep fighting. And look! Sibi cut my hair!"

Sibi grinned mischievously and hid a pair of scissors behind her back.

Hale peeled Sibi off Olligan's shoulder. "Sorry, Ollie, but it's just because they're going stir-crazy. Cooped up inside all day and having to be quiet isn't easy for them." Hale fluffed her fingers through Ollie's curls. "For what it's worth, she didn't do a bad job."

Three knocks rapped on the front door. Everyone froze and

looked at each other worriedly. Izzy tiptoed to the window and peeled the curtain back. A stoat sniffed the air in front of the house.

"It's just Selden." She whispered anyway, reminded that they were supposed to be keeping quiet. "Tom must have dropped him off and gone to hide his ship somewhere close by." She rushed to the entry hall and pulled open the door.

Selden slipped inside and Changed from the stoat back to himself. "If you're trying to be quiet, you're all failing miserably. I could hear you loud and clear from the outside."

Dree came hurrying down from Marian's room, looking very much like a ghost floating down the dark staircase of a haunted house. Izzy thought Dree looked a little funny, like she was upset about something, but she didn't want to ask in front of everyone.

"Did you guys see anything?" Dree asked Selden. "Any sign of Rine? The other witches?"

"No Rine—not yet," answered Selden. "But we think he's sent the Unglers out ahead. We found tracks near the City Road, down below the rim of the Edgewood plateau. Tom says they're fresh. He thinks they're only moving at night right now, but once they get to the Edgewood, the trees will give them cover, so they won't need to hide during the day."

"How many do you think?" asked Dree.

Selden's lips moved silently, counting. "From the tracks, ten, maybe twelve."

"Twelve!" gasped Lug.

Hale cleared her throat. She handed Sibi back to Olligan and said very calmly, "Ollie, will you please take Yash and Sibi upstairs? Play a game with them and the others, something that will keep them quiet. And, Sibi, no more scissors, all right?"

Ollie rolled his eyes and trudged up the stairs with Yash and Sibi clinging to his legs.

Hale watched until they were out of earshot, then turned to Selden. "First of all, don't give that kind of report in front of the little ones."

Selden put his hands up. "Hey, don't get mad at me. I was just answering the question. Besides, they don't know what's going on."

"They know more than you think, and I don't want them to get scared. Ollie too. He might be nine, but he still has nightmares." Hale flipped her braid from one shoulder to the other. "Second of all, we've got to figure out a plan for them. I know you asked for three days, but we haven't figured out anything about the King's Key. And now that you've seen the Unglers, we can't stay here any longer. It's not safe."

Selden's lips were pinched shut like he was trying to keep the words in his mouth from spilling out. Izzy knew he wanted to tell them not to give up—not yet. She felt the same way. They were so close.

Selden glanced at Dree, who stood on the bottom step of the stairs with her arms crossed. She gave him one short nod.

"All right then," said Selden, sagging a little. "Back into hiding we go."

Hale eyed him skeptically. "Are you being serious?"

"I don't want to run away, but the longer we stay here, the more likely the Unglers will pick up our trail," said Selden. "Our only hope of hiding from them is to get a long enough head start. Besides, you're right. We haven't gotten any closer to finding the Key."

"That might be the fastest you've ever agreed with me on anything," said Hale.

Selden shrugged. "I'm just trying to do what Peter would have wanted."

Hale smiled and held her hand out to him. "Thank you. I know it's not what you want to do. But it's the right decision."

As Hale and Selden shook hands, Izzy's eyes wandered up to the painting on the wall behind them. She reached out and clapped her hands around theirs. "Oh my gosh," she whispered.

"What?" asked Hale.

"Oh my gosh," said Izzy.

They let their hands fall away, and Izzy walked between them, up to the foot of the painting. She stood on tiptoe and leaned in close to the canvas. She spun around to face the others.

"Oh my gosh!" she cried.

"Will you stop saying that?" said Selden. "What's the matter?"

Izzy pointed at the painting. "This is not a handshake."

The others exchanged concerned looks. "Izzy," said Hale. "None of us have been sleeping well—"

"Come here and look!" said Izzy. "Green and Revelrun aren't shaking hands. They're *passing* something to each other."

Everyone else gathered around the painting. Lug picked Hen up under the armpits and lifted her so she could see over the others' heads. Izzy hoped they noticed what she had: a streak of gray and a glimmer of gold between the clasped hands. It wasn't much, just a couple of brushstrokes of paint, but the artist had definitely put them there on purpose.

"Huh," said Lug, squinting. "I think you're right, Izzy. I do see something there between their fingers."

Hiron adjusted his glasses and leaned closer. "And their hands are cupped funny, like they're holding something solid."

"All right," said Selden. "But so wh—"

Before he could finish, Izzy ran to the sitting room. She scooped up *The Book of the Bretabairn* and all the papers off the floor, then hurried back to the entry hall. She set everything down in front of the others and started shuffling through the pages of poem titles.

"Where is it…" she mumbled. "I know I saw it… Here!" Izzy held up the paper and shook it like a flag. "'Rejoice in the Making'! Peter told us that Green and Revelrun made the King's Key to help keep Earth and Faerie connected. What if this is a painting of the day they made it? The symbol of the clasped hands, you see it everywhere in

Faerie. It's important, right? Maybe it's important because it symbolizes that day."

Lug tilted his head at the painting. "They do look like they're having a party."

"A celebration!" said Hen.

"Exactly!" said Izzy. "And that same symbol is on the front of this book. A book written by one of Master Green's relatives. The book and the painting could be connected!"

Hale stepped forward and took the paper from Izzy's hand. "This is the title of Phlox's poem." She scanned over the child-faced animals in the painting and pointed to a greyhound. "Phlox can Change into a greyhound."

Hiron nodded down at the papers on the floor. "What if we try to match all the Changelings in the painting with the titles of their poems? We could see where that gets us."

Izzy jumped to her feet. "Yes, let's try!"

It took them the better part of an hour to go through *The Book of the Bretabairn* and find the poems that matched the animals in the painting. When they found a match, they laid the papers on the floor in a circle in the same order as the Changelings in the portrait. Some of their own group were represented—there was a squirrel like Ollie, a horse like Hale, a frog like Rusk, and a monkey like Sibi.

Some animal forms—like cats—were common to multiple Changelings. Dree, Luthia, and Chervil could all Change into cats. But they soon realized that the titles themselves formed a rhyming verse, and they could use the rhyme to choose the right ones.

When they had matched up twenty-three of the animals, Hiron stepped back and rubbed his injured arm with his good hand. "Well, that's all of them except one. The fox is the only one we don't have a match for."

"That's because Izzy's the fox," said Selden. Everyone got quiet and looked at him.

Lug nodded his head slowly. "My goodness, you're right."

Izzy tapped a finger over her heart. "We'll have to figure out what we can without mine for now."

"So where do we start reading?" said Hiron.

"If Izzy's poem was important enough to hide, I bet that means it's the last clue in the puzzle," said Selden.

Hen fetched a fresh sheet of paper and a pencil and gave them to Hale. Starting with the greyhound, Hale wrote out the twenty-three poem titles in order. When she finished, she read them aloud:

> *Rejoice in the Making*
> *To heal from the Breaking.*
> *When the sun rises waking,*
> *Enter Smythe's Hall.*
>
> *Follow the Mallow,*
> *East past the fallow*

Fields that lay shallow
Below red poplars tall.

Cross ground low and sinking,
To stones dry and drinking.
The Gift for a Spring King
Hides to your right.

The stream winds and wanders,
North it flows onwards.
'Neath a bride's veil of water,
Crawl through the night.

A tree for the fairy
Children so merry.
A stone for the wary
Men of the loam.

To find the great treasure,
Its worth you must measure.
Knock thrice with a feather

Izzy felt a tingle down her spine. She looked up at her friends, and they all had smiles spreading across their faces. This had to be it. The verse didn't make complete sense, but it was full of directions. After spending so much time wading through the book, this was the first time they'd found anything that seemed like instructions.

"Smythe's Hall," said Selden. "That sounds like where you're supposed to start. But where is it?"

"Smythe is the old word for a smith," said Hiron. "A smith is someone who makes things out of metal."

"Like a key?" offered Hen.

"Maybe."

Dree leaned toward the painting on tiptoe. "Lug, will you come take a look at this? Don't we know where that is?"

She pointed to a formation of large boulders in the painting's background. The stones leaned against each other, forming a dark corridor underneath.

Lug squinted at the picture. "Yes, of course! That's Brightsmith Hall." He turned to Izzy and added wistfully, "When we lived in the Edgewood, we'd go berry picking near there. Got caught in a thunderstorm once and had to hide under the rocks. They make a fairly good shelter."

"A brightsmith is another word for a silversmith," said Hiron, cleaning his glasses against the fabric of his sling.

"That's it!" cried Hen, bouncing up and down as if the floor was a trampoline. "That's got to be where you're supposed to start looking!"

Hale twisted her braid between her fingers. "But what about what we just agreed?" She looked at Selden. "About hiding? And keeping the little ones safe?"

"What about the people on Earth?" said Izzy. "If we can find the King's Key, we can keep everyone safe from Rine."

Selden's mouth twisted from one side to the other. "Dree, what do you think?"

"I think looking for the Key wouldn't be the stupidest thing we've ever done," Dree answered. "Though it's a strong contender. But Peter put you in charge. You have to decide."

"Peter," murmured Selden. Izzy could tell he was struggling with the decision. "All right, I think I've got a plan." He turned to Hale. "We'll split up. You and Hiron can go with Tom and the little ones up in the *Muscadine* and start heading east. The rest of us will go with Izzy—"

"And me," said Hen.

Selden smiled. "And you. If we can't find the King's Key in one day, we'll give up and join Hale and the others. We'll hide so deep in the Edgewood that no one will ever find us." He glanced at Izzy. "And we'll send Izzy and Hen back to Earth."

"Hold on," said Hiron. "You don't have the last clue, remember? You're going to tramp through the woods, but when you get to the end, you won't know what to do."

Footsteps shuffled softly down the staircase behind them. They turned to see Marian, who had come down while they had been debating their plan. She twisted her cap in her hands like she was wringing it out to dry.

"Don't gawk at me," she said gruffly. "I'll be ready. By the time we get to the end of this, I'll have that poem out of Izzy's heart."

ON THE TRAIL OF THE KEY

IZZY SWAYED SIDE TO side, perched on Lug's shoulders as he moved quietly through the undergrowth. The Edgewood was in the full leaf of summer, and the thick air hummed with tiny insects. The buzzy drone and the heat were starting to slow them all down.

Izzy pulled the verse of clues from her pocket. "Lug, are you sure this is right?"

Lug pointed down at the star-shaped purple flowers dotted among the ferns. "The instructions told us to *follow the mallow*. Well, we're following it."

Selden, in his stag form, trotted up beside them with Ollie and Hen riding on his back. "Haven't we learned not to question Lug's plant knowledge by now?"

"OK, you're right," said Izzy. "It's just that we've been heading east for hours. If we're going to *crawl through the night*, that means we'll have to get through these other clues by nightfall."

They had left Netherbee Hall early, when it was still dark, so they could pass through Brightsmith Hall at sunrise. They didn't know how crucial it was to get the timing right, but they didn't want to take any chances. They'd only have one shot at following the clues in the right order. If the Unglers picked up their trail, they wouldn't be able to backtrack.

They'd helped Hale bundle up the youngest Changelings the night before and tuck them into the *Muscadine*'s basket. It was Hale's idea for Tom to take them at night, so they would sleep while he flew them east.

Hiron had stood in the corner of the basket, looking frustrated. "Wish I wasn't so useless," he said, tugging at his sling. "What if you need another flyer with you, Izzy?"

"We've got Dree," said Izzy. "Besides, you'll be healed up soon, and Tom will need you in case—"

She'd been about to say, *In case we fail and something terrible happens to us.* But she smiled instead and patted his good arm.

Tom leaned over the edge of the ship to hug Izzy and Hen. "You girls both be real careful and send Dree for me if you get into trouble. I'll come back for you quick as I can."

Marian put her arms around the sisters. "These girls'll be just fine. You take care of that cargo." She nodded at the sleeping children in the basket.

"You're brave souls," said Olligan, shaking his head at Tom and Hale. "You couldn't pay me to get in that basket with all those babies at once."

The truth was that they had wanted Ollie to go with Tom, but he refused. He said it was because his friend the chipmunk was afraid of heights, but Izzy knew he wanted to stay with Selden.

Olligan smiled proudly, riding on Selden's back as the appointed lookout. His chipmunk rode with its nose sticking out of his pocket, nibbling bits of biscuit Ollie had saved from breakfast. Ollie also had a speckled salamander draped across the back of his neck and two chickadees, one perched on each shoulder.

"Haven't seen any fallow fields so far," he said, scanning the woods.

Hen lowered her flute from her lips. "What's a fellow field again?"

"Fallow," corrected Marian. "It means resting."

Marian brought up the rear of their party on foot. She carried a sturdy walking stick in one hand, the page with the heart spell written on it in the other. For most of the hike, she'd lagged behind. Not because she couldn't keep up but because she was still reading the spell, working on memorizing it.

Marian leaned on her staff and took off her cap, wiping her brow with it. "Fallow fields. That must be talking about abandoned farmland." She looked overhead at the dense canopy. "Though I can't imagine a farmer choosing to plant their crops here. Think of all that work, clearing the trees just to get enough sunlight."

Lug jolted to a halt, nearly pitching Izzy off his shoulders. "Oh goodness! I just realized something. Izzy, how old is *The Book of the Bretabairn*?"

"Dree said five hundred years."

"Well, any fields would be completely overgrown by the woods after five hundred years." Izzy held on to the top of Lug's head as he leaned back to look up at the trees. "We wouldn't be able to tell when we were crossing farmland, fallow or not."

"Oh," said Izzy, disappointed. "Then what should we do?"

"The next verse says the fields lie below *red poplars tall*," said Marian. "Farmers sometimes plant trees in a ring around their fields. Makes a natural fence."

"Poplars that were tall five hundred years ago have likely fallen down by now," said Lug. "But they would have dropped seeds onto that fallow field. With nothing else in the way, the poplars wouldn't have any competition. So we need to look for a thick grove of red poplars."

"You see?" said Selden, nodding at Lug. "The master of plants."

They walked on for another mile before they found what Lug was looking for—a large square area where the only trees were straight, bare-trunked poplars blooming with crimson flowers. Just to be sure, Lug dug his finger deep into the ground and tasted the soil. "Yup, this has to be it." He smacked his thick lips. "If I had to guess, I'd say this was once a field of beets."

"All right, Ollie," said Selden, turning over his shoulder. "Send Dree the signal."

Ollie turned and twittered something to the chickadee sitting on his left shoulder. The bird nodded and bobbed, then took off up through the canopy.

After a few minutes, the chickadee flew back down with a scissor-tailed bird following behind. Dree landed beside Lug and Changed back to herself. "Please tell me you found a giant *X* with a shiny golden key buried under it."

"Not yet. But we think this is the fallow field—or it used to be," said Izzy, pointing to the trees around them. "That means we've got to find *ground that lies sinking* next."

"That's got to be a sinkhole," said Selden.

"All right, give me a minute, and I'll see what I can find," said Dree. She Changed into a bird again and flew back up through the trees.

The rest of them took a break to eat what they had packed from breakfast. Hen sat against the trunk of one of the poplars, so absorbed in her flute that she even declined a biscuit loaded with jam. She could play short tunes now. They didn't sound as lovely as the songs Peter had played, but at least they had a melody. Suddenly, Hen jumped to her feet.

"Hen, you OK?" asked Izzy.

Hen walked through the trees, staring forward like she was in a trance.

Izzy followed her, worried. "What are you doing?"

Hen played another melody and stared again. She spun around excitedly. "I can see them!"

Izzy looked around nervously. "See what?"

"The paths!" said Hen with a giant smile. "Or the fairy roads or whatever you call them. Izzy, when I play the flute, I can see where the entrances are. They're everywhere!" Hen walked up to two poplars that stood a few feet apart. "The flute makes the entrances glow." She laughed, moving her fingers in the shape of a square. "It looks like they're covered in twinkling Christmas lights. Come see!"

Izzy joined her sister. Hen pointed to a spot on the ground between the poplar trunks. Izzy couldn't see the twinkly lights Hen was talking about, but when she leaned in at the right angle, she could see a dark hole in the ground that hadn't been visible before.

"Whoa," whispered Izzy. "Hen, it's like you've turned into Peter."

Twigs snapped overhead as Dree crashed through the branches and swooped into the glade. Her eyes were wide, and she waved everyone closer as she caught her breath. Her words tumbled out quick and anxious. "I found the sinkhole. It's not a hole—more like a bowl in the ground. A mile to the east. But I also spotted the Unglers. It must be the ones you saw before, Selden. They're about five miles west of here, moving slowly but definitely coming this way. They must have picked up our trail."

Hen rolled the flute between her fingers. "Sorry, was I making too much noise?"

"It's all right, child," said Marian. "You found a way to Earth just in time."

Izzy looked down at the flute in her sister's hand. Now Hen could guide them back to Earth, but if they left, Marian couldn't go with them. They would never get the poem out of Izzy's heart. "We're so close," she said.

"I'm with Izzy," said Selden. "Let's see how far we can get before we give up. Dree, you think you can try to get the Unglers off our trail? Lead them the wrong way and buy us some time?"

"All right," said Dree, Changing into a silver-flecked fawn. "But you guys better hurry. There's no way I can give off as much of a scent trail as the rest of you." She leaped into the trees and bounded away.

They followed Dree's directions to the sinkhole, a place in the forest where the ground sloped down into a wide depression the size of a city block.

"Listen," said Lug, pausing to let Izzy down off his shoulders. "I hear water."

They followed the sound down into the base of the sinkhole, where a tumble of boulders lay at the bottom. A woodland stream drained down from the higher ground, disappearing into cracks between the rocks and flowing into some underground reservoir beneath their feet.

"What do you think?" said Izzy. "Would you say those stones are *drinking* that water?"

"Slurping it right up," said Selden.

Izzy's pulse beat faster. She held up the paper full of clues. "The next part of the verse says *the gift for a spring king hides to your right.*"

"Sometimes, Revelrun is called the Spring King," said Selden. "The gift must be the King's Key."

The ground rose steeply as they followed the water upstream. Everyone had to climb down off backs and go on foot. Soon, the stream forked, and they followed the branch to the right. True to the verse, it turned north, winding out of sight through the trees.

"Follow me," said Selden, splashing into the creek. "Walk in the water so we don't leave a trail."

They trudged single file through the stream, trying to go as quietly as possible. Izzy looked up. The late afternoon sun shone bright through the leaves. If they were going to *crawl through the night*, their timing was off pretty badly.

They heard the quick clacking of hooves and turned to see Dree galloping up toward them. "It's no good," she panted. "I tried, but I can't shake them. They sent one Ungler after me. I lost him, but three more split off, following your trail."

"How far away are they?" asked Marian.

Behind them, they heard a distant shriek. The sound was

joined by another high-pitched squeal and another. The shrieks grew to a chorus.

"Come on!" shouted Selden, leaving the stream and Changing to a wolf. "We've got to move! Dree, you do what you can, then get up in the air if you can't shake them."

They ran along the bank of the creek, no longer trying to be quiet. Izzy pulled Hen up the slope by one hand. The gentle trickle of water grew to a swooshing rush.

"Look!" cried Olligan, pointing to a short waterfall that spilled over the edge of a shelf of moss-covered granite.

Selden charged into the pool at the bottom of the waterfall. He ducked under the falls, then popped back out. "There's space behind here. We could hide. Come on!"

They all waded down into the thigh-deep pool. Izzy took a deep breath and ducked through the falls. There was so much water, it pushed her down, and Lug had to grab her hand and help her up. Behind the waterfall, the rock formed a deep pocket lined with ferns and strings of algae that hung from the ceiling. They huddled to the back, cramming as far into the darkness as they could.

Izzy put one arm around her shivering sister. Thankfully, the rushing water masked the sounds of their breathing, but it also made it impossible to hear what was happening on the other side. Selden sat beside her, perfectly still except for his twitching wolf ears.

Izzy leaned close to him. "What about Dree?" she said quietly.

"Don't worry about her," said Selden. "Dree can take care of herself."

Izzy felt Hen's body tense up. She gasped and pointed. The wavering silhouette of a hunched figure loomed on the other side of the waterfall. Izzy squeezed Hen closer. The Ungler waded down into the water, standing a mere yard away. Its head swayed side to side as it smelled the air. Another Ungler joined it. The shadows crossed each other as they walked back and forth across the pool.

Izzy didn't dare breathe in case one puff of air would tip the Unglers off to their scent. Her heart was pounding as she waited, expecting the bony beasts to punch through the waterfall any minute and grab them with their long fingers.

Slowly, she scooted farther back, drawing Hen along with her. They were trapped, with their backs against the wall. But when Izzy put her hand behind her, she realized there was no wall to back against.

She turned and peered into the darkness. The pale light filtering through the waterfall was too dim for her to see much. She reached back as far as she could and still touched empty air.

She snapped her fingers softly to get everyone's attention, and they leaned in closer to hear her. "This is the next clue in the verse!" she whispered. She pointed at the waterfall where the two Unglers still lingered just outside. "That's the *bride's veil of water*. And there's a space behind us big enough to crawl through."

"But it's not nighttime yet," said Hen.

"I think when the clue says *crawl through the night*, it could mean crawl through the *dark*. And it's pitch-black in there."

Lug made a face. "I don't think I can fit in there, can I?"

"You're going to have to try," whispered Marian, pushing him forward. "Let's give it a go. It's better than sitting here waiting to be found. Izzy, you lead the way."

Izzy got on her hands and knees and started forward, with Hen right behind. Ollie came next, then Lug, Selden, and Marian. Lug had to Change into his badger form, and still he grunted as his body scraped against the walls on either side.

The sounds of the waterfall faded behind them as they crawled on. At first, Izzy's adrenaline pushed her forward. She was so eager to get away from the Unglers that she hurried down the tunnel without thinking about anything else. But soon, she grew worried. What if the tunnel got smaller and smaller? What if it opened up into a bottomless pit or a deep pool? The cave was completely black. Izzy opened her eyes as wide as they could go, but she caught no light whatsoever.

The ground beneath them seemed to be sloping gradually up, but they didn't pop out into the open. Izzy's palms and knees burned from the scratchy gravel underneath. Her breath started to get panicky and fast. Just when she thought she couldn't go any farther, the darkness grew one shade lighter.

"You guys! I think I see something!" Izzy scooted along faster. "Yes, there's an opening up here!"

"Slow down." Selden's voice sounded small and faraway at the back of the line. "There could be Unglers waiting there when we come out."

By this point, Izzy had become so claustrophobic that all she wanted was to see the sky again. After a few minutes, they all huddled up top, dripping wet, scratched, and filthy. They stood in a wide clearing of rocky ground padded with clumps of moss.

In the center of the clearing stood a boulder the size of a garden shed. A tree with deep folds of blackened bark grew out of the top. It had the thick trunk of an old tree but was short and stunted, with low, drooping branches. The tree's roots spilled over the top of the boulder and cascaded down the sides. In some places, they grew right through the stone itself.

Izzy's pulse drummed in her ears as she pulled the clues out of her pocket. She smoothed the page out on her thigh and read the second to last stanza:

> *A tree for the fairy*
> *Children so merry.*
> *A stone for the wary*
> *Men of the loam.*

"What's a loam?" asked Hen, circling the boulder.

"Good, rich brown soil," said Lug. "Farming soil. I think

the words mean the tree is for the fairies, the stone is for humans. That's what they symbolize."

Hen nodded. "Like those stone towers me and Izzy build. You stack a leaf and then a rock, one after the other."

"It's a very old symbol," said Marian, running her fingers along the tree's roots. "Leaf for Faerie, stone for Earth."

"This is it," said Izzy. "This has to be the hiding place."

They walked around and around the strange boulder, searching for crevices or anything buried under the rock. But the stone was seamless, and they found nothing hidden among the tree's roots.

Lug laid his cheek against the stone and knocked on it with his big fist. "I could be wrong, but I think there's a good chance this boulder is hollow inside."

"There must be a way in," said Selden. "Izzy, what does the rest of the poem say?"

"It says to *knock thrice with a feather*."

"You mean twice," said Hen smugly.

"No, I meant *thrice*," said Izzy. "It means three times."

"But knock what?" asked Ollie. "The rock? Or the tree?"

"I don't know," said Izzy. "It's definitely not very clear. And there's one more line that's missing. The last word should rhyme with 'loam,' but it could be anything. Roam, dome..." She turned to Marian. "Are you ready? We need that last line."

Marian unfolded the paper with the heart spell written on it. "I don't have all the words memorized. I tried, but I keep getting them mixed up." She sighed, and her voice trembled with frustration. "I'm no good at this, Izzy. I can't do what you're asking me."

Izzy reached for Marian's hand. "If our places were switched, you wouldn't let me give up. You just need a little more time, that's all."

A small shadow passed over them as Dree fluttered down into the clearing and landed at their feet.

She Changed back to herself. "Thank goodness I found you!" she said breathlessly. "When you disappeared under the waterfall like that, I didn't know what happened to you. I've been flying all over the place looking!"

"We crawled through a cave!" said Hen, hugging Dree around the waist.

"Did you see where the Unglers went?" asked Selden.

Dree swept one arm in a wide circle. "They split up and spread out. They must know we're around here somewhere, because they have the area surrounded. And I saw something else. On the City Road, south of here. Three horses."

Everyone drew closer together.

"Their riders are driving them fast enough to kill them," continued Dree. "Whoever it is, they're in a hurry and coming this way."

"It has to be Rine," said Selden. He looked at Izzy and shook his head. "That's it. We're beaten and we have to face it."

Izzy looked at the gnarled tree sadly. "We were so close."

"How close?" asked Dree.

Izzy quickly explained to her what they'd found and how if Marian could just get a little more time, they would have the last clue in the puzzle.

Dree bit the corner off her thumbnail and spat it at her feet. She looked up at Marian. "What if we could hold Rine off long enough to give you the time you need?"

Selden tilted his head and stared at Dree down the bridge of his nose. "What do you mean *hold him off*?"

Dree folded her arms and looked sideways at Marian. "We've got a little secret. Something that gives us a big advantage over Rine. Something he'll never see coming."

Everyone looked at Marian for confirmation. She huffed and nodded. "He won't expect it, that's for sure."

"If we do everything right, we can stall him long enough to give Marian the time she needs to work the spell," said Dree. She grinned. "If we do it really, really right, we might actually mess him up for good."

Selden gaped at her. "Hold on, *you* want to fight the witches now? You sure Marian didn't cast a personality reversal spell on you?"

She elbowed him hard in the arm. "Oh, come on. Don't be such a baby. When am I ever going to try to convince you to do something this crazy again?"

"All right," said Selden, throwing his hands up. "Tell us your plan."

Dree held her arms out to gather them closer. She smiled slyly. "All right, everyone. Listen up."

SMOKE AND MIRRORS

THE EDGEWOOD WAS SILENT when the witches walked into the clearing, as if the trees were holding their breath, waiting for the strangers to pass.

Rine came first, his eyes bright and watchful under the locks of dark hair that fell across his forehead. Hyan followed, her black braids tied back in a thick ponytail. Delin lagged behind, looking skittish. The two junior witches had managed to escape from the Fillifut after all, though it must have been quite a struggle. Izzy noticed they both had scratches on their faces and forearms.

The witches had left their horses tethered near the City Road. Rine had traded his robes for simple gray clothes. The three of them would have looked like an ordinary group of friends out for a hike in the woods had it not been for their companion lurching into the clearing behind them.

One Ungler, its bagging skin slick with sweat, came to

stand at Rine's side, snuffling the ground at his feet. Rine reached out and petted the beast's neck. The sight of it made Izzy sick, but she held very still, trying to breathe shallowly. She crouched with her friends on top of the boulder, hiding between the tree's thick roots. From their vantage point, they could stay hidden behind the tree's low-swooping branches and still see down into the clearing.

Ollie knelt beside Izzy, breathing fast. He was nervous. Ten woodland animals—two chipmunks, three chickadees, a pair of rabbits, two larks, and a rock squirrel—sat around him. They held unnaturally still, watching his face, waiting for their cue.

Selden crouched on the other side of Olligan. Izzy caught his eye and nodded at poor Ollie. What they were asking him to do was both crucial to their plan and extremely dangerous.

Selden nodded at her and squeezed Ollie's shoulder. "You're going to do great," he whispered. "Just stick to what we talked about."

The witches were quiet, watching and listening. Suddenly, the Ungler in the clearing jerked its snout up and began wheezing excitedly.

"This is the place," said Rine to the witches behind him. "They're close by."

"Ollie, it's time," said Selden. "Now!"

Ollie sprang to his feet and stood on top of the tree roots. His animal friends leaped up to stand and flutter beside him.

"Look, the Changelings!" shouted Hyan, pointing to the top of the boulder.

Ollie looked down at the animals, his mouth hanging open. "Oh no, they've seen us!" he cried, a little overdramatic in Izzy's mind, but it was good enough. "We've got to run! Come on, guys!"

Ollie Changed into a squirrel and bounded down the side of the boulder into the forest. All the animals scurried and flew after him through the trees.

"Go," Rine commanded the Ungler at his side. "Bring them back alive if you can."

The Ungler vaulted across the clearing and tore through the woods after Ollie and the other animals.

Izzy crossed her toes inside her boots. Moments earlier, Lug had tramped through the forest, leaving a winding trail of his scent. The plan was for Ollie and his friends to follow that same trail for a hundred yards. Then Ollie would duck off the trail and hide, while the animals continued crashing and fluttering through the woods. If their plan worked, the Ungler would follow the false trail, away from the clearing.

Hyan started to run after the Ungler, but Rine held her back. He stood very still, sweeping his eyes warily over the clearing. Izzy's palms began to sweat. He looked suspicious.

Izzy glanced at Marian, who sat leaning against the tree's stout trunk, eyes shut while she murmured to herself. Marian's eyelids were papery and crinkled, squeezed tight in concentration. Izzy could tell the old woman still needed more time.

Izzy's heart pounded. Once they moved to the next phase of their plan, they wouldn't be able to turn back.

She looked at Hen and Lug, who crouched nearby. Hen gave her an emphatic thumbs-up. She took out a handful of cylinder-shaped fireworks from her backpack and handed two to Selden, two to Lug. With a soft click of her lighter, she lit the twine that spiraled out from the brown paper that covered each one.

Selden and Lug slowly rose onto their knees and chucked the fireworks down into the clearing. The cylinders thudded and rolled across the forest floor, coming to a stop at the witches' feet. They immediately began to fizz, emitting thick plumes of red, green, and purple smoke.

Hyan backed away as the smoke drifted up toward her. "What kind of sorcery is this?"

The witches, unaccustomed to the wares on offer at Bob's Fireworks Bonanza, had never seen a Swirly Smoker before.

"Everyone be ready," said Rine, raising his hands.

The colored smoke hung low in the clearing, obscuring the ground completely. Lug and Selden took advantage of the witches' confusion to lob six more fireworks down from the boulder.

Delin turned in a slow circle, watching the smoke. Suddenly, his body jerked forward. His hands slammed together, like he was clapping. "What—what's happening?"

he cried, trying to yank his hands away from some unseen force holding them down.

Izzy smiled as she watched him struggle.

This was Dree's secret.

Back at Netherbee Hall, Dree had asked Marian to perform the reverse invisibility spell on her to make her look solid. Marian had tried many times, but no matter what she did, Dree remained her translucent self. In the process, the two of them discovered that although Marian's spell couldn't make Dree visible, it could work in the opposite direction.

Marian had made Dree into a proper ghost.

Down in the clearing, an invisible Dree had cinched an invisible cord around Delin's wrists. Before he knew what was happening, she had tied his ankles as well. With a shove from behind, Delin toppled to the ground, vanishing beneath the fog of colored smoke.

"Help me!" he cried. "He—" Delin gave a muffled yelp, then went silent.

"Delin!" shouted Hyan, searching the smoke. "Where are you?"

Delin popped back onto his feet. "I'm here," he said, waving his free hands. "I'm perfectly all right!"

If it hadn't been so smoky, the other witches might have noticed that Delin's pale neck had sprouted thick brown hairs and he had the faintest coloration of a stripe across his face. Lug wasn't the best at doing Likenesses, but the smoke helped disguise his mistakes.

Izzy turned back to Marian. "Marian, are you ready?" she whispered. "I don't want to rush you, but we're running out of time!"

Marian opened her eyes and checked her spell one more time. "All right, I think I'm ready." She scooted closer to Izzy and held her hands up, palms out. The old woman's fingers shook as if she had tremors. She swallowed and took a deep breath.

Back in the clearing, Hyan screamed and sank to her knees. One hand waved overhead, barely visible above the smoke. She staggered up to her feet, the other hand drawn behind her back. Dree must have let one wrist loose.

"Rine! Something has me!" Hyan shouted, struggling. She grasped with her free hand at the air, swatting and pulling on the cord at her wrist. She tripped and fell down into the smoke.

Rine lifted his hands high, and shadows streamed out of the woods, looping around his fingers like ribbons of black mercury. He worked the shadows into two blades with sharp, jagged edges. He tossed one knife to Delin. "Help her up!"

Lug, in Delin's Likeness, caught the blade and bent down over Hyan. A muffled, confused struggle took place under the smoke cloud.

Then Hyan and Delin stood up together. Hyan whirled around, hands free. She backed up to Rine, breathing hard.

"Rine, something's here in the smoke," she said. "Some sort

of ghost or spirit. We have to get out of here! We're no match for this thing!"

A cry came from the forest floor, and a figure staggered up out of the smoke. It was another Hyan. This version had both hands tied behind her back, and she worked to spit out the invisible gag that had been shoved in her mouth. "That's not me!" she shouted. "This is all a trick!"

Rine's eyes grew wide. He turned his head back and forth between the bound Hyan and the one standing beside him. The version closest to him smiled a cunning, wolfish grin.

Selden Changed into a wolf. He lunged at Rine, dragging him to the ground before he could draw his blade back.

A flicker of heat in Izzy's chest startled her, and she turned back to face Marian. The old woman's hands held steady now. Izzy felt a pull at her ribs, as if a thread connected her to Marian's fingers. She shut her eyes and clamped her teeth together, bracing herself for the final part of the spell.

A painful cry rang out from the clearing. Izzy opened her eyes. "That was Selden!"

Marian stopped her spell, and they both turned to look.

Selden had Changed back to himself. He stood in front of Rine, who held his dagger out in front of him. They both looked bewildered. Izzy was confused too, unsure why Selden had cried out. He stood out of range of Rine's blade and didn't look hurt at all.

Then Selden held out his arms and staggered back under

an invisible weight. "She rushed in front of me!" he cried. "I didn't even see her!"

Lug gasped. "Oh no, no, no!"

Selden cradled his arms and sank down slowly. And then Izzy knew what had happened.

Rine had stabbed Dree.

THE KING'S KEY

"Dree!" cried Izzy.

Before Marian or Hen could stop her, Izzy climbed down from the boulder and rushed across the clearing toward Selden.

Rine held out his hand at her. "You stay right there."

Izzy halted. She stood still while Rine released the real Hyan and Delin from their binds. The smoke from Hen's fireworks had thinned and risen, filling the woods with a hazy color. Izzy coughed, her eyes watering.

Through the lifting fog, she saw Selden kneeling on the ground. He leaned over and whispered, "Just hold on, Dree. Hold on, all right?"

Izzy couldn't see Dree at all. She was still invisible. Lug crouched close by, his furry cheeks stained dark with tears.

Izzy turned to Rine. "Please. Don't hurt them. It's me you want."

Rine pushed a dark lock of hair out of his face. "That's very noble of you, but I don't need to choose."

"You don't get it," said Izzy. "Their hearts won't help you. Mine's the only one you need."

Rine tilted his head. His green eyes looked dull behind the screen of hazy air. "What do you mean?"

Izzy shut her fists tight. It was over. What had they been thinking? That they could beat Rine without Peter? That they were going to somehow save Earth and Faerie all by themselves? Izzy had been foolish and reckless, and now one of her best friends was going to die for it.

"Why do you think we were in the Norlorns?" she said bitterly. "We went there to ask the Fen Whelps a question—a question about me." Izzy pointed to her chest. "They told us everything. They said that your friend, Sasha, discovered how to find the King's Key. He took the clue and hid it in my heart, then asked Peter to take me to Earth, where you couldn't get to it."

A pained look flickered across Rine's face. "Don't you even speak Sasha's name," he hissed. "You know nothing about him."

"I know he was treated cruelly," said Izzy. "And I know you got revenge for him."

"I was in Lake Umbra too," piped up Hen. "The Fen Whelps told us all about you. The boy with the crutch hid a piece of paper in Izzy when she was a baby. He did it just before he got sick and—"

"Enough!" shouted Rine. "Sasha and I were searching for the Key together. We were planning to use it to return to Earth. If he knew where to find it, he would have told me."

Izzy swallowed, unsure if she should say what she was thinking. She was afraid of Rine's sharp flashes of anger. But his shoulders were curled in. He looked pitiable, sad. Maybe if she said the right thing, she could use his feelings for his friend to turn everything around.

"I don't think Sasha wanted to hurt you," said Izzy gently. "He was hiding the clue from you because he was afraid you might hurt someone on Earth. He didn't want that. He didn't want you to hurt yourself. I think he kept it a secret because he cared about you."

Rine bowed his head, staring at the forest floor. "When Peter selected us for the Exchange, he promised us we'd have a better life in Faerie. But our lives were nothing but sorrow. Work and sorrow. And then Sasha died." He lifted his face, and his eyes gleamed bright again. "And for what? For the sake of two worlds that didn't want us?"

Rine spoke louder now, biting out the words. "With Sasha gone, I have nothing. No one in this world or any other. Earth and Faerie could burn to ashes, and I wouldn't shed a tear for either one. In fact, I'll gladly be the one to do the burning."

Rine surged forward. Izzy froze, too surprised to keep him from grabbing her wrist.

Marian rushed in front of Rine as he pulled the shadow

blade back. "Stop it, you fool. You'll ruin everything! You can't get the clue by cutting it out of her. It has to be removed the same way it was put in. I know the spell. I can do it."

Hyan looked Marian up and down. When she noticed Marian's pointed ears, she curled her red lips in disdain. "A *fairy*? Casting spells?"

Delin sneered. "What do you know about witchcraft, old woman?"

Marian glared at him. "I know it's caused more trouble than good," she said gruffly. "And I know the spell to get that poem out is a tricky one. You get one chance, and if you botch it, she'll die, and you'll never get the last clue to find the King's Key."

Rine let go of Izzy's wrist and stepped back, sweeping his arm in a low bow. "Be my guest," he said without lowering the dagger. "I'm intrigued to see a fairy who can do any more with witchcraft than dye a shirt."

"First, you have to let me help the child," said Marian, nodding down at the place where Selden and Lug knelt beside Dree.

Rine stepped back to let her pass. She hurried to Lug and handed him a jar from her satchel, whispering instructions. He took the jar and swiped a finger through a thick black paste, then gently dabbed it onto Dree, feeling for the place where she was wounded.

Marian stepped in front of Izzy and took both her hands, squeezing them tight. Izzy could feel everyone watching them.

The old woman pulled the crumpled spell out of her pocket and read it to herself one more time. Delin snickered.

Marian held her hands in front of Izzy's heart. They were steady this time. Her mouth was closed, but her jaw bobbed up and down, forming the unspoken words of the spell.

Again, Izzy felt a warm flutter in her chest. She kept breathing steadily as the feeling grew stronger and stronger. She shut her eyes, trying not to let the pain show on her face. She didn't want to mess Marian up. The scratchy flutter tugged on her, like Marian held a thread tied around her sternum and was pulling, then releasing it, over and over. And then there was one long, painful pull. The warmth in Izzy's heart blazed white-hot, then went out.

Slowly, Izzy opened her eyes. In her fingers, Marian held a single clean white page ripped along one edge.

Izzy rubbed her sternum. The pain was fading quickly. Everyone stared at the page in Marian's hand. Izzy couldn't read it from where she stood, but she could tell it was written in Ida Green's swooping handwriting.

She couldn't believe it. There was her poem. That was her, written down in six lines on a sheet of paper.

"Well done, hag," said Rine coldly. He snatched the paper out of Marian's hand. His eyes scanned the words, then darted to Izzy. "What is this supposed to mean?"

Izzy brought out the verse of clues from her own pocket and held it out to him. "It's a poem from *The Book of the*

Bretabairn. When you arrange the titles in the right order, they give the clues to find the King's Key." She nodded at the page Rine held between his fingers. "The title of that poem is the last clue. The one we were missing."

Rine looked back and forth between the two papers as he read them together. He smiled and read the last lines aloud.

> *Knock thrice with a feather*
> *And say, "I am home."*

"I am home?" whispered Izzy.

Rine walked toward the boulder and the tree. His smile turned bitter as he ran his fingers along the side of the rock.

"Tree and stone. So fitting," he said in a mocking tone. He turned around and held his arms out wide. "We all get along so well, don't we? Fairies and humans, tied together by such strong bonds. Bah." He slapped the rock with his open palm. "I don't belong here. Neither did Sasha. We never should have been brought here. And you?" He pointed to Izzy and swept his arm out to the other Changelings. "You think you belong on Earth? You don't! The worlds split for a reason. We were never meant to be together. When I'm done, all this stupid mixing, this stupid *Exchanging*, will all be finished." He snapped his fingers, motioning for Izzy to come closer.

Izzy hadn't taken her eyes off the piece of paper in Rine's

hand. She could see the scrawl of ink through the thin paper, but she couldn't read it.

Rine caught her looking at it. He balled the paper into his fist and threw it onto the ground.

"Enough stalling. Time to get that Key. I'll let you open up this treasure box," he said, patting the boulder. "You can say those ludicrous words. This place isn't my home. But first, it sounds like we need a feather."

Izzy reached into her back pocket where she had kept the crow feather that floated into her lap on the day Peter left them. She smoothed out the ragged barbs between her thumb and forefinger and walked up to the boulder.

Izzy held out the feather and tapped it three times on the face of the boulder. She swallowed and placed her open palm against the rock. "I am home," she whispered.

For a long moment, nothing happened. The woods were still, and it seemed that everyone, Izzy included, was holding their breath.

And then the stone moved under Izzy's hand. A cut in the shape of a large square ran over the face of the boulder where it had been seamlessly smooth seconds before. Izzy pressed gently, and the square slid inward with a soft swishing noise, as if it hung on well-oiled hinges.

Rine ran his hands along the edges of the doorway. A soft glow lit up the space within. "Keep watch over them," he called to the other witches as he ducked inside. Izzy followed him.

A small room had been carved out of the boulder, not much bigger than Izzy's closet back home. The walls and ceiling had little hash marks all over them where the rock had been chiseled away. The roots of the tree emerged here and there, flowing in and out of the walls. Opposite the door was a rough ledge, about shoulder height with Izzy. A candle on the ledge flickered, though how it could have been lit, Izzy didn't know.

Rine walked up to the ledge. It was covered in a woven brown cloth, like the burlap sacks used on slides at the county fair. Lying on top of the cloth were the most exquisite treasures Izzy had ever seen.

A pale-blue jewel the size of a chicken egg sat on top of a heaping mound of other gems and stones. There was a polished silver apple that reflected a distorted image of Izzy's face, a stack of thick coins a dull gold color stamped with the symbol of hands clasping, and a thin gold crown set with bloodred stones. Izzy recognized it as the crown worn by King Revelrun in the painting at Netherbee Hall.

Rine looked over the treasures, breathless. But he didn't take any of them or pick them up. His hand went straight for an object in the center of the ledge. A tiny silver key with an intricately carved handle gleamed brightly in the candlelight.

Rine picked up the key carefully. "The King's Key," he whispered, holding it up in front of his eyes and turning it back and forth.

He was so mesmerized by the object in his hand that he seemed to have forgotten Izzy was standing behind him. She stared at the other beautiful objects on the ledge. They all looked priceless. All except one. Curious, Izzy took a step closer.

Nestled at the bottom of the pile of precious gems was a plain gray rock.

Rine walked out of the secret room and back into the clearing. Izzy picked up the rock and held it close to the candle. It was about the size of a sugar packet, oval and somewhat flat, like a pebble tumbled smooth by a river. But when Izzy looked closer, she realized it wasn't just plain gray. Ribbons of golden brown rippled through the stone.

They were thin bands of wood. Wood embedded in rock.

Its worth you must measure.

Izzy quickly slipped the stone into her pocket, then turned and followed Rine outside.

Rine held the silver key up as he walked toward Hyan and Delin. The key glowed brighter than seemed natural in the fading dusk, like it had its own tiny flame inside.

"Now we just need a road to travel down," said Rine. His eyes drifted to the flute in Hen's hands. "You'll oblige us?"

Hen planted her feet defiantly.

"Now!" shouted Rine.

Hen glared at him. She lifted her flute and played a simple melody that reminded Izzy of the song Peter had played when he showed up at Camp Kitterpines. When she was finished, she lowered the flute.

"Well?" snapped Rine. "Where is it?"

In the tree behind you, thought Izzy.

Hen held her chin high as she walked past Rine. She pointed to a standing dead tree. What before had seemed like a shadow on the trunk had become a dark hole as wide and tall as Hen.

Izzy saw the hole before her sister pointed it out. In fact, when she looked into the woods, she saw dozens more.

The Edgewood was full of passage openings, narrow ones sized for tiny pixies and wide, gaping entrances big enough for a horse-drawn carriage to enter. When Izzy squeezed the stone in her palm, she could see all of them. It was just like Hen had described. Their edges glowed as if ringed in Christmas lights.

The openings weren't the only things Izzy could see clearly now. She glanced at the wadded page Rine had discarded. The desperate need to read her poem was gone.

Who are you, Izzy? Who are you really?

Izzy smiled. It now seemed ridiculous that she hadn't known the answer before. She didn't need a poem to tell her who she was. There was no secret, hidden Izzy waiting to be revealed. She was herself, as ordinary and extraordinary as that was.

She was like the stone in her hand: part of Earth, part of Faerie. They all were: the Changelings, Hen, Tom, Marian, even Peter who had left them without really leaving them completely. Why had she ever doubted where she belonged? She belonged with them. And right now, they needed her.

Izzy backed up slowly, careful not to draw Rine's attention. It wasn't difficult, because he was so focused on finally getting what he had wanted for so long. He walked up to the dead tree and put his hands on the rim of the opening, setting one foot inside. He paused.

Spinning around, he held the key out to Delin. "You take the honor."

"Me?" Delin stepped forward and pinched the key between his fingers. "Are you sure?"

"I'm sure."

Delin placed his hands on the tree and ducked his head down inside the passage. He lingered in the opening with one hand still on the outside. He turned and looked worriedly at his companions.

"Go on," said Rine. "You have the key to protect you."

Delin nodded. He stepped farther in, and his entire body disappeared into the dark passage. His excited voice echoed inside. "I'm walking in... This is incredible!"

Izzy continued backing up, taking small unnoticeable steps.

Hyan ran to the dead tree. She started to duck inside when the ground began to shake like the rumble of an approaching train. Hyan stepped back. She called into the opening. "Delin! Come back!"

The entire clearing shuddered. Everyone braced themselves,

holding on to each other or kneeling on the quaking ground. Hyan fell onto her hands and knees as the ground surrounding the tree that held Delin cracked and sank.

When the quaking stopped, the dead tree leaned at a sharp angle. Hyan ran her hands over the bark where the opening had been. She tried to reach into the hole, but it was closed. "Delin?" She dug her fingers at the trunk, scraping away the dark wood with her nails.

Hyan turned to Rine. "What happened? I can't get back in!"

Rine's lip curled beneath flared nostrils. He spun around.

Izzy held up the gray stone, wagging it back and forth as she backed away from him. "I think you might have picked the wrong key."

She put the stone in her mouth, Changed into a fox, and ran.

IN BETWEEN

RINE BELLOWED. WITHOUT TURNING to look behind her, Izzy knew he was chasing her. She bounded through the woods, springing lightly over fallen logs on her nimble paws. With her keen fox hearing, she heard branches snapping and boots pounding the ground behind her.

Straight ahead, three Unglers emerged from the trees. They caught Izzy's scent and squatted down, ready to spring at her. Izzy put her head down and ran straight for them.

When she was ten yards from the bony creatures, Izzy dipped her snout down, then snapped her head up, flinging the stone into the air over their heads. She leaped up after it and swept her forelegs back.

The Unglers' wart-crusted heads craned up as Izzy flew over them in her blackbird form. She followed the arc of the stone and caught it in her scaly feet. The weight of it pulled her down, but with another pump of her wings, she was high in the air again, flying through the trees.

Rine shoved past the confused Unglers and tore through the woods after Izzy. She risked a quick glance behind her. As he ran, Rine pulled in shadows from the woods. The sun had begun to set, and the growing darkness gave him plenty to work with. The shadows trailed out behind him, dangling off the hem of his shirt, dripping from his fingers. He formed needle-sharp darts and flung them at Izzy.

But she had the reflexes of a blackbird now. She saw the darts in her wide peripheral vision. With a tilt of her wings, she dodged the darts with inches to spare.

Izzy rocketed through the trees with no fear that she would lose this form—or any of her forms—ever again. This was different than any other time she had Changed before. She knew who she was now, and she had no intention of forgetting again.

She could have soared straight up into the sky, where Rine couldn't follow. But she needed to keep him close. Entrances into Earth lit up all around her. Another hundred yards, and she spotted a large passageway, the entrance rimmed in stone. The opening was wide enough for her to fly through and for Rine to follow.

Izzy folded her wings back and dove at the passage. She landed inside on a dusty floor and Changed back to herself. Clutching the stone in one hand, she stood panting, catching her breath, her heart hammering so hard that it felt like it would break out of her chest.

Torches set in the walls flared on ahead of her down the passageway. This wasn't the same road Peter had brought her down. Thankfully, this one was shorter. She was too tired to run far.

Rine's silhouette appeared on the outside of the entrance. He stepped inside, looking overhead warily. He grasped for Izzy with one hand, but she stayed just beyond his reach. Cautiously, he stepped inside. He stood there a moment, catching his breath. With a snarl, he lunged at Izzy.

She jumped back—but not too far back. The earth rumbled, and the opening to the Edgewood began to buckle. Rine cried out and held his arms over his face. Izzy held the stone out toward him, and the cave-in stopped. The King's Key formed a dome of protection around him, holding the passage open.

"Give it to me," demanded Rine, his voice ringing off the passage walls.

Izzy backed up slowly. Rine followed her as more of the tunnel caved in behind him. She kept backing down the tunnel, luring him farther and farther inside.

Rine's breathing was ragged. Izzy could see his frustration boiling over. "Enough!" he cried. "Give me that key!"

He sprang at Izzy. She turned and ran, stumbling over the shuddering ground. Rine ran after her, the walls crashing in behind him.

Up ahead, a bluish-white light pooled on the walls. Earth.

Izzy sprinted toward the light. She was almost there. If she could get the King's Key out of the passageway, she could stop Rine forever. But twenty feet from the opening, Izzy tripped over the cracking floor and landed hard on her stomach. She turned her head and saw Rine closing the distance between them.

Wasting no more time, Izzy flung the King's Key as hard as she could out the passageway into Earth.

Rine's eyes widened with the realization of what she had done. But it was too late.

The sound of cracking stone was deafening. Izzy curled into a ball and covered her head with her arms, clenching her jaw to stop it from rattling. She shut her eyes.

She heard Rine scream, and then the cave-in became so loud that she couldn't hear anything else. Stones fell onto her. The passage closed in, tighter and tighter.

And then everything became very still and very dark.

THE MOST COMMON

The world was breaking.

Izzy kept her eyes shut tight, her body curled in on itself. She squeezed her jaw to bear with the horrible sounds of scraping and crunching around her. In the midst of the cracking and groaning of stone, Izzy dreamed. She faded in and out of consciousness. In her dream, she heard a familiar song. She couldn't place where she'd heard it before. The notes grew louder and louder. When they finally quieted, she heard voices, low-pitched and warbled, like they spoke underwater.

"I don't see her."

"Oh no…oh please, no…"

"Wait! You guys, look!"

And then the stone lifted away from Izzy. She could breathe more easily. There was space to kick out her legs. Her eyes picked up on light in the darkness, but she couldn't focus. Her head hurt so much.

"Do you think this could be…"

"Let me through! Let me see!"

Izzy's body rolled onto a cushioned pink pad. She took a deep breath. She smelled…grape jelly.

"Oh!" The voice sounded like Hen but deeper and very far away. "Lug, come here and look! Is this her?"

Slowly, the world came back into focus. Izzy looked up at a face as large and round as a planet, peering down at her, its lips stretched in a wide smile.

"L-Lug?" Izzy whispered.

"Oh, my dear Izzy!" Lug boomed. "You discovered your other form!"

FIERCENESS BENEATH
THE LACE WING

BEFORE, WHEN IZZY HAD daydreamed of what her fourth form could be, she hoped it was something magical and spectacular. It would have been nice to be a giant golden eagle like Hiron or a silvery fawn like Dree. She dreamed of being some special hybrid: half bird, half horse maybe. But she would have settled for something just plain unusual, like a platypus or a quetzal.

She never would have imagined she would be grateful for being able to Change into the most common insect in the world.

Izzy's last form was a beetle.

If it had been anything else, she never would have survived the cave-in of the passageway. But small as she was, she had tucked into a hole between the falling stones, safe until Hen came to clear away the rubble with her flute.

They never found Rine's body. Once they found Izzy, they took her back out to the Edgewood, and Hen closed the passageway up again. But Izzy knew what must have happened to him. He couldn't have survived the cave-in. Even as a beetle, Izzy had barely made it out herself.

Marian and the others took her back to Netherbee Hall to rest and recover. She had been banged around a good bit, but more than anything, she was in shock and needed sleep. When she finally woke up, alone in a bedroom at the top of the stairs, the house was quiet. With a sickening feeling growing in the pit of her stomach, Izzy knew they weren't keeping it quiet just for her.

She ignored her pounding headache as she slipped on boots and buttoned on a shirt. The curtains were still drawn against the light, even though they had nothing left to fear from the Unglers. Along with Hyan, the beasts had fled after Rine met his end.

Izzy walked down the hallway, following the amber light of candles. All the other bedroom doors were shut except the last one. When Izzy looked inside, she found Lug sitting in a chair at the foot of a bed, his chin dropped down to his chest, snoring. Selden sat beside him, his head lying on his crossed arms over the coverlet.

Lug stirred with a snort and looked up. "Oh, Izzy," he said with a smile. "You're up. That's so good to see."

"Is that…" Izzy swallowed and walked closer to the bed. "Is she…"

The bed looked rumpled and empty. Izzy reached out at

the mattress. She felt the smooth skin of Dree's arm lying on top of the covers. She was warm. Up close, Izzy could hear her friend breathing softly.

Lug strained to hold his smile. He patted the covers at the foot of the bed. "Yes, it's Dree. And she's all right. She's going to be just fine."

Selden lifted his head. Izzy could tell from his puffy pink eyes that he hadn't slept. "She's not all right," he said flatly.

Lug stood up and walked to the head of the bed. He flipped his hand over and gently rested the back of it on Dree's invisible forehead. "Marian and I did everything we could think of for her wound. Luckily, the sword missed everything vital." He pointed to his own chest, just below the shoulder. "And she hasn't had any fever. She's been breathing easy. Although..." Lug sighed. "More and more shallow throughout the day."

Izzy rubbed Dree's arm. "Marian should make her visible again. Wouldn't it be easier to make her better if you could see her?"

"That's exactly the problem," said Selden.

Lug cleared his throat. "Marian *has* made her visible again. At least, she's tried. She's performed the visibility spell on Dree many times. But it's like the spell won't stick to her somehow. Marian said there's nothing more to do. It's up to Dree whether she'll stay or go."

Izzy shut her eyes, remembering what Dree had said that

night in the castle. *Sometimes, I wonder if one day I'll just fade away completely…and no one will even notice.*

She felt for Dree's hand and squeezed it, folding her friend's fingers around her own. "We notice, Dree," she whispered. "We're here, and we want you to stay."

Lug dabbed at the corner of his eye with his thumb knuckle. "I've got to go get more fresh water and towels," he said, picking up a ceramic pitcher from the table beside the bed. "It's about time for Marian to come and do the spell again. She tries it every few hours, just in case."

When he reached the door, he turned around and said, "Izzy, could you come here a moment?"

Izzy walked to him, and he leaned down and whispered, "Try to talk to him." He nodded his chin at Selden. "He's barely spoken and hasn't eaten anything since we got back to Netherbee. I think he blames himself for all this. I'm very worried about what will happen if she—"

Izzy put her hand on Lug's arm. "It's all right. I'll stay with him."

Lug smiled and left. As Izzy walked back to the bed, Selden's body tensed, and he shrugged aside.

"I know what Lug told you," he said. "That he wants me to eat or something stupid like that."

Izzy pulled Lug's chair over and sat beside Selden. She held back from trying to hug him, knowing he'd bristle at anything like that right now. She folded her hands in her lap and looked down at the bed, waiting for him to go on.

"Everyone thinks I'm upset because I'm blaming myself for what happened," he said. "But that's not it at all. This isn't my fault. Dree did this to herself."

"You're right," Izzy whispered. "It's not your fault. It's not Dree's either though. It's no one's."

"She should have stayed back instead of rushing in front of me," said Selden, waving his hand angrily at the bed. "She's always telling me I make stupid decisions, but how stupid was this?"

"But you're not going to make anything better by making yourself sick sitting here."

Selden's fingers squeezed into fists. "I just want to be here when she wakes up. She has to wake up. She has to." He looked up at Izzy, his eyes rimmed with tears. He tilted his head back, but they spilled over anyway. "Everyone leaves. Family, friends. Peter left. And now—" He twisted the bedcovers with his fingers. "What are we going to do if she goes?"

Izzy reached out for his hand. There were no words, nothing that she could think of that would make him feel better, that would make any of it better. They sat together like that for a while, listening to the sound of Dree's quiet breathing.

Selden wiped his eyes and sniffed. "I keep telling her to get up. That's all she has to do, just get up. But Dree's always been so stubborn. She doesn't like to listen to anyone."

"Sounds like someone else I know."

"No," said Selden. "Dree's so different from me. If this were me, I'd be raging to get up out of that bed."

Izzy smiled. Selden would try to get out of bed even if he had both arms and legs in casts. That's just who he was: *Strongest, bravest, when wounded deep.*

They heard footsteps outside the door, and Marian came in, followed by Lug. Izzy suddenly realized that she and Selden were still holding hands. She slipped hers out of his and rubbed her palm over her knee.

Hen and Ollie came in a moment later, and each of them hugged Izzy.

Marian stood beside the bed and took off her cap. She took a deep breath. "All right, time to try again. Dree?" she said loudly. "I'm doing the spell again, child. You hold on to it this time, all right?"

"Why hasn't it worked before?" asked Izzy.

"The visibility spell tells the light to bounce off an object," said Marian. "But part of the spell is that the object goes back to '*what it was.*' I think that's the problem. I know this sounds odd, but a teacup knows it's a teacup, and a house knows it's a house. Part of this is on Dree. It's like she's forgotten who she was before. And if she doesn't know, the light can't find her."

They all took a step back from the bed to give Marian room. The old woman stood at Dree's side and raised her softly wrinkled hands over the blankets. She took a deep breath and began moving her fingers like she was playing a piano.

Izzy bit down on her bottom lip, watching hopefully. She glanced at Selden and Lug. They both stood with their heads bowed. They'd seen Marian do this before and fail at it. Izzy shut her eyes.

This is on Dree. It's like she's forgotten who she was before.

Izzy's eyes popped open. She turned and ran out of the room, past her grieving friends. Izzy hurried downstairs to the parlor. When she came back up, she had *The Book of the Bretabairn* tucked under her arm.

She laid the book at the foot of the bed and opened the cover.

"Izzy?" said Lug. "What are you—"

Marian shushed him. She gave Izzy a short nod. "Go on, child. It's worth a try."

Everyone watched Izzy as she flipped through the pages. She knew what they must be thinking. She was thinking it too. *The Book of the Bretabairn* wasn't a book of spells. But Izzy had learned that there was a certain magic in knowing who you were supposed to be.

Maybe Dree needed a little reminder.

Izzy found Dree's poem and started reading it out loud.

> *Butterfly, bird with scissored tail,*
> *Fawn and cat with sharpened nail,*
> *Cloaked in moonlight, skin like dew,*
> *Fiery heart, kind and true.*
> *For love, no trial she cannot face*
> *With fierceness hid 'neath wings of lace.*

When Izzy got to the end of the poem, she started over. Selden joined her. Hen scooted up beside her and held on to her sleeve. She started reading along with Izzy, stumbling over the longer words. Ollie didn't know how to read, but after hearing it a few times, he recited the poem from memory. Lug joined in as well.

They kept reciting the poem as Marian worked the spell. They spoke the words over and over until they ran on in a singsong, and even simple words, like *bird* and *true*, began to sound like nonsense.

Selden stood up. "It's working," he whispered. "Look, it's working."

The faint outline of Dree's body came into view, like someone had drawn her with a gray pencil. They continued reading, louder and faster.

Dree's arms appeared, lying on top of the blankets. Her face, eyes shut, hovered over the pillow. She was translucent as she'd always been, but she was there again. The bedcover stirred. They all stopped reading midsentence.

Dree's eyelids fluttered. She opened her eyes slowly and looked around the dark room. When her gaze focused on them, she cracked her lips. They all held a collective breath and leaned in.

"This place looks decked out for a funeral," she croaked.

"Dree!" shouted Hen and Ollie.

Lug clapped his hands together and sobbed.

Dree looked up at Selden. "What's wrong? You look like you've seen a ghost."

He laughed. Izzy laughed. And then they were all laughing and crying and hugging one another and hugging Dree—but not too tight.

Marian put her hands on her hips. "You're right, this place is much too gloomy." She went to the window and pulled back the curtain. Soft light flooded the room, shining through Dree's perfect, glassy face.

Izzy reached into her back pocket and pulled out the crow feather. Its edges were tattered now. She tucked it into the book's spine, marking the page with Dree's poem.

"Don't worry about us, Peter," she whispered. "We're all going to be fine."

HOME AGAIN

"SWEETIE?" CALLED IZZY'S MOM as she knocked softly on her bedroom door. "The mail's here!"

Izzy sat up on her bed and crossed her legs. "You can come in, Mom!"

The door swung open, and Izzy's mom leaned inside, holding out a small brown envelope. "Dad says dinner'll be ready in fifteen minutes, OK?" she turned to the other bed and added, "Dree, you like asparagus casserole, right?"

Dree sat on Hen's bed with Izzy's dog, Dublin, sprawled across her lap. "Love it, Mrs. Doyle."

"Good. At least someone does around here. Lug and Hen are making a big salad from what they found in the woods." Izzy's mom smiled and shook her head. "That boy knows more about plants than anyone I've ever met."

When she shut the door, Dree puffed out her cheeks and exhaled. "I still can't get used to that."

Izzy waved her hand. "You can relax. Hen's got Mom and Dad totally enchanted. They think you're solid, and they think Lug's just got early facial hair growth."

"And they think Selden actually combs and cleans his fingernails?"

Izzy grinned. "There's a limit to what even Peter's flute can do."

Actually, Hen was showing amazing self-control in not abusing the flute's power over humans. When they got home, she'd used it to make their parents think they should eat French fries and banana pudding at every meal, but even Hen got sick of that after a few days. Now she just used it to make them see the Changelings as regular children. Izzy's parents thought Dree, Selden, and Lug were kids from the neighborhood.

Izzy's mom did make remarks about how they didn't like to wear shoes and had awful table manners. And every now and then, Izzy would catch her watching Dree, her head tilted curiously as if she wasn't quite sure what to make of her. But overall, her parents were so glad that Izzy had finally made friends that if they suspected Dree of not being entirely solid, they never mentioned it.

Dublin rolled over so Dree could rub his tummy. She nodded at the letter in Izzy's hand. "Another one from Selden?"

"He sent one with Smudge just yesterday," said Izzy, flipping the envelope over. "I don't know what else he'd have to say unless they've found a new family."

Selden was now overseeing the Faerie side of the Exchange. But even though he took his new job very seriously, he had decided to do things differently than Peter.

They stuck to the ancient agreement of "*a Child for a Changeling*," but they no longer made it an exact trade. Hiron and Ollie scoped out Earth for kind families who desperately wanted children but couldn't have them on their own. They had already placed Phlox, Luthia, and Yash with good parents and had found a potential home for the twins, Mite and Mote. The new rule was that no Changeling had to be Exchanged if they didn't want to, and everyone was encouraged to come back to Avhalon to visit.

Dree was in charge of finding human children to bring into Faerie. She looked for misfits, unhappy kids who weren't loved at home. When she made contact with them and told them they could start a new life in a magical world, they almost always jumped at the chance. Hen rarely had to use the flute to lure anyone away, but she still played it as she led the way into Faerie, more to keep up with tradition than anything else.

Once in Faerie, human children lived with Hale and the other Changelings until Lug could find them a good family to live with—one that really wanted to take in a human child, not just get an extra helping hand around the farm. If he couldn't find a perfect match, they could stay with Hale in Avhalon or with Marian at Netherbee until they were old enough to live on their own.

Selden oversaw the entire operation from Peter's old desk. He worked with Smudge to keep all the details in order and sent messages to Earth through Izzy. The new system was way more complicated than the old one, but with all of them working together, they managed it somehow. The result was that Izzy's friends came and stayed at her house often now, and she and Hen went back to Faerie on a regular basis. Selden had made her promise to come back for every major holiday, which for fairies meant every few weeks.

They had no idea where the King's Key ended up after Izzy threw it. All they knew was that it lay somewhere on Earth. Izzy wondered if anyone would ever find it, and if they did, if they'd even notice that it was no ordinary rock.

"So?" asked Dree, nodding at the letter. "What did he say?"

Izzy opened the envelope and pulled out the paper tucked inside. She rolled her eyes and passed it to Dree. "He's drawn all of us at the starting line of the Thripplemas races. It says, *Two more weeks. Get ready to lose.*"

"Everyone's in this picture but you," said Dree.

"Can't you see, there at the bottom?" Izzy leaned over and pointed to the corner of the paper. "He's drawn me as a shrimp."

Dree grinned and handed the letter back to Izzy. "Good old Selden." She hopped off the bed, and Dublin followed her to the door, tail wagging. "Should we go down to dinner? Lug won't leave us anything if we don't hurry."

"Sure. I'll be there in just a second."

Izzy went to her desk and took a thumbtack out of the drawer. She pinned Selden's drawing on the wall, next to the other letters from him and Lug and the other Changelings. As she leaned back, she smoothed her hand over a wrinkled piece of paper tacked next to her bed. Ollie had gone back to the clearing and found it for her.

Izzy didn't need her poem to tell her who she was or where she belonged. But she liked reading it anyway.

> *Blackbird, beetle, mouse, and fox,*
> *Uncommon gifts in a common box.*
> *Slow to action, swiftly clever,*
> *With head and heart in equal measure.*
> *A worthy friend to stand beside,*
> *At home wherever love resides.*

Izzy smiled. Then she turned off the lights and went down-stairs to join her family for dinner.

ACKNOWLEDGMENTS

This is a story about wild and magical children, and it was greatly inspired by my wild and magical nieces and nephew: Iliana, Verena, Eoin, Beatrice, Leonora, Lucia, Mae, Neave, and Anne Louise.

This is a story about noticing the value in something that appears ordinary. Thank you to my wonderful editor, Steve Geck, for finding the value in this story when it was just an ordinary manuscript in your inbox.

This is a story about hard work and perseverance. Thank you to John Aardema, Beth Oleniczak, Alex Yeadon, and to all the team at Sourcebooks who work so hard to put stories into the hands of young readers.

This is a story about friends who would walk through fire for each other. I am grateful for my friends, especially Shauna, Lynn, Carolyn, and Soraiya, for your unending support. I would walk through fire for you.

This is a story about family, and I am fortunate to have a family that has encouraged me at every step along this journey. Thank you, Bob, Liz, Marvin, and Peggy, for your big hearts. Thank you, Dad, for being my greatest champion. Thank you, Mom, for *everything*.

Finally, this is a story about love and finding home. Tom, Elowyn, and Aven, you are my home and my love and the source of all my strength.

ABOUT THE AUTHOR

Christina Soontornvat may or may not be a Changeling in disguise. She hates to wear shoes. She would rather live in a tree than in a house. And she has gotten up to plenty of mischief in her lifetime. At the moment, she lives on Earth with her husband and their two mischief-making daughters in Austin, Texas. Find her online at soontornvat.com and @soontornvat.